FIRST DAUGHTER

Royals of Dharia 3

SUSAN KAYE QUINN

First Daughter
(Royals of Dharia, Book Three)
fantasy steampunk romance

IT SAYS we're at war.

Aniri's own words haunted her. How could she wage war with a single, limping skyship, when the enemy supposedly commanded an armada? How could she fight the Samirians at all while they held her sister and husband captive? It was too great a price. It was too much to ask of anyone. But as she gazed out over the snow-dusted mountain peaks gliding thousands of feet below her skyship, she knew the answer: she couldn't betray her husband's country while saving his life. She couldn't exchange a crown she didn't want for a man she loved more than anything.

He would never forgive her for it.

Aniri gripped the edges of the skyship bridge

window with both hands, crumpling the sheer netting that had replaced the glass blown out by the Samirians' bombs. Her Jungali sailors had hastily patched the ship, using steel beams and wooden planks and yards of royal tablecloths when necessary to stem the loss of the lighter-than-air navia gas that kept them afloat. Their skyship, the *Prosperity*, was hardly living up to its name—the gas bag was still leaking, the command center was a laughable skeleton, and there was only a half-load of fuel on board.

"We're well into Dharia now, Captain," Master Tinker Karan said from his station at the plotting table.

"Very good, Mr. Karan." He had fallen into the habit of calling her *captain*, even though she was no such thing, and her ship was barely afloat. Yet she had no choice but to hurry aloft as soon as Natesh, Second Son of Samir, made his demands:

SURRENDER NOW AND I WILL SPARE EVERYONE

He wanted the crowns of both Jungali and Dharia. In exchange, Aniri could win the lives of both her sister, Second Daughter of Dharia, and her future husband, Prince Malik of Jungali. But Aniri knew it was a fool's choice: any royal would soon find the point of a saber through their backs, regardless. She would be no exception, being the Third Daughter of Dharia, but more importantly, she knew Natesh would kill whomever necessary to win the crown in his own country of Samir—waging a war was just a means to that end.

Besides, his message could easily have been meant to stall them, keep them grounded while he brought his Samirian skyship, the *Dagger*, back to Jungali to bombard the capital with death once again. Aniri hadn't bothered with a reply—she simply dropped everything and bundled her injured mother, the Queen of Dharia, aboard the *Prosperity*. The Queen's Jungali healer made a fervent protest about moving her, but her loyal *raksaka* protector, Janak, didn't argue. Given that he loved the Queen and could easily enforce his will with lethal assassin skills, she knew he understood the danger all too well. Once her hand-maiden Priya and Master Tinker Karan had boarded, Aniri ordered them up into the sky, where the ship would no longer be a sitting, wounded target for Samir's black, bullet-nosed bombs. Those bombs had already blown holes in the streets and hearts of the Jungali people. She wouldn't let them take the only weapon they had left to fight this war—or the few royals left with the authority to wage it.

"My fix puts us at the capital of Dharia in less than an hour, Captain," Karan said, still bent over his papers.

Since boarding, Aniri had changed out of her soot-covered and blood-stained adventuring clothes —partly because they were filthy, but also because they were a too-constant reminder of the carnage wrought on the streets of Jungali. Her ever-resourceful handmaiden had quickly hemmed a spare Jungali naval uniform to fit Aniri's shorter frame. It was baggy in the middle, and the sleeves were too long, but the twin rows of steel buttons down the front and the uniform's brilliant blue color—bright as the Jungali mountain sky—fortified her with a sense of military purpose. Only her crisp new attire seemed to encourage Karan in calling her *Captain*, despite multiple protests on her part.

"Is there any command I could give you, Mr. Karan, that would keep you from referring to me as the captain of this ship?"

"Well, ye could stop giving orders and dress like the Third Daughter of Dharia."

Aniri cut a sharp look to him, but the humor in his eyes made her relax more than anything else had managed to since they had left the bombed-out dock of the palace in Jungali.

"I'll be sure to don a corset as soon as we arrive, then."

Karan's deep *hmpf* expressed his lack of faith that she would carry through on that threat, and honestly, she couldn't stomach the thought herself. As long as they were at war—which may be as long as many of them had yet to live—she would rather be in attire suitable to doing *something* to end the madness that was spinning out around her.

The window netting billowed with the wind just beyond it, each gust threatening to work loose the tattered edges hastily bound by nails to the frame. A fog of despair constantly threatened to close in on her mind, held at bay only by the boiling anger that simmered in her chest for all that had been stolen from her and her people. The sad state of her ship only made her situation more plain. And the depths of her heart cried out against it: any war she cared to wage faced terrible odds. They would fight, but it was likely to end in all their deaths, regardless. And then Natesh would gain the thing he wanted anyway: rule over all three Queendoms.

Why had this burden fallen to her? Why not her sister, First Daughter Nahali, who was raised from birth to bear the weight of the Queendom? Aniri had crumpled the aetheroceiver message from Natesh, but the terse demand from the impersonal wireless device would have to be answered in some way eventually. Even the non-answer she had given was an answer of sorts. One that may have already cost her future-husband Ash and beloved-sister Seledri their lives.

Their next steps would be critical—she needed to speak to her mother's raksaka about them before they arrived in the capital. Aniri searched the horizon for the pink-tinged sandstone walls of her homeland's capital city of Kartavya. It was a home she had thought she had finally left—to claim her place as Jungali's Queen—but that wish was also blown to pieces, along with the bomb that stopped her and Ash from exchanging their vows. The only good thing to come out of Natesh's threats was discovering that Ash had actually survived the blast and was still alive.

At least, for the moment.

Tears that had been strangely absent through most of the trauma suddenly threatened to make an appearance. She blinked them back, gaining her vision just as the first parapets of the Dharian capital showed themselves in the hazy distance below.

Karan was still bent over his maps, checking the fix of their position. It was nearing eve, but the stars had yet to come out, so he must have sighted the sun with his new celestial navigator. The original aetherscope-like device—which had been destroyed along with the front half of the bridge—had been adapted from the Samirian Navy and modified for use in the sky. Fortunately, Karan had a spare from the time when the *Prosperity* was a joint, secret project between the Samirians and the Jungali, not an instrument of war between them.

Aniri cleared her throat before attempting to speak again. "I presume you have things well in hand, Mr. Karan. I'll be in the captain's quarters if you have need of me. I need a word with Janak before we arrive."

When she turned to him, his intelligent eyes held too much concern. She ducked her head away, turned on the heel of her boot, and strode from the bridge.

The true captain of the skyship, Mr. Tarak, still kept his station in engines, and with Karan on the bridge, they had no need of a captain anyway. But she had commandeered the captain's quarters for her mother. In her state, recovering from the Samarian raksaka assassin who had tried to take her life with a bullet, the Queen needed any small comfort the skyship had to offer. Aniri knew Janak would be at her side, as he had remained constantly since the attack.

The hallways were crowded with tubing and hand rails, but empty of sailors. It was a wonder they had enough crew left to fly, but Karan assured her they were fit. Or fit enough. Aniri climbed the metal-racked stairs and stepped through the bulkhead door to the hallway that held the captain's room. She paused before knocking on the door. Her mother's injury still required Aniri to put on a brave face that was nowhere near reflecting the tormented, hollowed-out state inside her. She rested her hand on the hilt of her saber, strapped on one side with a pistol on the other. The sword was Ash's gift to her—a present for a wedding and a promise for a future that seemed less likely with every passing hour.

But that was precisely why she needed to speak to Janak. And before they arrived at the capital and had to face her sister, First Daughter Nahali. With the Queen in no shape to command in peacetime, much less in war, it would fall to Nahali to decide how to deploy Dharia's efforts in fighting it. Aniri feared she knew all too well how the life of a Jungali prince would stack up against the concerns of Dharia in Nahali's eyes.

Aniri knocked softly on the door. Janak swiftly opened it.

The raksaka was dressed in the same royal jacket he had been wearing when the attack occurred, since he had been unwilling to leave the Queen's side and thus unable to change. Past Janak in the doorway, Aniri glimpsed a nest of mattresses and blankets cosseting her mother on the floor of the small cabin. Given the skyship's bunks were completely inadequate, it made sense to position her there, but the travel must be aggravating the gunshot wound in her side: her mother's normally creamy brown skin was ashen, drained of color and life. It was even more deathly than when they departed, and Aniri's heart seized with uncertainty. Janak slipped through the thin opening of the door and closed it quietly behind him, leaving the two of them in the hall alone.

"Is my mother sleeping?" It was a demand for reassurance as much as a question. A terrible fear rose up to choke her: that in whisking her mother away from the danger of the Jungali palace, the travel itself might kill her.

"Yes." Janak's voice was grave, his face as nearly as drawn and gray as the Queen's. "I've given her some of the vapors the healer sent with us. She was in too much pain."

Too much for Janak to endure, not her mother, Aniri suspected. But the ghostly look on her mother's face… Aniri didn't want to think about the expression it might have held *before* Janak had sedated her.

"The ride is too rough for her." Janak's scowl grew deeper. "I'm afraid it may have aggravated her wound, perhaps caused more blood loss. And she's already lost too much."

Aniri's breath was trapped in her lungs. If her mother died… she couldn't even put those thoughts into words. Instead, she managed, "I would smooth the air for her if I could, Janak."

He nodded tightly, and Aniri's heart wrenched even more for the pain he must be carrying, watching the woman he loved suffer, with her recovery not at all certain. All the worse that she was his Queen and he was her raksaka… and that he failed to take the bullet himself. Aniri couldn't imagine the turmoil churning inside him.

"In spite of the difficulty of the transport, I agree that leaving Jungali was most prudent," Janak said. "However, I'm not entirely convinced that returning to the capital of Dharia is the same."

They had already had this discussion, in the haste of the evacuation, but apparently they weren't done having it. "We could have flown to Sik province," she said, "but the Samirians know where the airharbor is. They would, no doubt, go there first, assuming we would seek to repair the skyship. And it *is* in desperate need of repairs, but that's no place for the Queen."

"Agreed. And she will have the finest healers in Dharia at her bedside in Kartavya. But the capital of Dharia is the first place they will look for her. And it is also a symbolic target, should they choose to strike at the heart of the country."

"You can secret my mother away with a dozen of our best healers once we arrive." Aniri crossed her arms and leaned against the bulkhead wall. The weariness of the day was turning her knees to jelly. "But I also need to speak to Nahali about our plans going forward. And the skyship must be kept in motion, stopping only for fuel and supplies. We must not let it be a target for the Samirians, should they come looking for one."

"The entire country is a target."

"I realize that." Aniri sighed, the weariness climbing its way up her bones. "Although I expect them to attack our navy—the sea-going one, not the single skyship we possess—and the capital first. If they attack at all."

Janak frowned. "You think they're bluffing?"

"I think they only brought one skyship to attack the Jungali capital. And I would like very much to know why."

His eyes widened.

Aniri was sure he would have seen it, had he not been so consumed with worry for the Queen.

"You suspect the armada is a ruse, in spite of what your father claimed," Janak said. "That they indeed have only the one ship."

"I suspect it's simply a matter of time before they have an armada. Exactly how much time could mean the difference between a war we can win and one we cannot."

Janak nodded. "What are your thoughts on this, my lady?"

Aniri blinked and was speechless for a moment. Janak mostly tormented her with his wit, and occasionally gave her a grudging respect, but she had never heard him address her so... formally. As if she were the Queen now, instead of her mother. It tore at her, an unwelcome reminder of the tenuous hold on life her mother had. Or perhaps it was merely his concern for her mother that had him looking to Aniri for guidance.

Still, it took her a moment to respond. "My thinking is that if they have an armada, we cannot hope to prevail by attacking them, either by air or by sea. That leaves stealth. Which, as it happens, could well be the way to free Ash and Seledri as well as restore the rightful leadership to Samir."

"You think Pavan could still take the crown?"

Pavan was the First Son of Samir and Seledri's husband. "I think Pavan *should* have the crown," Aniri said. "I think we can't win this war on Dharian soil with one skyship, but we might win it on Samirian soil with a fight from within. And we won't need to fight the Samirians at all if the proper Son wears the crown. But I don't have a gauge on where the Queen Mother falls in this royal family drama. Or the true temper of the people."

"Civil war is quite the antidote to a war among neighbors." Janak's tone was approving.

"If it comes to that," Aniri said.

Janak's eyes narrowed. "Working within the

country on sabotage would also be an excellent way to rescue the Second Daughter."

"And the Prince of Jungali," she reminded him. Aniri knew Ash's life was less important to a raksaka committed to defending the crown of Dharia, but he needed to understand Ash's importance to *her*. And to any war effort. "It *is* the prince's skyship in which we're flying. And that is the only thing at the moment keeping the Samirians from simply bombing any part of Dharia they wish."

"Understood." Then his voice tempered. "I *am* sorry, Aniri. That Ash has been taken prisoner. I know that's a burden that must weigh heavily on you."

His soft tone threatened to spring back tears that had no place in this moment. "Then help me, Janak. I need to convince Nahali that subterfuge and stealth are the way to attack this problem. But I fear she will not see it in that light."

"She would not be unreasonable in this." Janak frowned. "Your mother—"

"My mother is in no shape to conduct a war!" It came out harsher than she intended, and suddenly, she had to turn away, examining the length of the skyship corridor as if it held great interest to her, not that she was simply trying to hide her tears of anger. And fear. A cold fire of hatred for the Second Son of Samir burned deep in her chest and beat back those other, softer feelings. She would have time for them later. Or there would be no need for them at all.

"I understand well your mother's condition." Janak's voice didn't have its usual bite, and this time Aniri almost wished for it. Longed for him to rebuke her silliness, to tell her that she was foolish to worry that the Queen might yet succumb to her wounds. That the Queen's assassin might yet succeed in his mission.

But there was no room for that, either.

"Once the First Daughter sees your mother and understands fully the situation," he continued, "I believe she will act in accordance with the Queen's wishes. Nahali has been training for this job all her life, Aniri. Have faith that she will act rightly when it falls to her."

Aniri looked back to him, searching his face. Where was this softer side of Janak coming from? Was it hidden by the tough raksaka exterior, now peeled back, exposed and raw by her mother's near death?

"I hope you're right. But I'm not sure you quite know Nahali the way I do."

He gave the barest of smiles. "No, I'm certain that I do not. A blessing of the gods, to be sure."

That almost wrenched a smile from her. Which only brought the tears rushing back to her face. She ducked her head away again. "I think I will retire to my cabin until we arrive. You should avail yourself of a short rest before we reach the capital as well." She said it, even though she knew he would ignore it.

"Yes, my lady." A whisper of sound, and when she looked up, Janak had slipped back into the captain's quarters. Back by her mother's side, where he would no doubt remain until the Queen was able to order him away herself.

Aniri drew in a deep breath and slowly walked the corridor toward the stairs and the room she shared with Priya on the deck below. She needed to pull herself together before she could hope to face her imperious eldest sister with anything close to the determination she would need to stand up to her.

And to win this fight that had found her in spite of all her efforts to prevent it.

Chapter Two

THE STIFF COLLAR of Aniri's Jungali sailor uniform chafed against her neck. Or perhaps it was First Daughter Nahali's cool stare that made her feel like a child in grown-up attire… and ready to crawl out of her skin with the scrutiny. For her part, Nahali was impeccably dressed in a deep red corset and muted orange skirts, with a proper traditional sweep of fabric draped perfectly over her shoulder. The corset was short, leaving plenty of room for the next-generation-Queen that Nahali carried in her growing belly. The large, blood-red jewel hanging to her forehead looked suspiciously like one of the royal ones their mother had commissioned especially for matters of state.

Aniri and Nahali stood on the highest tower of

the Queen's estate. Beyond the walls of the palace grounds lay Kartavya. Unlike the colorful streets of Bhakti, Jungali's capital, or the crowded, smoke-soaked avenues of the Samirian capital, Mahatvak, her home seemed sparse and scrubbed clean—an artificial emptiness, devoid of the nation's people or flavor.

In all her time growing up in the seclusion of the Queen's court, she had never given note to the fact that the city of Kartavya lay *outside* the walls of the palace—a sprawling metropolis kept at a distance from the royal compound—whereas the Jungali palace was snug within the fortified walls protecting Bhakti. Ash's balcony overlooked the streets where the people danced and traded and, in war time, fled to the security of his home. Even in Samir, the royal family lived in intimate contact with their people, with a mountain on one side and grand walls on all the others, protecting the people within their embrace. Of course, Dharia had always been a peaceful nation, united under a single Queen from the earliest days when nomadic tribes settled and started farming. Her country's past wasn't filled with warring provinces which finally united—as had been the case in the distant past for Samir, and more recently for Jungali. Still... the detachment of the royal court from the Dharian people seemed to place it hopelessly out of touch with the realities of the world.

Just like Nahali.

"I'm breathless with the speed you've taken to the Jungali ways, Aniri." Her sister shaded her eyes against the glare of the setting sun and peered up at the Jungali skyship. Although, for the moment, it was *Aniri's* ship—and apparently a warship, although ill-equipped for battles of any kind.

She decided to ignore Nahali's snide remark and get straight to the point. "The *Prosperity* is in desperate need of repairs. And if we're to have any hopes in another attack, we'll need armaments as well."

"Perhaps if we send the ship away, the threat of attack will recede as well." Nahali turned her cool stare back on Aniri.

She frowned. They didn't have time for this back-and-forth, pointless goading.

Their mother had already debarked, accompanied by Janak and a troop of six royal guards carefully carrying the stretcher with their injured Queen. The country's best healers were no doubt attending to her now, which lifted a burden from Aniri's heart and allowed her to focus on the dangers at hand. The narrow tower bustled with Jungali sailors bringing supplies to the skyship and returning empty-handed to the nearby stairwell to fetch more food, medicines, and the various clockworks and machinery Karan had ordered for a multitude of critical repairs. Fuel resupplying would have to wait as the tower was ill-equipped for moving crates of coal. A small fleet of pamgari would have been very useful in that effort. A reminder, once again, how Dharia would profit so much more from the Samir as partners, not enemies. And how ensuring Pavan took the crown was key to everything.

"We'll send the ship off for fuel soon enough," Aniri said. "We need to keep it moving so that it does not become a target. But sending it away only leaves the capital defenseless." How could her sister not see this? Why was she playing games?

Nahali glanced at the skyship again. "Is your burning glass operational? You seem to have joined the crew, so perhaps you can answer that question? Or should I consult with the captain or your Master Tinker?"

Aniri ground her teeth before answering. "The burning glass is one of the few undamaged parts."

"Excellent," Nahali said looking back to her. "Then our next steps are clear."

They are? Aniri's heart lifted, like a rush of ascent into the sky… but then she took her sister's meaning, and her hopes sunk just as quickly. Nahali couldn't possibly intend what Aniri thought.

"Don't look so shocked, little sister." The sneer on Nahali's face said she had every intention of shocking Aniri, hoping to get this inarticulate rise of outrage from her. That only added to Aniri's disbelief, but it finally dislodged the words from her throat.

"You mean to attack Samir with the burning glass." Even as the words floated like vapor in the evening air, she couldn't believe them. The burning glass rode on top of the skyship like a beautiful but deadly copper insect that collected the sun's heat and focused in one intense beam below the ship. It had nearly been used to burn the capital of Dharia to the ground. Surely, this was some taunt on Nahali's part, not a serious proposal to use the weapon. It was madness. An outright act of war. Not to mention that countless innocent people would die in the most horrific way. And the first on the list would be her future husband.

Their sister Seledri wouldn't be far behind.

No. Aniri head physically shook with the horror of it. "You can't possibly mean that." The words escaped without her permission. "What about Seledri?"

Nahali's demeanor changed, but only to gain a certain haughtiness that Aniri couldn't even fathom. "We will, of course, threaten the destruction of Samir's capital with the burning glass first, before actually carrying through with the act. They wouldn't dare touch Seledri, knowing we will burn down their palace in return."

"You don't know that! Or what capabilities they have." Aniri flung her arm at the half-broken skyship. "We barely have the means to stay afloat, much less carry through on that threat. And Natesh *knows* that. He personally conducted the bombings." Aniri gritted her teeth again. It was foolish to tackle Nahali on her own. She should have waited until Janak was able to join them. He would buttress her arguments and keep Nahali at bay with his wit, but Aniri couldn't bring herself to tear Janak away from the Queen's side just yet.

"What would you have me do, Aniri?" Nahali's glare became even more arrogant. "Give up the Queendom to save Seledri? I don't have the childish luxury of running off on adventures or risking war for my own whims. *You* are the one who brought this upon us, by interfering in the internal politics of another country. And Seledri knew the risks when she married Pavan."

"*What?*" Outrage stole Aniri's breath. "Seledri had no choice in that. None. She never did! How can you say—" Inarticulate anger choked off her words. Only the hint of a cruel smile on Nahali's face worked her tongue free. "She's your *sister*, Nahali!"

"She is *your* sister." A reddish color finally rose in Nahali's creamy brown cheeks. "Always it was the two of you. Always allied against me. The Third Daughter could get away with anything. And the Second Daughter… who ever expected anything of her but to be beautiful? And eligible. It was Seledri's duty to cement a bond between our countries…. a duty she apparently failed to perform. Yes, she managed to carry the First Son's child, but she never truly returned his affections. Don't tell me *that* didn't weaken our alliance. And me? I've always done what was asked. I've always carefully adhered to the labyrinth of rules, ones you could blissfully ignore. Because I was to be Queen, Aniri, and Queens don't play childish games or get caught in affairs with courtesans."

Aniri's mouth hung well and truly open, shocked into wordlessness again. Her fists curled tight. How could Nahali believe any of that was actually true? "I… how can you…"

"And now this war you've brought upon us. Don't think for one minute that I will risk a single Dharian life to save that barbarian husband of yours."

"I… we… we're not yet wed." Somehow those were the only words that could make it out of her mouth. And they were utterly wrong. Correct in fact, but completely *not* the lashing retort she wanted to unleash on Nahali.

"All the better."

It was hopeless. Beyond hopeless. Aniri would be better served trying to take on the entire Samirian sky navy with her bare hands and a cross bow. She straightened her back, uncurled her fists, and turned away from her sister with as much dignity as she could muster. She marched after one of the sailors disappearing into the darkened door of the palace tower.

"Do not run to the Queen like a child, Aniri," Nahali called after her. "She is in need of her rest, not your fanciful plans, whatever they are."

Aniri clomped down the stone steps, her heavy

boot sounds lost in the clatter of a dozen sailors traversing the same open sandstone stairwell.

Do not run to the Queen like a child… Of course, that was exactly what she had intended to do. The Queen, Janak, anyone who could make Nahali see reason.

Aniri stopped mid-flight on the stairs and pressed her back against the wall to let a sailor pass. She should go to the skyship now—*right now*—and fly away with it before Nahali could bend it to some purpose that would only result in more death: Ash's, Seledri's, who knew how many Dharians and Samirians. If Nahali threatened them with the fiery destruction of their capital, the Samirians would have no choice but to bring war to Dharia's doorstep as quickly as possible. Aniri had no doubt the Jungali sailors would fight bravely, but their ship was in no condition to wage anything but a losing battle.

She had always thought Nahali was so clever. She was so competent in all her studies, without effort mastering all the physicks of the inventive steamworks that were constantly changing their world. She could have been the most ingenious of tinkers. In fact, were she not preoccupied with matters of the court, she could easily captain a skyship. Or design a new and more capable one.

How could she be so insensible about matters of life and death?

It seemed a puzzle with a skyship-sized piece missing.

Aniri had never questioned Nahali's wisdom before. Perhaps because their mother had always been such a rock that Aniri never noticed the Queen's steadiness underneath them all, including Nahali. Aniri had assumed her sister would simply follow in their mother's confident footsteps, but now she could see she didn't know Nahali at all. Her sister had always been inscrutable, aloof, holding herself separate from her sisters. And, apparently, Aniri and Seledri had only made matters worse with their childhood slights. But that left Aniri without the tiniest understanding of what was driving the First Daughter into so eagerly embracing war. Nor the first idea of what to do about it.

A deep emptiness took hold of her. There shouldn't be such a gulf between her and her sister. Echoing in that chasm was a sharp whisper of fear—Natesh and Pavan were similarly torn apart, two brothers pitted against each other for the crown.

Dharia couldn't afford that, and Aniri wouldn't allow it to happen. Nahali was Queen, if only a temporary one, and Aniri would respect that, no matter the strife between them. But her sister was unmistakably angry in her newfound power, and that was a dangerous thing. Aniri had to find a way for Nahali to become the Queen her country truly needed.

She leaned back into the smooth, cool support of the stairwell wall. This day was impossibly long, and the weariness of it was taking hold of her. What she needed was rest and a clear head. And perhaps counsel from Janak… or her mother, once she had rested as well.

Then she could begin to piece together how to deal with her eldest sister.

Aniri waited for a clearing in the traffic of sailors servicing the ship, then made her way down to her room. Priya was already there, fussing through Aniri's things. The appointments of her room seemed like someone else's set of gowns and jewels and trinkets—they had no relevance to her life now.

"My lady!" Priya rushed over to her, carrying a dozen yards of gold-trimmed fabric that probably constituted a dress, but which was too bunched up in Priya's arms to be sure. Her handmaiden frowned at Aniri's Jungali uniform. "I'll find a suitable change of clothes for you immediately."

"I think I'd sooner be shot than put on whatever you have there, Priya." Aniri slowly unbuckled her saber and pistol and laid them on the mirrored table where Priya had prepared her a hundred times before—for teas or parties or other nonsense of the court. A sudden wash of weariness threatened to topple her where she stood. "In fact, I can't find a bed soon enough. I'll change in the morn."

Priya looked aghast. Aniri braced herself against the table, unsure if she could withstand even the slightest approbation from her handmaiden at the moment. Priya's horror faded into concern, and she tossed aside the gown to come stand by Aniri.

"Are you well, my lady? Should I fetch a healer?"

"Wearing a uniform to bed isn't cause for medical intervention, Priya." But Aniri's knees were balking at her orders to keep her standing. When she looked in the mirror, she could see Priya's source of concern. Aniri's face was scratched with a thousand small cuts, thanks to the briared bush outside the temple where the explosion had caught her and Ash about to exchange their vows. And she had the same drawn expression, the same gray tone, she had seen on Janak's face. The tears she thought she had hidden had somehow left shiny trails from the corners of her eyes.

She was looking at the war and its ravages, and it had only just begun.

Aniri pushed away from the table and stumbled to her bed with every intention of falling into it and hoping to awake into a world where her sister wasn't bent on worsening a war that had already torn apart Aniri's heart. When she reached the stout wooden post of her bed, she held onto it, steadying herself. Her head buzzed with the motion. She felt sick. She closed her eyes, waiting for it to pass.

When she opened them, Priya had appeared at her side, holding silken pajamas, black as night, and a soft, brown washcloth damp with something that smelled sweet, like flowers. The scent made Aniri even more light-headed when Priya pressed the cloth to her face, dabbing at her tiny wounds, but it soothed an ache she didn't know they were causing. Some oil or ointment must be in the cloth.

That knowledge revived her somewhat. "Nahali is going to use the skyship against Samir," Aniri said, her words dull and flat.

Priya finished her ministrations of Aniri's face and set the cloth down. "They have stolen your sister. And your husband." Her voice was soft, her gaze cast down to Aniri's uniform as Priya worked the dozen buttons loose. It melted Aniri's heart how her handmaiden referred to Ash as her husband even though it wasn't true. Or maybe it was true enough, in the ways that mattered.

"She will get them killed." Aniri lifted her arms so Priya could work the stiff fabric of the sailor's jacket free.

"The First Daughter isn't so skilled as my lady in the affairs of state." Priya slipped the silken pajama top over Aniri's head, momentarily blocking the shocked look on Aniri's face. First Daughter Nahali had spent her entire life training in the *affairs of state*, as her handmaiden put it. Even the Second Daughter, her sister Seledri, should know more than the Third. Aniri had never been expected to perform any royal duties. And yet, Priya was right in that Aniri had been thrust into more political situations in the last few weeks than she ever expected—or wanted—to deal with. Aniri composed her face again before her head emerged from the midnight fabric.

But she was certainly more awake now. "What do you mean, Priya?"

"Only that the First Daughter would not be Queen if it weren't for a Samirian raksaka assassin in Jungali." Priya kept her gaze to straightening Aniri's silk top, even though it had no need of it. "Nahali hasn't had the advantage of travel and circumstance the way my lady has." She raised her gaze to meet Aniri's. "Everyone knows it, my lady."

Aniri frowned. "You don't think she has the confidence of the people? But she's First Daughter..."

Priya picked up the silk pajama bottoms from the bed and brushed imaginary dust from the shiny fabric. "My lady has already been more of a Queen than the First Daughter of Dharia will ever be."

"That's not true, Priya."

Priya's face filled with mock outrage. "Is my lady calling mc a liar?"

Aniri let out a small huff of air. Then the weariness returned tenfold. "Priya, Nahali is Queen, at least for now. I have no official say in any of this. I'm not the Queen of anything. Ash and I are betrothed, not wed. The Jungali crew might listen to me, but even if I could command the skyship, I can't use it to threaten the Samir any more than Nahali can—that will only lead to more bloodshed. My sister doesn't understand all that is at stake here. Nor does she seem to care, at least when it comes to my future Jungali husband."

Priya held up the pajama pants to her. "My lady will find a way to make things right."

The resolution in Priya's eyes... the faith that somehow she could do this... bolstered Aniri. It was a tiny ray of hope. "You've never been wrong before, have you, Priya?"

"No, my lady. A lesson Mr. Karan is still learning."

A smile finally worked its way onto Aniri's face. "We must find a way to have you wed. He will surely learn it then." Aniri slipped her legs into the silken night clothes, and the feel of them against her skin was like breathing in a cloud of vapors. The weariness dragged her toward the bed.

"Don't let me oversleep, Priya," she said as she climbed onto the down-filled comforter.

"Bright and early on the morrow, my lady." She held up Aniri's Jungali sailor uniform, inspecting it. "I will have a uniform suitable to your work by then."

Aniri attempted a nod, but the pillow interfered,

so she simply closed her eyes instead. She would solve the problems of the world in the morn.

Chapter Three

THE MORNING CAME IN A BLINK. At first, Aniri thought Priya was waking her in some cruel insistence that she change into her night clothes. But then she remembered she had *already* changed. The sun assaulted her eyes through the thrown-open windows. She curled away from it, but awareness crept in anyway. The morning was here.

Time to face it.

Priya nearly dragged her from the bed, then helped her stumble through a haze of tasteless breakfast, a painful hair brushing and plaiting, and finally getting dressed. Aniri thought Priya had simply washed and aired her Jungali sailor uniform, but now the sleeves came to neat cuffs at her wrists and the coat tucked trimly at her waist. It fit her frame perfectly.

Aniri's eyebrows lifted. "You altered my uniform."

Priya stepped back to admire her handiwork. "It took a good part of the night, but my lady required clothes that befit her command."

A quick glance showed two small brass bars had been added to the collar—the designation of a captain. "Mr. Tarak will not be pleased about this." Aniri grinned, then quickly unclipped the bars and slid them into her pocket. "I'll be proud to wear these, if the need arises. For the moment, a simple uniform is more than sufficient. You're a wonder, Priya."

Her handmaiden made a small curtsey. Aniri nearly laughed, but instead she took a deep breath. "I would like to see my mother, if she's accepting visitors."

"I expected you might, my lady. Mr. Janak says she has awakened and is well enough for a visit whenever you have arisen."

Aniri let out a low breath. Simply the fact that her mother was awake worked fingers of relief through the tensed muscles of her back. She nodded, hesitated, then hugged Priya briefly. Her handmaiden was smiling broadly when Aniri turned and strode from the room.

The long walk to her mother's office brought stares from the household staff. Wearing a Jungali uniform in the palace no doubt made them wonder where her allegiances lay—was she still the Third Daughter of Dharia or would she wage war as a Jungali? The truth, she hoped, was *both*… and that she could convince First Daughter Nahali that Dharia and Jungali should be the strongest of allies, not just the newest ones.

With any luck, her mother would be roused enough to help convince Nahali—if not, Aniri would have to pull Janak from the Queen's side and enlist his aid.

Two guards were stationed at the door to her mother's office, a precaution no doubt put in place by Janak. And bitter reminder that assassins may yet seek to take the Queen from them. The guards' faces were impassive, but their eyes lingered a little too long on her uniform. She pushed open the door without answering their unspoken questions.

The Queen's office was empty, just the normal scattering of papers on her desk and the shrine of trinkets on the shelves from her father's voyages, including a vase of black sand that glittered in the morning light. Aniri's father had brought it back from Chira, the seaside resort where volcanic mountains edged the rocky eastern shores of Dharia, spilling inky lava and creating black diamond beaches. Her father had promised to take her there, but instead, her first visit had been in the dark of night as the *Prosperity* had refueled on the way to Samir. The country her father had chosen for a new home, and which now held him prisoner.

Aniri forced herself to look away, but a parade of emotions trampled her heart: anger that her mother still held onto these mementos, when her father had so clearly abandoned them long ago; bitterness that he had left them for the love of another woman; and guilt and fear that, if he still lived, he might be languishing in a Samirian dungeon, perhaps being tormented for any knowledge he may have.

Aniri blew out the burden of her feelings on a huff of air, then strode across the room to her mother's adjacent bedchamber and knocked on the door. Janak answered, pulling it open a small crack, then farther, once he saw it was only her.

"How is she?" Aniri asked quietly.

"Well enough to hear you whispering at the door," her mother called from inside the room.

Janak's ever-present scowl morphed into a hard-set frustration that ironically lifted Aniri's heart. If her mother was well enough to annoy Janak, then she was faring much better than Aniri had dared to hope. She pushed past Janak, hardly holding back her smile, and hurried across the room to her mother's enormous four-poster bed.

The Queen was cocooned in a ridiculous heaping of silk pillows—so many they couldn't be contained on the bed and spilled onto the floor. But the rosy hue on her mother's face wasn't simply a reflection of the red-tinged blankets and rose-tinted wall drapings. The gray grip of death had fled. Aniri paused at her bedside, barely restraining her urge to throw her arms around her mother. But when the Queen held out her arms, Aniri melted into her embrace, taking care not to squeeze anything that might give her pain.

"Mother," Aniri whispered into her unbound waves of dark, shining hair. "You gave us quite the scare."

Her mother squeezed her, weakly, before releasing her. "You'd be amazed what a little rest and a competent Dharian healer can accomplish."

Aniri pulled back and frowned.

"Oh!" her mother rushed to add. "Don't take

that as an affront to Jungali medicine, Aniri. It's just that we have more… *experienced* healers in Dharia."

Before Aniri could respond, another voice spoke up from the back of the room. "For which I am very grateful."

It was Nahali, standing near a Dharian healer. A cart of potions and medical instruments stood between them. Aniri had been so intent on the Queen, she had somehow missed them on the way in.

"Nahali." She tipped her head, not quite a bow, but enough recognition. She hoped.

Her sister didn't respond, just dismissed the healer with a flick of her hand. Janak held the door while the elderly woman scuttled out of the room.

As Nahali strode over to join her at their mother's bedside, she said, "So nice of you to join us, Aniri. I see you haven't had a chance yet to change. But I understand wanting to check on Mother first."

Heat rushed Aniri's face but she refused to let Nahali provoke her. This pointless warring between them had to stop. "The health of our mother hasn't left my thoughts since I found her bleeding in Janak's arms." Perhaps they could find common cause in their concern for the Queen.

Nahali sent a narrow-eyed glance to Janak at the door. "A failure that almost cost our Queendom dearly."

Or maybe not.

It took everything Aniri had not to come to Janak's defense. But as she struggled for words, her mother rustled quietly in her nest of pillows, drawing Aniri's attention and diffusing the anger building in her chest. The Queen was still frail, in spite of her words and apparently improved health, as each shaky movement revealed. She sat a little straighter, adjusting the pillows that fell to each side.

"Nahali," the Queen said quietly, not looking at her First Daughter. "I will not hear you cast aspersions on my raksaka again." She looked up, face serious but calm. "Is that understood?"

Aniri's eyes went wide. She couldn't recall her mother ever rebuking Nahali so coldly.

Nahali's jaw worked for a moment. "As you wish, Mother."

The whole interaction soared Aniri's hopes. Perhaps their mother would yet rein in Nahali's misguided ideas about the war and how to wage it.

"I didn't expect to find you awake," Aniri said in a rush, "much less so quickly recovered, Mother." She glanced at Nahali, who was still working to cool her anger. "I merely wanted to assure myself of the quality of your care. But if you're well enough…" Did she dare to just rush into it?

"Yes, we should absolutely discuss the war." Her mother's voice carried a level of gravity that settled Aniri's heart even further. The Queen may be in her sick bed, but surely this meant she was still in charge, not the First Daughter.

Her sister finally found her voice. "The Samirians have perpetrated an outrage, Mother. We can do nothing but respond with everything Dharia can bring to bear upon them." She glanced at Aniri. "Which, at the moment, includes the most feared weapon in three Queendoms. We would be remiss to not act swiftly. Indeed…" This time her look for Aniri was more of a sneer. "I do not understand why we haven't already made haste for the Samirian border, giving chase to those who would dare to assault our Queen. An immediate price should have—"

"Nahali." Again, a single word from the Queen stilled Aniri's eldest sister, choking her words off in a way that turned her bronzed cheeks red.

"We were unable to pursue at the time," Aniri said softly, reminding her mother, in case she didn't remember in her sickness all that had occurred in the aftermath. "We were badly damaged. We were in no condition to answer Natesh's demands with a military rebuke." She left unsaid that Seledri and Ash were on the *Dagger*. She couldn't harm the Samirians' ship without risking their lives as well.

"Yes, the Second Son made his demands." Nahali's anger still seethed in her voice. "And we have yet to respond. He makes a mockery of us." She turned to the Queen. "Mother, you have to see that every moment he holds Seledri captive, every hour in which there is no price for assaulting our Queen, they grow stronger. Bolder. If we don't retaliate—"

Their mother held up her hand, and Aniri's heart clenched to see it shake. But it stopped Nahali in her tirade.

"We can't simply burn down their capital, your Majesty," Aniri said, trying to keep her voice from rising like Nahali's. "Even the threat of it is a risk to Seledri and Ash. We don't know the Samirians' skyship capabilities, not truly, or even the actual state of the fight for the crown. It might still be possible to avert the war altogether. If there were a battle from within, one encouraged by our assistance to the First Son, the rightful heir, we could turn the Samirians back into allies. We don't even know where the Queen Mother falls in her temper about this. She has been quiet throughout."

Her mother let out a long sigh. "I imagine the Queen Mother is despairing that her sons are battling for her crown."

Aniri's hopes lifted again. "Perhaps she can rein in the Second Son—"

Nahali cut her off. "Perhaps the Second Son is carrying out her wishes."

Aniri faced her sister. "Would she allow one Son to assassinate her grandchild in the womb? This can't be—"

"You don't know what's actually happened—"

"And neither do you—"

"Enough." The Queen's quiet voice silenced them both. "We will answer the Samirians' attack, but in our time, in our way. We will not rush to act. Especially any action for which we are ill prepared and which may have consequences that we cannot properly estimate as yet." That rebuke was for Nahali, who withdrew from it and appeared ready to storm from the room… yet she held still a few paces from the bed. The Queen turned to Aniri. "How soon can the *Prosperity* be ready for whatever mission we may give it?"

Aniri was tempted to stretch the truth—to say

that the *Prosperity* was irreparably damaged in order to stop Nahali from using the burning glass—but her mother's rosy glow had already started to fade. She didn't know how long her mother could endure their fighting… or this planning for war while still in her sick bed.

Instead, Aniri rushed out the truth, as well as she knew it. "A few days, maybe more. We were slowed by a lack of proper facilities and the need to get aloft again in case Natesh returned to attack. A stop just over the border gained us fuel enough to reach Kartavya, but we didn't have time or resources for repairs. Given those, I'm sure Karan could repair the ship within a few days, maybe a week to completely replace all the damaged parts of the hull and bridge."

"These repairs," her mother said, wearily. "Do we need to return to Jungali or can they be made here in the capital? Or would the naval ports be more suitable?"

The naval ports. The eastern shores of Dharia, where the distance between Dharia and Samir was shortest and where the sea-going Dharian Navy resided.

"Definitely the ports," Aniri said. "When they were building the skyship, Karan and his tinkers used modified naval machinery retrofitted for the *Prosperity*." She was thinking of the star navigator, but the ports should have everything Karan could wish for. Plus diverting the skyship for repair would delay any action Nahali might convince her mother to take.

"Very well." The Queen took a breath, and guilt wrenched Aniri's chest for the toll she could see this conversation was already taking. "I will begin making diplomatic overtures to Samir, starting with an announcement that their raksaka have failed in their attempt to assassinate me."

"Diplomatic overtures!" Nahali stepped forward again and caught hold of the sheer ruffle above the Queen's bed, as though the filmy fabric were the only thing holding back her outrage. "They tried to kill you, Mother!"

"Yes, I'm well aware of that," their mother said. "Although my understanding is that Second Son Natesh is behind the attempt, and for all we know, he has a tenuous, possibly unapproved, command of their nascent Sky Navy… however many ships strong that may be." She took another deep breath, only this one seemed more of a wheeze.

Aniri's heart clenched at the sound.

Janak appeared by her side. "Amala?" It was less

a question than a warning filled with tender concern.

Nahali frowned at the familiarity, looking rapidly between Janak and their mother. It reminded Aniri how little her sister knew about the state of things, not only between Janak and her mother, but regarding their father as well.

The Queen held up her hand, then put it down when it trembled. "I will rest in a moment, Janak." She looked up at Nahali. "Dharia will not throw away a hundred years of peace on one attack by a belligerent Second Son who may or may not have been sanctioned by the crown or have command of his nation's military. I will demand that our ambassador in Samir meet with the First Son—to make sure he is still alive, and in preparation for a full-scale diplomatic mission, as soon as I am able to travel."

"And while you are making full-scale *diplomatic* demands," Nahali said, voice full of righteous anger, "the Samirians could well be launching a full-scale *military* attack on Dharia."

"Which is why, my First Daughter, I will be sending you with the *Prosperity* to our naval ports. Not only do we need a fully operational skyship capable of devastating retaliation in the wake of an attack, but I need your evaluation on how quickly we can build a skyfleet of our own. As well as how fast we can modify our current ground cannons, build more of the floating mines we deployed previously, and develop any other weaponry we can turn into defensive measures against an incoming fleet of skyships. You will take the Jungali Master Tinker with you and have every resource that you need."

"You're… you're sending me to the *docks?*" Nahali couldn't be more incredulous if the Queen had suggested she fly directly to one of the twin moons hanging in the aether. "While you call for diplomatic talks with the Samirians."

"If I cannot yet avert this war," said the Queen, "then any hope of surviving will depend on your success in developing war machines to win it." Her voice softened. "I am sending you, Nahali, because you are most capable of saving us in this way. You have a brilliant tactical mind, my First Daughter. Please follow my wishes in this."

Aniri watched Nahali's face transform into a mask of steely determination, the kind their mother's usually wore like royal armor. She had no doubt Nahali would go to the docks, as ordered, and use every means at her disposal to assemble the weapons necessary to defeat the Samirians.

But she was *not* happy about it.

"Of course, your Majesty," Nahali said with a small bow.

Aniri tried to keep her relief inside, so as not to provoke her eldest sister any further.

"You may leave as soon as you are ready." The Queen waved a weary hand in Nahali's direction. Her sister bowed again, then hesitated, as if she were unsure whether their mother was dismissing them from the room or not.

Aniri looked to Janak for guidance.

He was already at the door to let them out.

Aniri turned to go, but her mother's tremulous voice stopped her. "Aniri, wait. I would have a word with you."

The anger in Nahali's gaze felt like a burning glass trained on Aniri's back. Her sister let her glare linger before turning and nearly stomping from the room. Janak quietly closed the door behind her, then quickly crossed the room to return to the Queen's side.

"Amala, you need to rest. Let me send for the healer again. She can give you…" He trailed off when her mother shook her head.

"Janak, dear," she said with a small laugh.

"Even for a raksaka, you have become an excessive worrier."

Aniri was surprised at the endearment, but that gentle rebuke didn't deter Janak in the slightest. "I only worry for Queens who overestimate their recovery." He eased to sitting on the bed at the Queen's feet, another familiarity that made Aniri raise her eyebrows. It wasn't her business to know what had transpired between them, but that didn't keep her curiosity from nearly leaping from her lips to ask.

"I promise to rest again soon," the Queen said with a sigh. Then she turned to Aniri. "I need your help, my Third Daughter."

"Anything." Aniri said it without hesitation, although she wasn't at all sure what her mother was going to ask.

"Your sister, Nahali… she's not quite ready to be Queen."

Aniri's shoulders relaxed. "I'm glad I'm not the only one who sees it."

"Do not misunderstand me. She will make a very capable Queen, one day. But she sees you and your accomplishments… and she is very threatened. She thinks you have my favor, and she is not far wrong." Her mother grimaced, then closed her eyes.

Aniri feared she was in pain again. She shuffled closer and laid a hand on her mother's limp one, lying in her lap. "Is there something I can get you, Mother?"

She opened her eyes and turned her hand to hold Aniri's. "I need you to help Nahali."

Aniri frowned. She was probably the last person in the world Nahali wanted help from. "Help her at the docks? Perhaps I could be of more help in your diplomatic endeavors. I've just returned from Samir —" Aniri cut herself off when her mother's hand gave her a weak squeeze. It was so shaky… a lump formed in Aniri's throat.

"I need your help in more ways than one." Then she wheezed and pressed her eyes shut again, as if fighting pain.

Aniri's heart seized. Was her mother worse off than she thought? Was the rosy show of good health just an act she put on for Nahali? As Aniri bent closer, it became clear that the pink tinge in her mother's cheeks was entirely artificial. Makeup covered the gray pallor that lay just below the creamy tint… and now it was fading, just like her mother's voice.

"Mother." Aniri's own voice was a gasp. This time it was Aniri's hand that shook, a tremble taking hold of her entire body.

The Queen took a deep breath, one that seemed to reach to the very depths of her being, then opened her eyes. "I am still recovering, Aniri. With any luck from the gods, I will fully regain my health. In case I do not, I need you to assist your sister in becoming the Queen she is capable of—and that Dharia needs."

Tears threatened Aniri's eyes. "You are our Queen."

"Someday, maybe soon, that will be the First Daughter's job. And I'm afraid it may not be in the best of circumstances. You must help your sister find her way, Aniri."

Aniri nodded, pushing back the tears.

Her mother shifted again, obviously seeking comfort and not finding a spot that would bring it. "I will endeavor to stay alive until she is ready. In the meantime, I will pursue my diplomatic efforts with Samir, but mainly as a cover for you and Nahali in your work."

"I will assist Nahali in any way I can in building our military readiness."

"I have a different mission for you." The Queen

coughed, a movement that shook her entire body. "I am relying on you to defeat the Samirians from within."

"A civil war?" Aniri glanced at Janak, who gave her an encouraging nod. So… he *had* been working to help her after all. "You want me to work to ensure Pavan wins the crown."

"Whatever it takes, Aniri," she said, softly. "I want our Seledri back home. Or safely in her own country by her husband's side. But no matter what, you cannot let this war proceed. In spite of what I said to Nahali, if we are forced into war, I fear that we will not survive it. The Samirians have many advantages against us. We will, of course, fight them with everything we have, and Dharia has many resources as well. But there will be much bloodshed on both sides, and the chances are good that Samir will prevail in the end. You must do everything you can to stop it from coming to that."

Aniri's head spun. How would she do this? Infiltrate the country? Find Pavan? That was a good place to start. But then she would need to discover the hiding place of the skyship… or *skyships* if there were several. Which also meant finding the source of their navia… "I have several ideas of how to accomplish this. We could—"

Her mother held up her hand. "I knew you would, Aniri." She gave a small smile that almost brought life back to her face. "But you needn't tell me. And if you're to be successful, your mission should remain secret... even from your sister. She may not see the wisdom of pursuing both paths at once."

Aniri nodded, her thoughts racing even faster on a wind of hope.

"By your leave, your Majesty," Janak said, his voice cool. "I will accompany Aniri on her mission. There is a Second Son I would very much like to assassinate."

The Queen's hand still lay in Aniri's, and she urged Aniri closer with it. Ignoring Janak, her mother whispered in a voice Aniri was certain Janak could still hear. "He will want to avenge me. Very badly. You must not allow it. Unless it is your only option or if war looms regardless. Then take him out."

Wide-eyed, Aniri gave a slow nod. Janak's dark eyes were hard as coal. Would he heed Aniri's order to stop? Should she even give it? Her heart understood exactly the desire for vengeance that burned in Janak's eyes. She wasn't sure she could stop *herself* from running a blade through Natesh, given a chance. But looking back to the Queen, Aniri could see she was still waiting for her agreement.

"I'll do my best, your Majesty." It was all she could truly promise, anyway.

The Queen leaned back against the headrest of her bed with a satisfied smile. "I knew I could count on you, Aniri." Her mother's eyes drifted shut, and her smile went slack.

The lump in Aniri's throat prevented her from saying anything. Which was just as well, as words had fled her. A soft touch landed on her shoulder. Janak tipped his head away, motioning Aniri to follow him. They both quietly eased away from the bed. The Queen didn't stir, apparently already captured by sleep, or at least a deep fatigue.

Janak walked her to the door, but clearly had no intention of going farther.

Aniri asked a silent question. *Are you coming?*

"In a few moments." He said it with mournful eyes that begged for understanding. He was lingering to say his final goodbyes. As if he didn't expect the Queen to be here when he returned. *Or he didn't intend to return from the mission at all.*

Aniri's breath caught in her throat, but she nodded, and quietly left, giving them room for their farewells.

She lingered outside the closed door, back resting against the wall, eyes closed. Her orders were to destabilize the Samirian government and ensure Pavan wore the crown. With any luck, they would rescue Ash and Seledri in the process. Failing that, she would let Janak eliminate the threat of Natesh.

You must help your sister find her way, Aniri.

It shocked her that the Queen would ask this. When did Aniri become the one the Queen confided in? The one she turned to? It was as though Aniri and Nahali had switched places. Her mother said Nahali was threatened by her, and Aniri could see it in the cold stares, the bracing retorts. Her sister's tongue had never been so sharp. But the First Daughter had always been the one destined to be Queen. Even now, that is what her mother insisted would happen. Just like Seledri, Nahali's fate had always been predetermined. Of the three Daughters, only Aniri had ever been free to make her own choices. To pursue her own fate. Even when she felt trapped by duty, or the possible neglect of it, she had always had the *choice*.

And now... now, the First Daughter was being upstaged by the Third. Aniri could suddenly see it: her eldest sister feared Aniri would take the one thing that had always been hers, and hers alone. *The Queen's favor.*

Aniri's heart softened. She didn't want the crown... any crown, really, but especially not the Dharian crown. It belonged to Nahali. Aniri merely needed to convince her sister that she had no intention of stealing. And help Nahali become the Queen Dharia needed in the face of the first war in a hundred years.

Somehow, that last order seemed most daunting of all.

Chapter Four

ANIRI WATCHED the golden waves of Dharian wheat turn into hazy blue waves of water in the distance: the *Prosperity* was approaching the eastern shores of Dharia, where they would land at the naval ports and attempt more substantial repairs than Karan had been able to effect at the capital. The bridge windows were still sheer fabric and the chilled air at their altitude kept the crew warming their hands in between their duties.

"How long until we land, Mr. Karan?" Aniri asked.

He gave a final quiet instruction to the crewman at the bank of instruments along the back then strode over to the plotting table. With a glance to the timepiece lying there, he said, "We should start our descent in about a half an hour, fresh. Ease her down slow this time. I still don't like the leaks we have in the gas bag."

Aniri gave a nod. "Do you expect Mr. Tarak to be done giving my sister her tour by then?" Nahali had disappeared with the captain shortly after she boarded, and Aniri hadn't seen her since. But before they reached port, she needed to have a word alone with her.

"I expected Mr. Tarak to be done an hour ago." Karan rubbed the back of his neck. "Not sure what's of such interest to the First Daughter in engines."

Aniri frowned. Her sister was probably instructing Mr. Tarak in all the deficiencies of his boilers and controls. But she was trying to respect that Nahali was the heir-apparent for a very injured Queen. "I can only imagine." She looked back to the window, avoiding Karan's questioning look.

The long piers of the naval port stuck out from the coast like white pillars fallen into the sea. To the north was a rise of dark mountains, the beginning of the chain that led to the Jungali provinces. Farther up the coast, to the north of the ports, she could just see the black sand beaches of Chira sparkling like jeweled snakes washed up on the waves. This was the closest she'd come to seeing them in the daytime, so she took a moment to admire their exotic beauty from afar. Someday, she wanted to bring Ash here. It would make for the perfect honeymoon. They could hide away in a tiny cabin perched among the lava flows that spilled like frozen black rivers into the sea. Chira was filled with cozy inns accustomed to granting privacy to couples on getaways.

An ache in her chest crept up and threatened to crush her heart. That sort of daydreaming was dangerous to indulge in. She tugged her Jungali naval uniform smooth and stood straighter.

A shuffle of boots and a soft whisper of silk skirts drew her attention from the beaches below. Captain Tarak stumbled onto his own bridge, his feet dragging while the rest of him desperately tried to make room for Nahali's wide skirts as they passed through the narrow bulkhead door. The First Daughter steeled her expression and checked her pace, allowing Tarak to gain his balance again before proceeding. Her silk slippers were silent, and her head held high as she strode onto the bridge. She glanced around as if she expected a trumpet to announce her presence.

Mr. Tarak's gaze met Aniri's, and she had never

seen him more desperate. Or terrified. Or possibly harried beyond reason. Even more so than back in Jungali, when he thought Aniri had come aboard to relieve him. He took three steps back, disengaging from Nahali's sphere of influence and glancing at the bulkhead door as if longing for escape.

Aniri sighed. *What has Nahali been putting the crew through?*

Nahali cleared her throat and sent an imperious look to Aniri, as if she expected *Aniri* to announce her highly royal presence.

Very well.

Aniri resisted the temptation of a smart remark and merely said, "Nahali, may I present Mr. Karan, Master Tinker of Jungali."

Karan lifted a bushy eyebrow at the whole interplay. Her sister's intense gaze raked across the full height and breadth of the man, which was impressive by any standards, but certainly loomed larger than poor Mr. Tarak. Karan coolly returned Nahali's examination of him with skeptical look for her jewels and corset and voluminous skirts.

After a tense moment, he politely said, "Welcome aboard the *Prosperity*." Then he gestured to the cramped quarters of the bridge. "She's a right wreck at the moment—ye should watch yer step with those silk shoes—but don't let that throw ye. We'll have her in top shape not long after we've made port."

"I certainly hope so, Mr. Karan." Nahali's gaze locked into some kind of contest of wills with the massive tinker… which only made tension crawl up Aniri's back. "We don't exactly have time to spare."

Karan's returned her stare with a rock hard one of his own. "Right ye are about that, missy."

Aniri bit her lip.

Nahali looked like she wanted to skewer Karan with the closest blade. "What did you call me?"

Karan's eyebrows both rose this time. "No offense intended." He gave the barest of bows with his head. "*Yer Majesty.*" A small smirk danced across Karan's face and then disappeared. "We don't stand much on protocol here on the *Prosperity.*"

Nahali gave a look of disgust. "Perhaps, once we arrive, the Dharian Naval officers can give your crew a few lessons in how a true navy operates."

Karan's eyes narrowed. "Lessons in protocol don't rate highly on the list of things that need fixin' around here. And, as I hear it…" Karan glanced at Aniri. "… we've got a bit of a war to wage. Thought maybe we'd be working on that together. Perhaps I understood wrong. In which case, I'll be dropping ye with yer Naval Officers and taking my ship to a proper skyharbor for repairs."

"*Your* ship?" Nahali asked archly.

"Aye. Or Prince Malik's ship, if you prefer. But I'll be hanged before I hand it over to the Dharian Navy." He folded his beefy arms across his expansive chest. "Yer majesty."

Aniri scrambled to save the situation. "No one's said anything about handing the skyship over to the Dharian Navy, Karan. We're just getting needed supplies from them. They can *help*."

"Not sure yer the one to know, fresh." His stare was for Nahali.

Her sister blinked. The glance she threw to Aniri was, for the first time, uncertain. Like she had just realized she was rapidly snarling the entire plan the Queen had laid out for them. After all, if the crew of the *Prosperity* weren't willing to cooperate—in protecting Dharia with the skyship or helping the Dharian Navy design skyships of their own—Dharia was dead in the water. And completely vulnerable to Samir.

Nahali swallowed, then inclined her head. "Of course, Aniri is right. I didn't mean to imply that the Dharian Navy would, in any way, be appropriating the skyship. You have my assurance that will not happen."

Karan softened his stance, but his arms remained locked over his chest. "We could just refuel and be on our way. Prince Malik isn't here… however, if he were, I'm sure he would favor us working with the Dharian Navy. He'd say we've technology to help ye win this war, and ye have a bounty of resources we're a bit short on. It'd fare us both well to work together."

Aniri held back from saying something, a lump rising suddenly in her throat. Karan was exactly right: Ash would want them working together, not sniping at each other on his broken skyship bridge.

Nahali glanced to Tarak, still hovering by the bulkhead door. "You have done an impressive job of adapting sea-going technology for the air." She looked back to Karan. "There is much we can learn from you. Indeed, the Queen sent me here to do just that. Mr. Tarak was helpful in engines, but I'm very concerned about the operation of the gas bag."

As she spoke, the arrogance in Nahali's voice slowly faded, replaced by the lecturing voice Aniri remembered from numerous "lessons" the First Daughter liked to give the Second and Third, back when they were just children dashing around the palace and pretending at running the Queendom. Only for Nahali, it was never pretend—it was always serious business and strategy and, apparently now, aeronautics.

And it was exactly Karan's language.

"Aye, I've been a tad concerned as well," he said, eyes widening a bit. "But it's not as dreadful as it looks. The ship's got more than one gas bag, ye see. There's a host of compartments, cells all fed by a central reserve."

Nahali stepped closer, resting one hand on the plotting table. "So if you sustain a hit, you're not likely to lose all of this lighter-than-air gas that gives you lift. What is it called again?"

"Navia," Karan said with a smile. "And it's right precious, so yes, we strive to keep what we've got. The outer cells are filled with air, which helps with ballasting, while the inner ones hold the navia. Hit the bag deep enough, and yer going down, but minor damage it can sustain and still keep afloat."

Nahali nodded, one finger tapping her chin in thought. "Kartavya's nearly at sea level—the air is thicker, which gives the navia even more float. But I can't imagine you vent out the gas in order to land…"

"Aye. Ye know yer physicks." Karan grinned, nodded his approval, then glanced to Mr. Tarak. "I bet ye were running the captain through his paces in engines."

A blush crept up Nahali's cheeks. Aniri's mouth dropped open.

Nahali dipped her head. "Mr. Tarak was most helpful in appeasing my curiosity."

Karan nearly snorted a laugh. "I'll wager he was." Then he tamed his smile. "But yer right about landing being a challenge. And when we burn fuel, the ship just keeps getting lighter as well. We'd darn near lift up to the sun if we didn't keep a careful control over our float."

"But how do you accomplish it?" Nahali was completely absorbed with Karan now. It was as if the rest of the bridge, including Aniri, had ceased to exist.

"Usually by routing the steam through a set of tubes to heat the navia itself. Cooling's just the opposite. We flush the tubing with air. It's a bit of a dance, and it doesn't always respond as fast as I'd like. When we need a right quick lift, we can dump our water ballast..." He glanced at Aniri. "... or something a tad heavier, like an entire load of coal."

"That sounds… problematic," Nahali said.

"Aye. But it's not a problem unless someone starts blasting holes in my ship. You'll see it in action as we descend into the naval port." Karan turned to the captain. "Mr. Tarak, how about you start that landing procedure now?"

Tarak scuttled across the room to the instrument panel and the sailors working it.

Karan returned his attention to Nahali. "Ballasting's one of the trickier parts of shepherding this beauty through the sky."

"I'll be keen to look at your drawings, if you have them," Nahali said.

Karan beamed as if she had just handed him an unexpected birthday present. Aniri was very tempted to let them continue their technical parrying—they shockingly had both landed in their element, and together, might yet accomplish Nahali's mission of preparing for war—but she still needed to speak with her sister before they reached port. And before Aniri departed on her own mission.

"Nahali," she said, drawing both their attention. Aniri tilted her head toward the hall. "May I have a word with you?"

Nahali stiffened, her royal demeanor apparently

flushing back with the reminder that Aniri was still standing nearby, but she didn't argue.

Instead, she tipped her head to Karan. "We'll have to resume this discussion once we've docked. I've several ideas for armaments as well."

"I would imagine." His smile quirked as he bowed in return. "Yer Majesty."

Nahali's skirts swept the bridge floor as she turned toward the hall. Aniri gave a pointed look to Karan before following her out, but he was already examining his maps on the plotting table, chuckling to himself.

Nahali stopped just outside the bridge, waiting for her.

"Not here," Aniri said. "I have to stop by my room to change before we debark anyway. Let's talk there."

Nahali frowned, hesitated, then followed Aniri as she hurried down the metal-grated stairs to the next level. "I don't understand—"

Aniri cut her off with a raised hand, and then a finger to her lips.

Nahali pursed hers but didn't speak again until they reached Aniri's cramped sailor's cabin. It was small, but plenty large enough for the short trip. With the door closed, and her aetheroceiver case occupying the small bench, there was only the cot on which to sit. They both remained standing.

"I'm not staying with you at the naval port," Aniri said.

Nahali scowled. "Of course not. You wouldn't want to do something *useful*, like help us prepare for this war you've tipped off."

Aniri gritted her teeth. The Queen wanted as few people in their confidence about Aniri's mission as possible, but her mother didn't understand... Nahali *needed* to know.

"I'm going to Samir," Aniri said. "My mission will be to destabilize the country and possibly win our sister's freedom." *And Ash's...* but that wouldn't be helpful to emphasize.

"You're *what?*"

"It's by the Queen's orders."

Nahali took a step back and bumped her head into the low-lying brass tube running along the ceiling. "She didn't mention to me anything about—"

"She wanted it kept from you."

Nahali's jaw worked, her face pinking up with anger, but she didn't say anything. Finally, she pressed the back of her hand to her lips and turned half away from Aniri, hiding her face.

In a hoarse voice, she said, "The Queen favors

you now." It was said with a despair that wrenched Aniri's heart.

She closed the space between them and touched Nahali's arm. Her sister jerked away from her, shoulders caving in, as if she would melt into the closed bulkhead door.

"Nahali, the Queen doesn't favor me. And even if she did, I don't want the crown. I never did and I never will."

Nahali flinched, then slowly uncurled and faced Aniri. "I am still First Daughter."

Her eyes were shining with tears that further clamped a vise around Aniri's heart. How could she make Nahali understand?

Before Aniri could think of what to say, Nahali thrust her chin forward. "If Mother wants to confide in you now, fine. If, from her sickbed, she chooses you to lead Dharia, I will respect it. But she is ill, Aniri. Gravely so. She may not live long enough to do so."

Aniri's eyes widened.

Nahali's face twisted into a pained smirk. "Oh yes, I know… I know her better than you ever will. She did not fool me for one moment with her makeup and her false bravado. She may well die, and instead of attending to her, I have to be *here*. As much as that pains me, I will follow her wishes and do the one thing she would truly want: defend Dharia at all costs. Regardless of whatever adventure you are chasing in Samir, if our mother can no longer act as Queen, I will step in and do what's right for Dharia. *No matter what.*"

Nahali stopped in her tirade, her eyes flashing, daring Aniri to defy her. That *no matter what* included Seledri's life, Aniri was sure of it. She had to fight to hold the cry of protest welling up in her chest.

"Of course," Aniri said, keeping her voice calm. "Dharia is lucky to have a future Queen who loves her country so much."

Nahali blinked, a confused twitch flashing across her brow.

"I know that Mother may not be alive by the time I return." Aniri's voice broke. She coughed to cover it. "I know that you will, sooner or later, become our Queen. This is why I'm confiding in you, Nahali. You need to know everything, so you may govern effectively."

The twitch took hold of Nahali's shoulders, and she leaned away from Aniri.

A small lurch in the floor and a drop in Aniri's stomach signaled they were descending from the

Dharian skies to the naval ports below. They hadn't much time left.

"Nahali," she said softly. "You're the Queen Dharia needs. And I will back that with everything I have, I promise you. But for now, I need to follow our mother's wishes, too. Which means going to Samir and doing all I can there. But before I go… there's one more thing you should know. Something I suspect the Queen would rather take to her grave than tell you."

"More secrets just for her Third Daughter?" Nahali's anger was rising again, but it was weaker, confused.

Aniri let out a small laugh. "No." She shook her head. "She would never have told me either. I discovered it myself."

The anger fell off Nahali's face then, and it opened in curiosity. It was almost girlish in this intrigue, and it reminded Aniri of the time when Nahali discovered that the automaton in the fencing hall could actually be taken apart. She had looked upon it with wonder. It was Nahali's wide-eyed need to know that gave Aniri hope—perhaps she might hear this without being crushed by it. Regardless, she needed to know, especially if the Queen passed away. And it was entirely possible Aniri would never return from Samir.

"What is it?" Nahali asked.

Aniri swallowed and braced herself. "Our father is alive." At least, Aniri hoped that was still true. "And he's been captured by the Second Son of Samir."

Chapter Five

THE DHARIAN PORT smelled of commerce, not war.

Aniri leaned on the salt-covered wooden railing of the pier and inhaled the pungent mix of sea spray, ocean creatures freshly caught, and coal-burning ships chugging in from their journeys across water. The sea lapped calmly on the pylons below her, but the wharf that embraced it was a hive of activity. Fishermen in rubber boots unloaded cargo-laden skiffs, merchants in cloaks inspected their clockwork goods just off-loaded from trade ships, and sailors in Dharian uniform grabbed land-based chow from vendors before heading back to their ships. A myriad of fishing boats and trade ships glinted brass and puffed steam in the noon-time sun. In the distance, the few warships of the

Dharian fleet suddenly seemed small and wholly insufficient to Aniri.

Like targets for a passing skyship.

The *Prosperity* had docked inland, tied down in an open field not far from the piers. Its billowing blue gas bag was easily seen over the small village that surrounded and served the port, but most of the townspeople were busy in their work and either didn't notice or gawked for a moment before returning to their business.

Aniri only wished a skyship could be so easily disregarded and not feared.

Janak strode across the pier toward her, scattering water birds in his approach. Even with his heavy, steel-riveted boots, his footfalls were silent. He no longer wore his tell-tale raksaka uniform, trading his light-stealing black wrappings for the high-collared linen shirt, rough leather vest, and billowing cloak of a Samirian merchant. The low-slung pistol holster and daggers strapped to his sides only marked him as someone who traded valuable goods that might need protection from the unscrupulous. Aniri was similarly armed and clad, her Jungali sailor uniform safely stowed onboard the *Prosperity*. Her new attire seemed to disguise her well enough as she hadn't yet attracted attention on the pier. Then again, perhaps it was the dozen small scratches crisscrossing her cheeks that made her appear more sea-faring merchant than royalty.

She brushed back the hood of her cloak as Janak approached. He set down the small case that held the aetheroceiver they would use to keep in touch with Karan. They would carry little else, to stay light and able to move quickly.

"Has Karan had any luck contacting our fellow merchants in Samir?" she asked, speaking somewhat in code. There were too many people nearby to speak openly about the spies Prince Malik had at the Samirian docks, some of whom would also trust Karan, especially once news had spread about the prince's disappearance.

"One remains on good terms," Janak said, and Aniri's heart sunk. Ash's spies wouldn't be much help in finding the prince if they had been captured as well. "He's agreed to meet us upon our arrival, but beyond that, I'm not sure what business we'll be able to conduct."

That didn't sound good.

"We may have to seek other business partners, then," Aniri said. Perhaps they could call on Riva, Devesh's friend. She had already helped them once, and she seemed the type to have an ear to the ground. Outside of her, the few people Aniri trusted in Samir were most likely languishing in a dungeon somewhere.

Janak nodded. "In related news, many of the day's trade ships have already departed for Samir, and passenger vessels present the difficulty of Samirian customs on the other end. I've found one trade ship that has been delayed and may yet grant us passage. However, they're departing shortly. We need to make haste."

He turned without waiting for her agreement, picking up the case again. She followed on his heels, weaving through the bustling commerce that made Dharia the richest and most stable of the three Queendoms. The ship Janak spoke of turned out to be a muscular steamer, as large as any Dharian naval vessel, but built for hauling cargo across the short sea to Samir. Black clouds chugged from the thick smokestack in the center of the metal-clad ship, and a steel crane lowered bulky wooden crates into the hold. Samir held an advantage in clockwork and new technology, but Dharia held her own in the standard steamworks. Their nation was driven to prosperity by not only the transport of crops, but manufactured goods across the land and sea.

Aniri and Janak boarded across a shaky but wide walkplank only to be stopped by a stocky sailor with arms like tree trunks. He wore the snug wool cap and high-necked work shirt of a merchant marine—the kind who manned commerce ships that could be counted on in times of war to aid the Dharian Navy in the transport of goods and personnel. They hadn't been called upon to do so in a hundred years, and Aniri suspected they took advantage of aid from the crown mostly to fortify their hulls and arm their ships against pirates—not that they truly expected to serve in wartime.

That may change sooner than they think.

"I would speak to your captain about gaining passage to Samir," Janak said.

"We're not a passenger vessel." Aniri could barely make out the man's words. They were more like grunts.

"Understood," Janak said. "But we've business to conduct that I'd rather didn't go through Samirian customs."

The man's weathered face carved out a scowl. "We're not smugglers either."

"We'll pay you handsomely." Janak's voice tipped up. To anyone else, he probably still sounded cool and collected, but Aniri could hear the tension beneath it. How many nights had he been without sleep? How many hours had he sat by the Queen's bedside, watching her in pain? Even a raksaka had his limits, and this sailor was standing between Janak and his opportunity to seek vengeance on Natesh—something Aniri knew lay at the heart of everything that moved Janak now. It was a dangerous thing to do.

"Nor are we profiteers." The merchant marine took a step forward and flexed his beefy hands. "You best be on your way."

Janak's hand twitched but otherwise he didn't move.

Aniri worked her way between the two glaring men. She stared up into the face of the merchant marine. What kind of man was he? The kind who refused smuggling at any price. The kind who served on a ship that may be called to defend Dharia, even if it had been a hundred years since a war. He was as stout and unmovable as a shashee, but it was in the defense of something honorable, not mere stubbornness.

"My sister is in trouble," Aniri said softly.

The man didn't say anything, but his eyes quickened with interest.

"She and my mother both are Samirian and associated with the court in Samir."

The interest turned into a narrowed expression. But he let her continue.

"With the recent events…" Aniri glanced over her shoulder to the skyship still looming over the wharf. "Well, you must forgive my father's brusque manner. He's only concerned that we will not be able to get them out of country and back home to Dharia in time… before tensions become greater and…"

"You're fearing for their lives." It wasn't a question. But with it came a slight softening of his stance.

Aniri didn't have to fake her relief. "Yes."

Janak had gone on high alert with a hard glare for her skating so close to the truth, but she ignored him.

"If we travel by normal means," Aniri said, "the court will hear of us coming. We can't have that if we're to spirit them away. And now that my sister is with child…"

At this, the man's face relaxed. Aniri would have felt a twinge of guilt, except that almost all of it was true.

"My father and I are Dharian," Aniri said,

letting pride creep into her voice. "We would rather her baby be born on Dharian soil, far from the vagaries and stupidity of the Samirian court."

The merchant marine nodded, threw a quick look to Janak. "We're short on crew, but we'll be departing soon without them. There's like to be an extra cabin no one's using."

Aniri's smile was all gratitude, and even Janak's tension level stepped down a notch.

The sailor turned half away, then said over his shoulder, "Follow me."

The man led them past rusted railings and salt-crusted cargo holds to the main cabin of the ship. Perched above them was the bridge, its wide glass windows looking out across the sea toward Samir. Aniri glimpsed a few crew members inside before the merchant marine led them down into the rela-tive dark of the crew quarters. The passageways were even more narrow than the *Prosperity*, crowded by steel tubing, wooden handrails, and coiled ropes fixed to the walls. Two levels down, the merchant marine led them to a miniscule cabin. It barely had room enough for Janak and Aniri to both stand. Two bunks were stacked on one wall with a tiny sink and closet built into the other.

"I'll tell the captain about your situation," he

said, "but it'd be best if you stuck to your room. Sorry there's only the one."

"It will be more than sufficient," Aniri said. "Thank you."

The man gave a short nod. "We're getting a late start, so we won't be arriving in Samir until well into the eve."

Janak set their lone case on one of the bunks. "Arriving under cover of darkness will suit our purposes well."

"I figured as much," the man said. "I'll bring you something to eat so you don't have to cross paths with the rest of the crew. Probably best to stay low."

Aniri stepped closer and peered up into his face. "Your kindness is greatly appreciated. Please let us know what a fair price would be for our passage."

A tight smile brought lines to his eyes. "Just bring your sister home, Miss."

The man's kindness and his words formed a lump in Aniri's throat. She just nodded. He left, closing the bulkhead door behind him, leaving Aniri and Janak with a single gaslamp lighting the cramped cabin.

"Your skills in negotiation have improved." Janak attempted to sit on the lower bunk, but there wasn't room to clear his head, so he stood again and braced his hands against the top bunk. The tension was back in his shoulders. "I'm not so sure about your talents for stealth."

"Sometimes, you have to trust people, Janak."

He gave a huff, shook his head, then crossed the two feet of distance to the sink and leaned against it.

"Once we're in Samir," Aniri said, "we will have to trust *someone*. We won't be able to find and help Pavan without assistance."

Janak folded his arms across his chest. "The latest message from Karan said the Queen's request to meet with Pavan has been rebuffed. He is not in charge, Aniri. The Second Son could not keep the First from meeting with the ambassador without the Samirian Queen Mother's tacit agreement."

Aniri leaned against the slender closet, edging closer to Janak and lowering her voice even though they were alone. "I think there are more Samirians who favor the First Son than the Second. If Pavan had our assistance, he would be able to foment the people against Natesh."

"Against their Queen's wishes?"

"With talk of peace, instead of war, yes."

Janak pulled in a breath and looked away from

her. "People love war more than you might think, my lady."

Aniri frowned. Her ex-lover Devesh had spoken of the unhappiness of the Samirian people with Dharia—always feeling second class, less powerful, while being technologically superior in their clockworks. And now their skyships. But was that enough to inspire them to war? "They cannot long for the kind of destruction and death that Natesh rained on Bhakti. And they must fear what we can do with the burning glass."

"It's been a long time since the last war," Janak said, his voice tight. "No one remembers the cost."

The last war was lost in the haze of history, but it left a legacy of arranged marriages to knit together the fabric of the Dharian and Samirian peoples through blood and love. That legacy was what prompted the young prince of Jungali to seek an arranged marriage with the Third Daughter of Dharia... and that led to all that came after. It was a strategy that had prevailed for a hundred years and complicated war even today.

"Which is why we have to help Pavan," Aniri insisted.

"Even with our help, I doubt he will sway Samir

from its course. Not once the people realize they have the ability force Dharia to their will."

Aniri frowned. "Well, we have to *try*."

Janak glanced at her, then resumed staring at the bunk across from him. He said nothing.

Then she realized… his priorities were entirely different. "You're going to kill Natesh."

Janak didn't look at her, didn't move, didn't react in any way. He was motionless in the way only a raksaka could be.

"Janak." Aniri was tempted to lean forward and shove his shoulder to force him to answer her. Instead, she said, "My mother asked you to wait—"

Janak whipped his head to her. "Natesh nearly killed her." Suddenly his chest heaved as if he had run a mile between one sentence and the next. "He may yet accomplish his goal. No matter what, Natesh *will* pay for it with his life."

Aniri's eyes were wide. "Even if it tips Samir's Queen Mother toward war?"

Janak looked away from her. "There will be war regardless." He paused. "And your mother has been secreted away from the capital with the best healers in Dharia. If she survives her wounds, she will survive an attack on the capital as well."

Aniri bit back her response, imploring him not

to give up on peace. But how could she ask it of him, when she hardly felt it in her own heart? When all she wanted was to find Ash, free him from whatever dungeon Natesh had thrown him in, and then run her blade through the Second Son herself? Working to forestall a war when the cost might be Ash's life… it was what Ash was willing to give, and he might hate her for rescuing him first, but she couldn't convince her heart it was the wrong thing to do. There were some prices that seemed too high to pay for one's country.

And Janak's heart was just as much a prisoner in this as hers.

She reached out to lightly touch Janak's shoulder.

He flinched as though her hand were a hot poker.

"You will have your chance at Natesh." She waited until he slowly turned his head to look at her. "But first we both must follow the Queen's wishes."

The muscles in Janak's face twitched. He took a long moment before responding. "We will find Pavan. And support him as well as we can. Beyond that, I make no promises."

"I will tell my mother that Natesh's death was necessary."

Janak blinked and turned away from her again. Only this time, she suspected it was to hide something, not to steel himself against her.

"In the meantime," Aniri said with a sigh, "we will contact Ash's remaining spy at the dock and see if he has knowledge of what's happened to the First Son. How we can assist Pavan, or effect a rescue if that's necessary, is beyond me, but we will devise a way to make it happen."

Janak cleared his throat, still reining in whatever emotion he had been trying to disguise. "The Queen has made arrangements to facilitate our mission. A team of raksaka are likewise on their way to Samir at the moment, traveling separately and under cover as we are."

Aniri raised her eyebrows. "And when were you planning on telling me this?"

Janak ignored her. "We've made arrangements to coordinate our missions."

"Arrangements?"

"Prince Malik is not the only one with spies in Samir, Aniri."

Aniri nodded her approval. "Do they know anything about Pavan?"

"Unfortunately, no. They are mostly located in the capital—we should be able to coordinate through the embassy. And once we ascertain the situation with Pavan, the Queen's raksaka can help him with his struggle for the crown and for the people's favor." Janak held her gaze. "It is possible the First Son will know the location of the skyships as well."

Hope rose in Aniri's chest. "And if we know where their skyships are…"

Janak tipped his head. "… then your talents for espionage may become useful yet again."

Aniri grinned. "I thought my skills lay in negotiation."

"They are not so dissimilar." The small quirk of a smile on Janak's lips quickly faded. "You will need all your skills, Aniri. I will not be accompanying you in that effort."

Aniri's grin fell away as well. "I understand." And she did, all too well. Because if she had to make a choice between freeing Ash and running after Samirian skyships, her heart had only one answer: she would save the man she loved.

Chapter Six

It was well past the dinner hour and into the night when they arrived at the Samirian port. The merchant marine who had given them passage said they made a regular run, every other day, between the two ports. Then he kindly offered a return trip as soon as they had secured her sister. Aniri could only hope she would be able to make use of that offer.

She stepped off the swaying walkplank onto the steady ground of the Samirian pier, breathing in the salt-laden air and relishing the release from their tiny cabin. Both moons had already set, and the only light on the boardwalk was cast off gaslamp flickerings from the ships. Raucous sounds of late night tavern-goers echoed out to the waves and were lost in the perpetual slapping of ocean against vessel and vessel against dock. A furtive dark figure made his way between ship and port and disappeared into the darkened warehouses.

Janak stood next to her, carrying their case with the aetheroceiver.

Aniri gestured with her chin to the fleeing shadow. "Someone else seems to think night is the best time for their work."

"There is a lot of technology that Samir is keen to keep within their borders," Janak said softly. They were away from the ship, taking quiet steps toward the waterfront, but their voices could easily carry. And who knew how many ears there were to listen. "I can imagine many who would profit by helping it across the sea."

"How are we to meet our friend?"

"He awaits us at the *Veruna Dive*." When Aniri raised her eyebrows, he added, "A local drinking establishment."

"For sailors."

"And Jungali spies, apparently."

Aniri smirked, glad to see Janak recovering some of his humor. His brooding during their ten hour journey across the sea, trapped in their tiny compartment, nearly drove her mad. When they reached the end of the boardwalk, Janak used a heavy iron key to pass through the gated entrance to the dock. There was no attendant on duty, and the key came courtesy of the merchant marine, who said they might need it for the return trip. It made Aniri proud that Dharia produced such men, the kind who would step forward to help a family in danger. It was the kind of thing she admired so much in Ash and which stopped her from just handing over his country merely to save his life. Like the merchant marine, Ash would be disappointed in anything so ignoble. No matter its effect on her heart.

The *Veruna Dive* lived up to its name, even before they entered. A bawdy wooden cutout of Devruna, goddess of the sea, leered from her perch above the door. The beast she rode draped tentacles around the doorframe, giving the impression that entering was akin to giving yourself over to a watery death. A sailor burst from the inn before Janak could pull open the salt-and-grime crusted doors. The man nearly stumbled into Aniri, stopped only by Janak's lightning quick arm across his chest. With an ale-scented whisper of apology, he stumbled on.

Aniri watched him go. "And how are we to tell our friend from the drunken sailors?"

"We won't," Janak said. "Our friend will find us."

Inside was a rowdy assortment of sea men and merchants, drinking, arguing, laughing, and occasionally falling off stools. The stench made Aniri wish for a salty-bite of ocean air to sweep in through the now-closed doors. Janak edged slightly in front of her, sweeping the room with his gaze, no doubt looking for threats first and Jungali spies in Samarian sailor clothing second. There were a few women, largely captains holding court with their crew, but most of the inn's occupants were men well-muscled with the hard labor of the sea.

Aniri and Janak began to attract attention with their relatively clean cloaks and unscuffed boots. Janak found them a small, empty booth, but they hadn't been seated long when one of the sailors broke from his group to saunter over. His bronzed face was made darker by a lack of shave, his dark eyes sparkled with mischief, and he smelled of fish… the dead and slightly rotted kind.

"Lost yer way, mate?" he asked, his voice heavy with drink. "Tourists usually stay at the *Sea Bird* down the wharf."

"Last I checked, the door was open to anyone," Janak said tightly. His hand drifted down to the handle of one of the daggers belted under his cloak.

"Well our *door man* has stepped out for a bit of fresh air," he said loudly, clearly for the benefit of his friends who were watching from the table across the way and hoisting their bottles to him. "Guess it's up to me to keep the Dharian trash out."

Aniri flinched. What gave them away? Dharians are not so dissimilar to Samirians in their features. But then their clothes, their late arrival… their stumbling into the wrong bar…

"We arrived late is all," Aniri hurried to say, "and we're weary. Just stopping for a quick drink, then we'll be on our way."

Janak's gaze was glued to the sailor's smirking face. The sailor's friends watched them with keen interest, snickering at their expense. Aniri scanned the inn, heart pumping. If Ash's spy would just make himself known, they could depart.

The sailor braced one muscular arm against the back of Aniri's seat and leaned in close. "Well now, I'd be happy to buy you a drink, Miss. Maybe even two for a pretty thing like you." His words were slurred, but his breath was ale-free. Up close, his eyes were quick and intelligent, not the dull kind she expected from a drunken sailor. He reached for her hand on the table and scooped it up to his lips before she could think to jerk it away. She almost belatedly yanked it out of his grip, but now there was something clasped between their hands—a thing that crinkled with rigid edges and felt very much like a folded note.

Janak was on his feet and in the sailor's face. "Remove your hand from the lady." The danger in his voice zinged alarm through Aniri's body.

The sailor dropped her hand and stood straight again, facing Janak. "That right? Maybe the little Miss can decide for herself."

Janak was a coiled snake ready to strike.

"I most certainly *can* decide for myself." Her words forestalled whatever Janak was planning. Aniri hauled herself out of her seat.

Janak's dark brows pulled together, silently questioning her.

Aniri ignored him, tucking the note into her cloak pocket as she stood to face the sailor... who she was almost certain was Ash's Jungali spy. "These Samirians' manners are apparently even worse than their smell." She said it loud enough to be heard by the man's friends. They answered with loud protests of indelicate sounds.

With his back turned to them, the spy seemed

to struggle to hold back a smile. He gave her a quick wink. Janak looked at her like she was crazed.

She tipped her head to Janak. "Father, I believe we will find more decent company at the *Sea Bird*." Then she turned on her heel and marched toward the door in a huff. She didn't look back, but Janak was by her side again before she reached it, covering her back.

"Come back anytime, Miss!" the spy called loudly after them. "Just leave your father at home!"

A round of rude laughter followed them out of the inn.

Janak was silent, keeping close by. Aniri continued to stroll away from the *Veruna Dive*, waiting until she was sure no one was following or watching. Then she ducked into an alley that stank of fish and coal but that had enough gaslamp light shining from a nearby post to read the note. She pulled it from her pocket.

"Would my lady care to explain—" Janak cut himself off when he saw her peering at the note and angling it to see the charcoal lines in the dim light.

"Our spy found us," she said. "And apparently he wishes us to meet him here." She handed the note to him. It said *Room 14*, but nothing more. "Only I don't understand where *here* is, exactly."

Janak's eyebrows pulled together again. "Indeed." He examined the note and then returned it to her. "I can't imagine he expects us to revisit the *Veruna Dive*. Although I can see why this spy is the only one remaining of your young prince's nest of Jungali spies."

Aniri smirked. "He's clever. Although rather lucky you didn't take too much offense."

Janak shook his head and swept a glance around the docks, but they were empty and quiet. "I expect the location is not far off. Our spy wouldn't send us scouring the port city, checking rooms."

"Perhaps he told us exactly where to go."

Janak lifted an eyebrow. "The *Sea Bird?*"

"It certainly would be worth a try," she said. "And it's a consistent cover, in case anyone else decides to take an interest in the late-night arrivals from Dharia."

Janak led the way out of the alley, the small case with the aetheroceiver clutched in one hand. The *Sea Bird* was a well-lit establishment at the end of the wharf, near the passenger boats and closed customs offices. Their rumpled but clean clothes fit in better here. A few tourists still populated the parlor in the lobby of the inn, and a sleepy clerk manned the desk, but Aniri and Janak strolled in as if they had already obtained a room and had no need of assistance. Finding Room 14 was a small trick—it lay at the farthest wing of the inn on the first floor, near a door that led to the outside.

It took another half hour of waiting, but then the outside door creaked open, and the man from the *Veruna Dive* slipped inside.

"My lady," he said quickly to Aniri, "my apologies for the liberties I took—"

Aniri smiled and held up a hand to stop him. "Your little show was quite clever, Mr…?"

He didn't provide a name, instead he pressed his hands together and gave a quick bow. "By your leave, my lady, perhaps we could step inside?"

He produced a clockwork key that fit the door, pushed it open, and led the way. Janak went first, although she couldn't reason why he would be suspicious at this point. The room must have been clear, because he quickly gestured her inside.

Once the door was closed, the Jungali spy spoke again. "My name is Akash, my lady. It is an honor to meet you. Even more so to play a small part in your mission."

An awkward blush crept up Aniri's cheeks.

"The mission is larger than just myself. But thank you, Akash, for your assistance. We have vital work to do, important to both Jungali and Dharia."

He beamed, and now that he had dropped the drunken sailor persona, Aniri could see he was quite handsome. And apparently intelligent and accomplished in his spy work. She only hoped all of it would be sufficient to actually help them in their task.

Janak set the aetheroceiver case on the single bed contained within the sparsely decorated room. "What information do you have for us?"

Aniri loosened her cloak, now warm inside the stuffy room. "I am most eager to know the whereabouts of your prince, Akash. Do you have knowledge of where the Second Son may have taken him?"

He grew serious again. "No, my lady. At least, not directly."

Aniri's heart sank.

Akash hurried to add, "But, I assure you, I have a plan to find him, my lady. Please allow me to explain."

He gestured to the bed for her to take a seat. She shook her head and remained standing, crossing her arms. Janak returned to her side.

Akash spun his words out quickly. "No one saw the Samirians' skyship until after word had spread about what happened in Bhakti." His mouth opened to say more, but nothing came out. He seemed caught off guard by a sudden surge of emotion. He dropped his gaze to the floor, then shook his head and blinked rapidly.

Aniri glanced to Janak, but he looked as confused as she felt. Then she remembered the condition the Jungali capital was in when she fled, afraid of another attack.

She reached out a hand to gently touch Akash's arm. "Are you from Bhakti?"

Akash looked up. "I'm sorry... I just..." He cleared his throat. "There's been no news about who died in the attack, just numbers. And a description of the toll."

Aniri's heart squeezed. "I'm sorry, Akash." It was completely inadequate, but she didn't have anything more to offer him. Even *she* didn't know the names and faces of the lost. They had been forced to flee before there could be a proper accounting. Proper burials. "If we accomplish our mission, we may yet avert more attacks, more lost lives."

"Yes, of course." A determination seemed to

rise up and take hold of him. "As I was saying, no one here at the ports saw the skyship leave Samir. It must have traveled in darkness on the way to Jungali. But on the return… my lady, you should have seen the excitement in the streets and on the docks. We saw it coming from over the sea. At first, some thought it was the *Prosperity* returning, but those red and black colors against the blue evening sky—it was clear that it was no Jungali ship. The people cheered and waved and followed it inland, but it didn't linger or land. The ship sailed right over us and continued over the coastal mountains. We lost sight of it then."

"Do you think it was headed to the capital?" Janak asked.

"It certainly was heading east, but there's been no further word of it." Akash gave a tight smile. "Trust me—if there were a triumphant unveiling of Samir's newest skyship weapon, I would have heard of it."

Aniri nodded. "But then where did it go?"

"That is precisely the question, my lady." Akash reached deep in a side pocket of his loose sailor pants and pulled out a tightly folded square of paper. As he unfolded it and laid it flat on the bed, next to the aetheroceiver case, it became clear it was a map. "Given the direction it was heading…" Akash trailed a finger from the Samirian ports, heading inland, due east. "And the smaller villages, here, here and here." He tapped a triad of mountain villages, nestled in between the series of mountain ranges that peppered the entire country of Samir. "There is no way they wouldn't have been spotted if they continued heading east."

"So they changed direction after you lost sight of them."

"Definitely," Akash said, "but more than that: there's a fairly well defined range of visibility for any given Samirian town. They're nearly all surrounded by mountains on one side, often all four. There's a certain amount of sky they can see, just like here at the ports, where we lost sight of the ship once it disappeared over the mountains."

Aniri scanned the map—it was a myriad of small boroughs and nestled villages. She knew Samir was a patchwork of these rural towns, with only the occasional larger city like the capital, Mahatvak, but looking at it now, she couldn't see how a ship could sail undetected over almost any part of it. "And *no one* has reported seeing the skyship?"

Akash's smile returned. "Exactly, my lady." He

returned his finger to the map. "There are several mountain ranges, especially to the north, where a skyship could be hidden away. But only a few that could be reached undetected."

"Perhaps it landed at one of these rural villages," Janak said. "They wouldn't gossip about it, if it was their central base of operations."

"That is possible," Akash said. "But I've already journeyed to two of the closest, and there have been no sightings. It's as if the thing simply disappeared."

"That's not possible." Janak glared at Akash, as if the Jungali spy were making up riddles just to annoy him.

"No, of course not," Akash said. "But they wouldn't have to disappear, merely to stay out of visual range."

"Flying low," Aniri said.

Akash snuck a smile to Aniri. "Yes. And following a precise route to avoid detection. One, I imagine, they have flown more than once."

"But why sail directly over the ports if you desire to avoid detection?" Irritation was scraping the edges of Janak's voice.

"For that, you have to understand the Samirian temper in this," Akash said, the smile dropping off his face. "After such an attack, a battle of unprece-dented glory for Samir after a hundred years of submissive peace, the crew of the skyship would need to do two things: show that they survived, but more importantly, to flaunt that survival by making an appearance. By feeding the national pride, even if only for a moment before disappearing for more tactical reasons. As you may have detected from your short time in the *Veruna Dive*, there is no love lost for Dharians, at least for many Samirians. Nor do they love the Jungali people, although they have less animus toward us, mostly because we present less of a threat. And, until recently, we were working closely with them, on the skyship itself." He nodded to Aniri. "But now that Jungali has allied so closely with Dharia, and our prince has brokered a marriage with the Third Daughter—"

"It's not a brokered marriage," Aniri interrupted him, her face suddenly hot.

Akash paled. "Of course, my lady, I didn't mean—"

"He only meant the marriage was arranged," Janak said, his voice calm.

Somehow that irritated her even more. She faced Akash full on.

He looked desperate to pull the words he had spoken back into his mouth.

"I love your prince with all of my heart," she said, in a voice that dared him to deny it.

"Of course, my lady." His voice had a small quiver.

"I want nothing more than to bring him home." She didn't know why the words were so forceful or why she had such a need to say them.

"I will do everything in my power to free your beloved, my lady." The strain in Akash's voice nearly matched hers.

Aniri nodded, heat still suffusing her face. She was here to avert a war, to save lives, but for some reason, she needed Akash to know her feelings for his prince. Janak already knew, but if there came a time when she had to make a choice… she ducked her head away, pretending to examine the map.

"Do you have a guess, Mr. Akash," she said, forcing the emotion from her voice, "as to where the *Dagger* may be hiding?"

"The dagger, my lady?" His voice still held a heap of trepidation.

Aniri looked up. "The Samirian skyship. Its name is the *Dagger*."

Akash's face twisted in derision. "The *Dagger*? Clearly subtlety is not a Samirian strength." He reached out to trace a line along the map. "But I do have an idea where they might be hiding the ship. I plotted out the few routes it could have taken and still avoided detection." He glanced to Janak. "And wherever their final destination, I suspect it must be near a navia mine."

Janak nodded. "It makes sense they would have developed their own supply."

"Which rules out any boroughs not known for mining operations. And given the location of the mines in the northern provinces of Jungali, I suspect one of these three Samirian villages near the northern ranges are most likely where we will find our skyship. Or in the mountain canyons nearby."

"And once we've found the skyship…" Aniri said, thinking they would be able to sabotage the mines or the ship or, at the very least, force Natesh into a position of negotiation.

"Then…" Akash smiled. "We will have found your prince as well."

Hope whispered through Aniri's heart. Of course, he was right. If the *Dagger* had to elude detection, for whatever reason, they certainly wouldn't be stopping to drop Ash and Seledri off at the nearest Samirian hamlet. Plus Natesh might want to keep his most valuable hostages nearby.

When Aniri and her fellow spies found the skyship, they would likely find Natesh's captives as well.

"Well done, Mr. Akash." Aniri tried, and failed, to keep the hope out of her voice.

Akash beamed again.

Janak's scowl remained firmly in place. "As much as I would like to find the skyship—and I suspect Natesh will be there as well, so my desires there are as strong as yours, Aniri—our objective is to find the First Son and assist him in taking the crown. We must focus on that."

Aniri's heart clenched. "But if we can sabotage the ships—"

"*If* being the operative word there," Janak interrupted. "We could easily be caught, foiled, with no recourse—"

"We can call on your legion of raksaka—"

Janak's jaw set. "They are *raksaka* not an *army*—"

Aniri's hands curled up. They couldn't just leave Ash lying in Natesh's brig. And who knew what he would do to Seledri. "Are you saying a half dozen raksaka are incapable of infiltrating a skyharbor?" Aniri's voice was clipped. "Because I know a certain princess who managed to accomplish it well enough."

"I'm saying we have orders from the Queen."

"We have orders to stop this war, Janak! We could do that just as easily by—"

"If I may interrupt?" Akash's gentle voice stopped her cold. He had been watching the words bounce between them, staying out of it, but now he edged forward, giving both Janak and Aniri a tentative glance in turn. "I think there is another option."

Janak's eyes narrowed. "Do you know how to find the First Son?" With a sideways look to Aniri, he added, "The question we should have been asking from the start."

Aniri bit her tongue to keep the harsh words on it from spilling out.

Akash smirked. "As it turns out, I might."

Chapter Seven

ANIRI FOUND the seafood car of their cargo train to be even less comfortable than it sounded. The ice-filled wooden crate below her had worked its chill through her cloak during the hours-long ride. Janak had alternated between peering through the slim cracks of the train car doors and throwing his daggers against the crates—usually in the opposite direction of where Akash sat, but occasionally a blade sunk into a wooden slat uncomfortably close to the Jungali spy. And Janak's temper grew worse as the train ride wore on. Akash, for his part, seemed to be meditating—he sat cross-legged on the highest crate, his head barely missing the roof with each bump of the gently rocking train car. He had changed into black leather boots, slim canvas pants with a low-slung holster for his pistol, and a high-necked jacket that reached to his knees and signaled his status as a trade merchant. Now clean-shaven, his hands were upturned and still, his breathing slow and even. He hadn't spoken in an hour.

Maybe he was actually asleep. If so, Aniri envied him.

The first half of their ride had been in complete darkness. She had tried to sleep then, but the dust of the crates, the stench of the fish, and the constant motion of the train prevented any kind of true rest: she'd managed a twilight state, but that was all. Then the light of the rising sun filtered through the slats and slowly turned into blades of brightness—they found her no matter where she moved, and all hope of sleep was lost.

It didn't help that the train was heading to Mahatvak, the capital city of Samir, and not to wherever the *Dagger* had taken Ash and her sister. Aniri was going in *the wrong direction*. Her heart kept pounding that message through her mind. She tried to silence it with reason, but each mile down the tracks gnawed further into her, carving an ache deep in her chest.

They had departed from the docks as soon as

Akash had revealed the swirl of rumors gripping Samir: that an attempt had been made on Pavan's life, but he was still alive; that he was taking refuge with a group of loyalists within Mahatvak while his younger brother flew skyships to rescue Samir's future-Queen from the enemy who had stolen her away; and that the Queen Mother was not pleased with the quarrels between her sons. It was well known that the King favored his own child, Second Son Natesh, over Pavan, son of the previous, now-dead King. But now there was talk that Natesh might rightfully be considered First Son, given he was the first child of the union of the Queen Mother and the current King.

Which was dangerous talk, especially with Pavan in hiding.

Akash claimed to have a way inside the loyalist group, which had tipped Aniri and Janak away from following the skyship and toward going to Mahatvak. If there was a way to bolster Pavan's bid for the throne—and distract Samir from war, if not end the possibility altogether—they had to take it. But as soon as Aniri had fulfilled her mission there, she was determined to head north to the boroughs that were the most likely hiding place for the skyship… to find Ash and Seledri.

Before it was too late.

The endless, repetitive clacking and creaking of the train car was suddenly interrupted by a mechanical racket from the aetheroceiver. Janak had laid it out on a crate, one hand holding it still against the vibrations of the train, the other transcribing a message. The shift in noise roused Akash: he stretched and yawned before opening his eyes and regarding Janak's device and Aniri's huddled form nearby.

"Is that word from your fellow raksaka?" he asked.

Janak didn't answer, just continued to transcribe the symbols into letters. The tiny strip of paper gave Aniri a chilling flashback to the last aetheroceiver note she received: from Natesh, threatening to kill the people she loved.

While Janak transcribed, Aniri filled in the awkward non-response by asking Akash, "How long have you been working in Samir?" Of course, by *working*, she meant *spying*.

He frowned, still watching Janak, then finally turned his gaze to her. "Long enough."

Aniri grimaced. He was a Jungali spy, accountable to Ash first and foremost, but she thought she had his loyalty. Or at least his cooperation. She didn't want Janak snarling that with his churlishness.

"We have the same goal here," Aniri said, hoping that was true.

"Do we?" Akash clambered down from his perch, surreptitiously glancing at Janak's notations. "Yet we're going to Mahatvak, where Prince Malik is almost certainly *not*."

His words were daggers that sliced open her heart. It must have shown on her face, because Akash's demeanor softened immediately.

He edged closer and dropped his voice. "I can see my lady has a conflict in her heart… but don't worry. We'll quickly dispense with our business in the capital. Then we'll continue on with my lady's true mission."

His kindness was a balm she desperately needed. "Thank you. For understanding."

He gave a short nod. The clacking from the aetheroceiver finally ceased, leaving a wake of relatively quiet train noise behind.

"Please tell me we have some good news," Aniri said to Janak.

"*Good* is a relative term, your highness." He scowled at the slip of paper.

Aniri's nerves were already rubbed raw. "Janak."

The warning in her voice drew his gaze up. He glanced at Akash, who arched an eyebrow, challenging him, but Janak's gaze didn't settle there… instead he turned back to stare at the aetheroceiver, as if he could conjure a new, and better, message from it. She sensed his conflict wasn't with the Jungali spy, or even the aetheroceiver message, but with the same immutable duty that tormented her: going to Mahatvak wasn't the mission he carried in his heart, either.

Janak drew in a breath, and when he faced her, the momentary doubt was gone. "A dozen of the Queen's best will meet us in Mahatvak. They will assist us in our efforts to find the First Son and strengthen him in a bid for the crown. We are instructed to protect him as if he were a royal of Dharia."

"A legion of raksaka on the streets of the capital?" Akash asked, humor in his voice. "I'm sure that will pass without notice."

Janak curled his lip. "I can see how hard it would be to imagine, given the Jungali have not developed the discipline necessary to train raksaka."

Aniri flashed a look to Akash, but there was

nothing but high amusement on his face. "Perhaps our raksaka are so incredibly competent that you've yet to even detect their presence."

Janak just shook his head, like Akash was a child, but Aniri had to bite back her smile. When she had the chance, she should explain to Akash about the conflict in Janak's heart... then again, perhaps the Jungali spy had already guessed it, with the teasing smirk he continued to throw at Janak. Perhaps he was even more perceptive than she had originally thought.

Aniri chided Akash. "Once we've found the First Son, having the support of a dozen of the Queen's raksaka *would* be somewhat helpful."

Akash folded his arms, the humor fading a little. "I'm not sure bringing a legion of Dharian raksaka to a secret den of Samirian loyalists is the best approach."

Janak scowled. "You said you had access—"

"I said I *may* have access... but it will require a delicate touch."

"Meaning?" Aniri asked.

"Meaning it would be preferable to make contact first," Akash said, "and bring out the deadly human weaponry second."

Aniri looked to Janak. A stone-coldness had

settled on his face. She turned back to Akash. "The others can hold back, but Janak must remain with me. Besides, the First Son knows him."

"But the others will not. And the First Son is unlikely to be present, at least at first." Akash pulled in a breath, paused, then said, "All right. You will be my lowly assistants in trade." His smirk returned. "You're rather well dressed for the title, but that will simply be a reflection of my success as a businessman."

Janak's frosty look settled into his normal scowl. He started folding up the aetheroceiver.

"So we'll be meeting with other tradespeople?" Aniri asked, glad to see Janak's temper calming. "Who exactly are these loyalists and how do you know them?"

Akash unfolded his arms and brushed crate-dust from his jacket. "Well, that's a bit of a story."

"I believe we have time," Aniri said, trying to keep her voice calm.

But it didn't provoke him. Akash only smiled. "There has been much heated talk since the *Prosperity* was revealed. The Samirians weren't simply afraid, my lady… they were *angry*."

Aniri frowned. "Angry?" It wasn't like the *Prosperity* had attacked Samir. In fact, it was some covert group of Samirians who had helped build the ship and encouraged the attack on her country of Dharia. What did the Samirians have to be angry about?

"They're a nation of tinkers." Akash said this as if it explained something, but she didn't quite take his meaning.

Janak finished with the aetheroceiver and joined them. "The Samirians knew no Jungali had designed the skyship," he offered.

Akash nodded. "The Samirian people didn't have to be told—they instinctively knew someone within Samir had aided the Jungali not only with designs but manufacturing as well. Speculation flew about who could be involved. The Royal Guild of Tinkers was immediately suspect, of course."

"Which meant the crown *was* involved." When Aniri's father spoke of it before, he certainly seemed to think Natesh was deeply engaged in the development of the armada.

"Perhaps," Akash said. "Except the crown immediately denied the ambassador was involved in the attack on Dharia. It was unclear whether this was simply posturing, a necessary position to take to avoid war with Dharia, or if there were some secret faction within Samir that had orchestrated the manufacture of the *Prosperity* without the knowledge of the crown. Which naturally made people question whether the Queen Mother was truly in charge. Either way, the people's anger only grew over time."

"I don't understand." Aniri scowled further, trying to piece it out. Fear was understandable, given the burning glass and its capabilities, but the source of the anger still eluded her. "Did they object to the crown developing such a powerful weapon?"

"Hardly," Akash said coolly. "It damaged their pride, my lady. To have such a technological marvel in the hands of *barbarians...*"

"Ah, I see," she said. "If it was of Samirian design—"

"Then why wasn't it in Samirian hands?" Akash finished for her. "There was much talk of who had designed it, how much the crown knew, whether it was the Guild tinkers, and most importantly... how long would it be before Samirians could boast of a skyship of their own?"

Aniri nodded. "So the people have suspected all along."

"Do you have knowledge of who designed the *Dagger?*" Janak asked.

"No. There is much conjecture, but no one truly knows." Akash sighed. "Although I'm certain the Guild was involved in some capacity. My lady is correct on one count—not everyone was pleased that Samirian technology had been used to create a weapon which could lay waste to an entire city. There is an underground group—they call themselves the *Free Tinkers*—who oppose the Guild's efforts to keep Samirian technology inside the country's borders. I have a contact there who assures me the Free Tinkers were not involved in the development of the skyship—which makes sense, as they're in favor of technology for commerce's sake, not for war. And both the *Prosperity* and the *Dagger* were most certainly designed for war."

"Perhaps these Free Tinkers can help strengthen Pavan's bid for the crown," Aniri said. "Peace is always more favorable to commerce than war." With the possible exception of weapons manufacturers, like those who built the bullet-nosed bombs the Samirians used on Bhakti—but Aniri had no love for that kind of commerce.

"Indeed, my lady. The Free Tinkers are very much in favor of peace as well." Akash smiled his approval at her logic.

"I fail to see how all this helps us find the First

Son." The agitation was again creeping into Janak's voice.

Akash folded his arms again. "And who might the loyalists be who are hiding the First Son in the capital?" he prompted Janak with a raised eyebrow.

"Free Tinkers," Aniri guessed.

Akash tipped his head. "If what my contact tells me is correct, we will find him there."

Chapter Eight

Several hours later, Aniri stood in a dusty warehouse with Akash, Janak, and a dozen raksaka —although she would never have picked them out in the crowded streets outside the textiles shop. A close examination showed them all to be lean and well-muscled, with coiled energy under their unnaturally smooth movements, just like Janak... but outwardly, they were vendors and shopkeepers and tinkers. Men and women both, some dressed simply with woolen cloaks, some with more elaborate embroidered jackets, for the supposedly well-heeled merchants, and the rest with belts laden with tools, for the mock tinkers. All had ample room in their attire for concealing knives and pistols.

They stood apart, fanned out across the room,

surreptitiously checking the entrance and exits of the warehouse while listening to Janak's whispered update on their situation.

Akash leaned close to Aniri. "So, the next time I'm in need of a Dharian spy, I should check the local fabrics shop?"

"When exactly would you be in need of a Dharian spy?"

"One never knows." Akash's smile was barely restrained. He seemed to find humor everywhere.

Janak broke from the group of raksaka, and they quickly dispersed, disappearing around the long racks of fabric bolts as if they intended to melt through the walls to leave the building. Janak dusted stray fibers from his merchant jacket and arrived at their side still carrying the small aetheroceiver case.

"They will follow us," he said.

"The entire lot?" Akash asked skeptically. He had dropped his previous objections to the well-camouflaged Dharian raksaka roaming the streets, but now he seemed uncertain again.

"You will not see them," Janak said coolly. "However, they will come to our aid at my signal."

"A secret whistle perhaps?" Akash grinned.

Aniri wished Akash wouldn't bait Janak quite so boldly. "I believe we have an appointment to keep?"

Akash's smile dimmed. "Indeed. We should be on our way."

He led them out of the warehouse, down an alley, and onto the bustling streets of Mahatvak. The midday sun gilded the drab metal and granite facades of the city's shops with its dazzling glare. Vendors' carts clogged the sidewalks, and three-wheeled pamgari ambled along the cobbled road, driven by the fervent pumping action of the drivers as they carried loads of goods across the city. Aniri looked in vain for the disguised raksaka they had left behind. A shopper selecting flowers might have been one, but she couldn't be certain.

Akash kept a steady pace through the streets, turning corners as if he were a native of the capital, bringing them finally to a tinker shop that seemed to specialize in mid-sized clockwork toys: the kind the ladies and lords of the court, or the wealthy in capital, might enjoy at parties. Two automatons dressed in frilly dancing skirts stood motionless at the entrance. Given steam, they would pirouette for the amusement of Samirian nobles, just like the one the ambassador had brought to show off in Dharia. But they were definitely not the kind of thing you could purchase outside of Samir.

Inside the shop, smaller clockwork toys sparkled

in the sunlight that managed to filter through the dust-filmed windows. There was a mechanical shashee big enough for a child to ride, dozens of ornate boxes and trunks with elaborate clockwork locks, and a fencing automaton tucked in the corner, its blade tipped down, awaiting someone to activate the brass button over its heart. The tinkling bell at the door drew out the shopkeeper, a wizened older man in a leather apron which was weighted with a double set of tinker tools. His belts bristled with bulky wrenches, fine picks, and a set of brass magnifying goggles—the lot seemed heavier than the man who wore it.

"Good afternoon to ye!" The old man sprouted a friendly smile. "My name's Rishi, and I've the finest entertainments in Mahatvak for yer pleasure. Is there something in particular my lord is looking for?"

"I'm in search of a key that will open any door," Akash said carefully.

The man's smile faded. He pulled down a pair of spectacles from its perch on his head to take a closer look at the three of them. "That would be a rare key indeed."

"The keys to peace usually are."

Rishi's expression fell even more serious. He

peered first at Aniri, then at Janak. They seemed to pass his inspection, because he gave a short nod to Akash and said, "I have just what ye need in back."

Akash smiled and gestured them to follow Rishi to the rear of his shop. His work tables in back were littered with shashee clockwork legs and splayed-open trunks. Once they were all inside, Rishi closed the door to the main shop. Then he pulled a pistol from somewhere in his multitude of tools and pointed it at Akash.

His face lit with surprise and his hands flew up. "Easy, friend. We're not here for any trouble."

"Oh, I suspect yer bringing trouble enough," the old man said. "Question's which kind, and if yer planning to make it here."

Janak tensed and edged in front of Aniri. The man glanced at them, but kept his gun trained on Akash.

"We have a mutual friend," Akash said quickly. "He said you supported free commerce for tinkers no matter the country wishing their goods. If I misunderstood—"

"And this friend? Did he have a name?"

"Yes—Sajjad. A young lad. But if he's no friend of yours, I apologize for our mistake—"

The old man lowered his weapon and sighed. "Aye, he was a friend of mine."

Aniri shot a quick look to Akash, but his frown was still fixed on the weapon. She took a step forward, in front of Janak. "Was?" she asked the shopkeeper, and apparently armed Free Tinker.

"Did Sajjad send ye?" the man asked her in return. "When did ye last speak to him?"

"It was only last night, at the docks," Akash said, eyes skittering between Aniri, the man, and the gun. "Why? What news have you?"

Aniri had already guessed, but it still shocked her when the man said it.

"He was found dead this morning. Hanged in his own shop, as if a tinker would do such a thing. Another mutual friend messaged it to me, first thing."

"Dead?" Akash's face paled. He ran a hand across it. "This is bad news, indeed."

"Yes it is." The old man waved the gun then tucked it away. "Sorry for the theatrics. Can't be too careful these days. Thought maybe ye were some of Natesh's people, come for me next."

"No, I assure you." Akash drew in a breath and let it out quickly. "My associates and I are definitely on the side of peace and the First Son. Sajjad had hopes you might help us find our way to the loyalists who are protecting him. We want to offer our services in aid to the cause."

The man relaxed with Akash's frank words.

Tension seemed to drain from Janak's body as well. "Do you know where we can find these loyalists?" he asked.

"It's a strange day in Samir when Free Tinkers are called loyalists." The man huffed an aged laugh. "But we'll be needing all the help we can get. What have ye to offer?"

"Jungali information," Akash said. "And Dharian forces."

"Aye, we could use some of that." He started unhooking his tinker belts. "Let's be on our way, then. The sooner the better. It's not a good day for business anyway. Not with Natesh's men tracking us. And finding some." He shook his head sadly.

Rishi closed his shop and led them through the streets of Mahatvak. It was growing hot, and the people along the walks had sprouted parasols for a tiny escape from it. The old man moved with surprising speed, dodging small children and vendors' carts alike to make a jagged path through the city. They quickly left the regular shops behind and wound through the industrial sector. The buildings were larger, less welcoming, but still gray with granite and steel. Finally, Rishi took them down a foul-smelling alley caked with coal dust and grease, and they arrived at the back entrance of a large, stone building.

Aniri glanced behind them, wondering if Janak's raksaka had managed to follow through all the evasions. There was no sign of them, but a small nod from Janak reassured her that he, at least, had confidence in their presence.

Rishi paused at the door, holding a clockwork key in his hand. "I'll introduce ye to our Master Tinker. Ye can explain yer offerings yerself. But I doubt she knows about Sajjad yet. Best leave that to me."

"Of course," said Akash.

As Rishi inserted the key and the lock whirred open, Akash gave a pointed look to Aniri and Janak and said quietly, "Let me lead with this."

Aniri nodded. Janak just pressed his lips together and glanced back down the alley, which made Aniri's stomach churn. Perhaps he wasn't so certain about the raksaka after all.

Rishi led them inside, followed by Akash and Aniri, with Janak bringing up the rear. It was a cavernous building, two stories tall, filled with racks of industrial mechanisms—a warehouse of ship-building supplies, as far as Aniri could tell. Enormous propeller blades lined up like children's twirlers with shiny brass steam boilers nearby, waiting to power them. It appeared empty of people. Their boot steps echoed off the stone floors, machinery, and walls, the only sounds in the warehouse… until a sudden clicking of cocked guns alerted them to five men emerging from the shadows.

Aniri and Akash raised their hands. Janak kept his at his side.

Rishi called out, "We be friends of the Free, foes of the Guild."

The men advanced on them, unspeaking, steel barrels still pointed at their heads. Janak shifted to a wider stance, readying. Aniri was afraid he might attack them before Rishi could clear their identity.

"I'll be the judge of that." A woman's voice came from the doorway at the end of the warehouse. She strode toward them, covering the space quickly with her determined strides.

As she got closer, Aniri recognized her. "Riva!" Her exclamation was both in surprise and relief. Aniri shot a look of *stand down* to Janak, but his pinched face still showed his uncertainty. Surely he would remember Devesh's tinker friend from their previous adventure in Samir, but Akash frowned at Aniri, and Rishi gave her a wary look, clearly wondering about her connection to Riva.

But Riva recognized her well enough and picked up her pace to close the last few yards between them.

"Ye gods, what are ye doing here?" she said to Aniri. As she reached the circle of men around them, she put a hand to the barrel of one of her men's guns and pressed it down. "Put those away. This is our lady's handmaiden. She's to be trusted."

Aniri's eyebrows flew up, and Akash's nearly left his forehead. Janak gave her a look of warning. So... Riva still thought Aniri was her sister Seledri's handmaiden. A deception that might not exactly serve them well at the moment. Riva didn't notice Aniri's surprise, or if she did, it didn't prevent her from stepping forward to embrace her.

When Riva pulled back, she said, "Please tell me ye have good news about yer lady. We only know what's come over the wire, plus the rumors that are each more wild than the next. His majesty is sick with worry."

"I... um..." Words tangled Aniri's tongue.

Akash's face was filled with alarm. Janak's body

bent with tension. Rishi's face wrinkled with even more confusion.

Aniri cleared her throat. "Riva, we're here to help. But I'm not Seledri's handmaiden."

Riva frowned and took a half step back.

"I'm the Third Daughter of Dharia."

Riva's face opened, as though that were the last thing she expected Aniri to say. Or possibly she thought Aniri had gone mad before her eyes. Then Riva squinted and took a closer look at Aniri's face. The tiny scratches on her cheeks seemed to gain heat under her scrutiny.

After a moment, Riva nodded. "Aye. I guess I should have seen the resemblance earlier." She leaned back and folded her arms. "Although it would have been easier had ye had simply told the truth."

Aniri grimaced. "I'm sorry for the deception, Riva. It just seemed…" …*easier.* She flailed for an explanation that wouldn't sound half as deceitful as that. And which wouldn't scuttle their plans.

Akash came to her aid. "I'm sure the princess had your best interests at heart. Surely it would have been a danger to you, knowing the Third Daughter was spiriting her sister out of the country."

Riva looked him up and down. "And ye brought a new smooth talker with ye this time." It wasn't a compliment.

Akash blinked. Aniri nearly laughed when his cheeks reddened. He appeared to be at a complete loss for words, surely a new state for him.

"I seem to find myself in the company of spies often," Aniri said, hoping the oblique reference to Devesh, the Samirian spy Aniri had once loved, might temper Riva's contempt. Devesh and Riva were friends… at least at one time, and perhaps again. "They're not all bad."

Riva's gaze was still fixed on Akash. "And a spy. Naturally."

Akash recovered his voice and seemed about to protest, but Riva had already dismissed him with a hand wave and turned back Aniri. "The Third Daughter of Dharia, then. All right." She chewed the side of her lip. "But yer here to help us?"

"Riva, she's my *sister*."

Realization stole over Riva's face, and it softened. "Of course. And when Natesh stole yer her sister, the princess, back to Samir, that's when yer prince went missing as well. At least, that's what the rumors are saying. Is it true? Did Natesh snatch them both?"

"Yes." Aniri's throat closed up. She struggled for a moment, then cleared it. "We only want what you want: Pavan as the rightful heir and peaceful commerce between our countries." Aniri tried to keep the desperation out of her voice, but Riva's knowing look said she wasn't fooling her. Aniri stood straighter. "Please tell me you have knowledge of where we might find the First Son."

"Aye, I do," Riva said, kindly. "And I can do better than that." She nodded to one of the armed Free Tinkers and tilted her head toward a far door. He hustled off, and she turned back to Aniri. "He's here. And ye just caught us. We were about to leave."

"Leave?" Aniri frowned. "Where are you going?"

"Why to rescue the princess, of course. And now, yer prince as well, gods willing."

"You are?" A wash of relief ran through Aniri's body, so strong her knees suddenly felt weak with the undertow.

Akash touched her arm, steadying her. "Are you all right, my lady?"

Janak's concerned look was a weight upon her. Aniri pulled away from Akash's support, standing straight. "I'm fine. Just a lack of sleep."

Riva's gaze sharpened as she inspected Akash again, as if trying to decipher his role, then it settled more gently on Aniri. "The First Son has been similarly troubled, my lady. It will be a comfort for him to have you with us."

On cue, a small retinue of figures emerged from the far door of the warehouse. As they approached, Aniri squinted to make them out in the hazy stabs of natural light spilling through the high windows above. Her heart quickened when she saw Pavan, but it seized up altogether when she recognized the man at his side, keeping pace with a slight limp and bent shoulders.

Her father.

She heard Janak suck a breath between his teeth. His face was impassive, but his body was rigid. She couldn't imagine the thoughts in his head. If her father had perished in a Samirian prison, she didn't think Janak would mourn him. But Aniri couldn't help but feel a rush of relief that he was alive, even if somewhat more battered than the last time she saw him, taking a bullet to save her from Natesh's guards.

By the time she turned back to the approaching figures, the four were nearly upon them: Pavan, her father, gaunt with some kind of abuse, the armed Free Tinker as their escort, and… *Devesh.*

Aniri blinked. Devesh had a flash of recognition, then dropped his gaze. A turmoil of feelings, acidic and sharp, boiled inside her chest. The last time she had seen her ex-lover and Samirian spy, he had unexpectedly kissed her and nearly broken up her marriage to Ash. And saved her and her sister by spiriting them out of Mahatvak. Aniri hadn't relished the idea of Devesh being trapped in a Samirian prison… but she hadn't exactly hoped to see him again, either.

Pavan's long strides quickly brought the group near. He wore rumpled adventuring clothes, scraped with dirt and creased with days of use. The other two—her father and Devesh—were similarly unkempt.

Pavan pressed his hands together and bowed quickly. "Thank the gods you're all right, Aniri."

She quickly took his hands in hers. "I'm glad to see you well, Pavan, but you have no idea how sorry I am. I failed in the most important promise I made to you: keeping Seledri safe." Tears threatened her eyes, and she worked to keep them at bay.

He gave her hands a reassuring squeeze, but his face was tormented as well. "I'm sure you did everything possible. I had better fortune in keeping my promise to ensure Devesh's safety." Pavan smiled.

Janak coughed, and Aniri forced a smile in return. Devesh's gaze was still fixed on the floor. Her father shifted from one foot to the other. She couldn't tell if he was awkward in the reunion or in actual physical pain.

"It wasn't easy to locate Natesh's secret prison," Pavan continued, apparently oblivious to everyone's discomfort. "It was buried in a catacomb beneath the palace, but we were fortunate to find your father imprisoned along with Devesh."

Aniri dropped Pavan's hands and stepped closer to her father, leaving Janak standing as stiff as a statue behind her. Her father seemed to have aged ten years since she saw him last, defending her and Seledri against Natesh's royal guard. He labored to stand straight under her scrutiny. She could see it caused him pain.

"I wasn't sure if you lived," she said softly.

"My injuries are rather minor." He gave a small smile. "It was nothing compared to the food."

A pain lanced through her heart. The leg he favored… had he been shot? Or were the injuries sustained in prison? She wanted to know, to hug him, to tend to his wounds… but in a warehouse full of spies and agitators, all eyes trained upon them, not to mention Janak laboring behind her to keep his stoicism, it wasn't the right moment. She gave him an awkward nod instead. It was inadequate, but all she could offer.

"Your father and Devesh have been extraordinarily helpful in obtaining information about Natesh's hideouts," Pavan said gently to her.

Aniri frowned, just now piecing together what Pavan had said before: that he had gone after *Devesh*, not her father. She faced Pavan. "Is that why you sought to liberate Devesh?"

"Yes. And my promise to you, as well. But Devesh's knowledge of Natesh's network, his agents within the Royal Guild… all of it was instrumental in finding the skyship operational base."

That snapped her out of her haze. *"You know where it is?"*

Pavan's face hardened. "Oh yes. And I'm going after my wife and child." His voice tightened at the word *child*. He had to work to swallow down the emotion clouding his face. "The Queen Mother is very concerned about her grandchild," he said more evenly. "She has insisted that Natesh send Seledri back to the capital."

Aniri's eyes went wide. "But Pavan… your brother was behind the attempt on Seledri's life. He tried to kill her right in front of me!"

"I know." Pavan ground his teeth. "Seledri told me before you left."

"You must tell the Queen!"

Pavan grimaced. "Unfortunately, the only witnesses to that are you and Seledri herself. And now my brother has performed an apparent rescue of the future Queen. Surely he could mean her no harm." The acid dripped in Pavan's voice. "*I have no proof*, Aniri." He balled up his hands, then ran both through his hair, pulling at it. "I cannot accuse the Queen's son of such treason without it. And now Natesh is sending Seledri to the capital in accordance with the Queen's wishes. On a very long train ride from the North." A fire burned in Pavan's deep brown eyes—if Natesh was within arm's reach, Aniri had no doubt he would kill his brother with his own bare hands.

"She won't make it," Aniri said weakly.

"We have to reach her before whatever contrived death he has arranged for her arrives."

Aniri nodded in vigorous agreement. "We've brought aid in that endeavor."

Pavan glanced over her shoulder to Janak,

Akash, and Rishi. "We will take any help you can give."

Aniri tipped her head to Janak. He raised his hand, making a circular motion in the air with one finger. The dozen raksaka under his command stole from the shadows of the warehouse, two for each of the armed Free Tinkers stationed around them. The tinkers jerked and spun to face the raksaka, but they were disarmed before they could fully turn.

Aniri winced. "Janak." Her admonition gained a nod from Janak. His raksaka returned the weapons and gave a small space to the shaken tinkers. But they still hovered nearby, an unspoken threat with their mere presence. The Free Tinkers edged away, weapons pointed at the floor, putting distance between them and the innocently-clothed raksaka.

Pavan was suitably impressed. "You do not disappoint, Third Daughter of Dharia."

Riva shook her head at the whole affair, then leaned close to whisper to Aniri, "I'm just glad you and yer friends are on *our* side, my lady."

Aniri gave her a tight smile, then turned to Pavan. "The Queen of Dharia sends you her full support in gaining your rightful place as First Son.

It sounds as though we have no time to waste in that endeavor."

He nodded, then said to Riva, "Gather the others. It's high time we were on our way."

A flush of elation ran through Aniri's body—it stampeded over the awkward feelings dredged up by her reunion with her father and Devesh; it drowned out any concerns about destabilizing the crown or ensuring that Pavan held it; the rush even momentarily subdued any worries of danger or skyships or war.

There was only one thought that held her fast: *I'm coming for you, Ash.*

Chapter Nine

THE SURREY WAS CROWDED, meant for four and carrying six. Every bump in the road, every puff of dust, made Aniri itch to go faster, arrive sooner. The minutes stretched to hours as they inched toward their destination: a train depot where they would attempt their rescue plan.

A six-legged beast pulled their surrey along a dirt path beside the railroad tracks. Two more of the lumbering animals drew two wagons filled with Janak's raksaka and Pavan's loyal guards. Pavan promised the trip would only take a few hours, and that they would arrive at the depot before the train which was transporting Seledri to the capital. But that event seemed impossibly far away as they rumbled through small valleys and between the many mountain ridges of the Samirian countryside. The beast pulling them was a Samirian breed not too dissimilar to those used for transport in Dharia, but this one was sturdier and shaggier… more akin to a miniature shashee than the sleeker, faster beasts that Dharia employed.

The ranges of Samir were not as closely packed as the Jungali mountains, with more plains and wide spaces in between—it appeared the cable carriages the Jungali used for fast transport between their mountain cities would be impractical here. Perhaps the beast pulling them was more acclimated to Samir's winding mountain roads than it would be for flat Dharian ones, but its speed, or lack thereof, left Aniri wondering if she would arrive at the train station sooner by getting out and walking.

The worst of it was the close company: there was too much baggage of the emotional kind between the passengers to have anything close to an ideal seating arrangement. Devesh apparently possessed valuable knowledge regarding the skyship's whereabouts, which necessitated him accompanying them, but Aniri still had no wish to sit near him. Riva and Akash had an ill-defined animosity fresh from their first meeting, which Aniri didn't understand, but which apparently was about to drive Devesh into skewering Akash for it. Pavan was as impatient to arrive as Aniri, from the looks of his bouncing legs and frequent checks on their progress, which inexplicably annoyed Janak.

Truth be told, none of them were fit company. But for seating, they had settled upon Pavan, Aniri, and Janak to one side and Devesh, Riva, and Akash facing them from the other. One of Pavan's guards rode in the driver's seat. At least Aniri's father had remained behind, recovering from his wounds and gathering more loyalists in support of Pavan within the capital. Aniri couldn't imagine how intolerable the trip would be with Janak and her father in a surrey together.

That thought had her breaking the silence that had fallen for the past half hour. "What injuries did my father sustain?" she asked Pavan.

Even though her question was directed to the First Son, Devesh answered. "His wounds will heal, Aniri. I made sure he was tended to, before we—"

Janak's glare cut him off. Devesh dropped his gaze to examine his boots in the footwell. Akash seemed highly interested in the whole exchange.

Pavan turned his head slightly to her. "Your father was shot in the leg. My brother's guards managed to bind it before throwing him in the dungeon. But I'm afraid his other injuries were sustained while in custody."

Aniri's heart wrenched. "Why would they…" But she knew. They wanted whatever information he might have to use against Dharia, especially since he had so recently been in contact with her, its Third Daughter. "Is he all right?"

"He is much better now than when we first recovered him," Pavan said softly. "I'm sure he will heal completely in time."

Aniri nodded. "Once we take the train and rescue Seledri, will you return with her directly to the capital?" The plan was for Riva to lead a team —including Devesh and apparently Akash, along with a small contingent of raksaka and guards—on to where the skyships may be hidden.

"Once I have my wife by my side," Pavan said, "you, Seledri, and I can return to the capital. Between the two of you, I have hopes you can convince my mother how dangerous Natesh is, and how wrong-headed he is in agitating for war."

Aniri nodded, although she hadn't actually decided what she would do once Seledri was recovered. Should she return to the capital to attack Natesh politically with her testimony to the Queen? Or go on with the others to attack him militarily by sabotaging his ships? Her heart was practically leaping out of her chest with its preference to go where Ash could be found.

Janak slipped her a sideways look, and she knew his thoughts were the same as hers: Pavan would have his wife, the half-dozen raksaka they would send with him, and his growing group of loyalists in the capital. That should be sufficient to help him regain the crown, and Aniri and Janak would have fulfilled their duty. They could justifiably travel on to wherever Natesh was holding Ash and hopefully disable some skyships in the process.

"Does the Queen Mother favor a war with Dharia?" Aniri asked. "Or Jungali for that matter?"

"No, not generally," Pavan said with a sigh. "And Natesh is skating a thin line with this bombing of the Jungali capital to supposedly rescue Seledri. The Queen is enamored of Seledri and the child she is carrying, just like her people —bringing her home is probably the one thing that could excuse Natesh's actions. But now that the skyship has been revealed to the people, there has been much excitement among the populace. A lot of talk about the resurgence of Samirian power."

Aniri glanced to Akash—Pavan's words proved

what he was saying before. Akash tipped his head in acknowledgment.

"However," Pavan added, "Samir is not quite ready for war. There's a reason Natesh only brought the one ship to Jungali."

"Do you know his exact capabilities?" Aniri asked.

Pavan nodded to Riva, that she might take the question.

"Now that the *Dagger's* been revealed," Riva said, "tongues are a little looser with information about Samirian skyships. As far as Devesh's sources know, there are four skyships under construction, perhaps three ready for combat. But the ships are going nowhere without the gas. We suspect they're low on it, which makes some sense given they've been mining the gas in Jungali longer than Samir. And it seems the *Dagger* is larger than the *Prosperity* —which means it can fly farther, but it needs more navia to give it enough float. And that's a mighty long trip across the sea to the capital of Jungali and back to Samir, especially if ye can't stop to refuel."

"How long will it take to mine enough gas to fill four ships?" Janak asked.

"No way to know without gettin' on the inside of the operation." Riva glanced to Pavan, and that appeared to be a topic they had discussed before. "But that's not the only thing holding them back from attacking Dharia with their armada."

Akash was nodding along with Riva's explanations. "There's also the risk of provoking a response from the *Prosperity*. Unless you've developed some defenses against the burning glass?"

"It's not *me* who's developing these weapons at all," Riva said, the annoyance still rumbling through her voice. "But, no, I can't see any kind of defense they could muster that would fight off that deadly fire from the sky. I'm sure they're lookin' for an opportunity to bring down the *Prosperity*. Which is a right shame. That ship's a thing of beauty." She shook her head with disgust. "But yer right, fear of the burning glass is the only true thing keeping the *Dagger* at harbor for the moment." Riva gave Akash an appreciative look that seemed to irk Devesh. Aniri wondered what exactly what was happening with the three of them… had they met before? Then she decided it was the very least of her concerns.

"Well, you can be sure that the Queen of Dharia, not to mention the First Daughter, are working diligently to prepare for war." Aniri looked at each of them in turn. "A war they believe is coming regardless. Unless we can stop it."

There were solemn nods all around.

"If it comes to it," Riva said, "the Free Tinkers have a few technologies the crown has yet to learn of." She bit her lip and glanced at Pavan.

He just smirked. "I certainly hope so, Riva."

She gave a small, slightly embarrassed smile. "If it's all the same to ye, the skyships are much easier to disable when they're on the ground."

Pavan nodded absently, glancing down the road. His heel tapped out impatience for them to arrive, a feeling that beat through Aniri as well.

"If we want to reach them while they're still on the ground," Akash said, "we will have to make haste. Once we recover the princess, our hand will be tipped."

Pavan's leg stilled in its bouncing. "You mean Natesh will know the Dharians are here."

"Precisely," Akash said. "We will have used a small legion of Dharian raksaka to recover Seledri and the Queen's grandchild. That won't exactly go without notice. Especially if you then seek out the Queen Mother regarding Natesh's fitness for the crown."

"Perhaps the assumption will be that they are

Samirian." Devesh's voice had an edge to it. "We have raksaka as well."

Akash scowled. "If the First Son had the confidence of that many raksaka, he would hardly need our help." He turned back to Pavan and Aniri. "I am certain Natesh knows you will be coming for your sister, my lady. You can catch him off guard once, but not a second time. He's certain to be awaiting your next move."

Aniri chewed her lip for a moment. "My mother's diplomatic overtures have been rebuffed. But there has yet to be a direct response to his threats."

"That is what he's waiting for. We will need to reach the skyships before Natesh realizes he has lost control of the situation with the princess." Akash glanced at the shaggy beast pulling their surrey. "And I fear this manner of transport will be entirely too slow for our purposes."

"We could take the train back to the airharbor," Riva said. "It's not a completely straight shot, but ye would be close. Another short train ride from there, and we'd catch him by surprise."

Akash smiled his approval. "The lady's idea has merit."

Devesh glowered. Riva looked on Devesh's foul temper with high amusement.

Janak scowled. "Yes, a wonderful plan. Except that it requires hijacking a train, not simply liberating a prisoner from it."

Akash raised his eyebrows. "A task I'm sure your raksaka are equal to."

Thankfully, Pavan interrupted their verbal wrestling before it escalated. "We'll discuss this further once we have my wife and child secured." His gaze was trained on the road ahead of them. Aniri twisted forward, and she could see why.

They were nearing the train depot.

There wasn't much to it. A small wooden platform extended to the tracks from a rough-hewn enclosed station. A few passengers milled about with their travel cases, awaiting the train. Judging from their simple attire and lack of carriages parked nearby, Aniri judged they had walked from the nearby mining town nestled against the granite ridge just past the depot. A small industry of buildings clustered together, but beyond those, an enormous structure of steel and timber pressed up against the mountain. It stood guard over an open wound in the rock where giant, clawed cranes scooped ore straight from the mountainside. Samir seemed to have an abundance of these mining towns along the train line, where they could easily transport their raw goods to the larger cities. The surrey had already passed several hamlets like this one along the dusty road during their hours-long journey.

At the near end of the train platform, a water tower waited with a spigot arm ready to lower to refill the train's tender car, once it arrived. In the distance, through a narrowed ridge cut in the mountainside for the snaking line of train tracks, a puff of steam slowly marched forward.

The train was nearly upon them.

The surrey, along with the two wagons full of raksaka and guards, ambled up to the water tower to park. The wagons were fully enclosed, so the legion of fighting forces they had brought to the depot weren't readily apparent, but the whole entourage was already gathering stares from the waiting passengers.

The screech of train brakes combined with the muscular chugging of metal wheels. Aniri was accustomed to the passenger trains of Dharia, with their stately wooden cars and glistening brass adornments, but this Samirian engine was twice the size, and its flat black face seemed an eyeless menace trundling down the tracks toward them. Steam hissed and a whistle sounded three times in a lonely wail to announce its approach. The clamor drew the attention of the few passengers waiting to board, giving Aniri and her band of spies, tinkers, and assassins, a cover of sound in which to gather by the wagons and attempt to plan their rescue.

"The passenger cars will be to the rear," Pavan shouted to be heard over the approaching train. "As soon as it stops, I'll have my guard take control of the engine and watch over the boarding passengers. Janak, I would like your raksaka to secure the rear cars. I expect Natesh will have sent at least a few guards along with Seledri, wherever they are keeping her."

"Guards?" Janak asked, raising his voice above lingering hiss of the train as it slowed. "I would expect raksaka to be guarding the princess."

"If Natesh intended her to live, yes," Pavan said darkly. "But you may be right. And if she's guarded by raksaka, it will be more difficult to recover her."

"There will not be a problem with that." Janak's confidence didn't seem misplaced. After all, they had a dozen of the Queen's finest raksaka to aid them.

Pavan held his gaze. "Seledri's safety is my paramount concern."

"Mine as well, your majesty."

"How can I help?" Akash asked, hand resting on his pistol strapped to his side.

"The surrey could use a guard," Janak said with an impassive face.

Akash and Devesh both protested with looks of disgust, but Riva beat them to it. "If we're to be hijacking the train, my lady," she said to Aniri, "I'd serve you best on engines."

Aniri couldn't agree more. "You will assist Riva," she said to Akash and Devesh. "Hang back until Pavan's guard has secured the engine, then I want you three up there, making sure we're ready to move as soon as my sister is recovered."

The two men eyed each other, but didn't disagree. Meanwhile, Pavan finished his whispered commands to the surrey driver, the lead among his guards, and the man hurried off to carry out his orders.

The train hissed and metal-squealed its way to a final stop at the station.

Their group broke apart, everyone going into motion at once. Guards and raksaka spilled from their wagons. Riva, Akash, and Devesh tucked behind the water tower, apparently choosing that as a suitable location to await the hijacking. Aniri and Pavan kept pace with Janak as he strode toward the backside of the station. The guards gathered at the front of their vehicles, then split apart, one group of four heading for the engine, the rest fanning out along the tracks and heading for the platform. The raksaka moved faster than anyone, breaking into two groups that scuttled along the near and far sides of the train, a human line of power traveling its length.

The train was comprised of a dozen cars, mostly bolted-shut cargo containers, but the last three were passenger cars. They had lined up with the station, and two were already releasing their riders, but the final car's windows were shrouded in drapes, and its doors had yet to open. Janak reached the rear of the station building on the side facing the dirt road and held Aniri and Pavan back with an outstretched arm. They watched from that distance as the raksaka reached the passengers on the platform. Startled cries rose up, but the raksaka wove through the travelers without stopping. Then their group splintered into three teams of two, one for each car, while Pavan's guards took up stations along the perimeter of the platform.

Aniri worried that only two raksaka would be insufficient for the final car. Then three more crawled like spiders onto the roofs from the far side, and she remembered the second team. In less than a moment, every door and window of the final car was covered by a dedicated raksaka.

They held still, awaiting some final signal.

The raksakas in the first two passenger cars started escorting passengers out of the cars and onto the platform. The voices on the platform grew more agitated and higher in volume as more and more people were crammed onto the small space, obviously not voluntarily. When the last passenger had debarked from each car, they were followed by a single raksaka who gave a closed-fisted signal.

The raksaka covering the final car took that as a signal to start attacking the two side doors with iron bars. The sharp crack of wood giving way to metal rent the air. Just as the doors cracked open, a close-packed volley of gunshots rang out.

Aniri's heart jumped to her throat. She couldn't tell where the shots had come from, but the two raksaka breeching the final car fell, landing across the now slid-open doors. Another raksaka near them likewise crumpled to the dirt next to the train car. Two black-clad figures melted away from the nearby rocky canyon walls and raced across the straw-like grass surrounding the tracks.

Aniri surged forward, pressing against Janak's

outstretched arm. He kept her back with one hand, the other bunched in Pavan's rough linen shirt, holding him back as well.

Then something grabbed her from behind, lifting her from the ground and choking off all her air. She dangled for a moment, boots pawing the air, before being dropped. She landed hard, hands and knees biting into the hard-packed dirt. She scrambled away, fighting to breathe and blink away the black spots swimming in front of her eyes. She got a couple of feet on her own when suddenly Pavan was at her side, lifting her up and shepherding her away with a protective arm around her shoulders.

Aniri caught a glimpse behind her and she gasped. Janak was engaged in hand-to-hand combat with a raksaka in midnight-black clothes. Silver glints of knives flashed and turned red, moving faster than she could track. Then she couldn't see the men at all as Pavan dragged her up onto the platform at the front of the station.

More gunshots rang out. Aniri jerked so hard, she thought a bullet might have actually found her. But it was just a reaction to the soul-splitting sound. The platform was in chaos. Passengers had dropped their cases and fled in all directions, screaming and searching for cover. Guards had their pistols out, but seemed uncertain what to do with them. Pavan wrapped his arms around her and pulled her against the wall of the station, covering her with his body. His head whipped back and forth, trying to take in all that was happening.

"The train car, Pavan!" Aniri's voice warbled in panic. Pavan's arms flinched and he twisted to look. One of the black-clad raksaka had joined the Queen's fallen raksaka, all four of them now lying dead in the dirt by the last train car. A Samirian raksaka fought at the door of the train car with a Dharian raksaka dressed as a tinker. Another of the Queen's raksaka, attired in merchant clothes, dropped from the roof and took them both down. A third arrived from another train car, pistol drawn.

Another gunshot clipped the air. The Samirian raksaka lay still.

Just then Janak surged around the corner. He was bleeding from a cut along his jaw, but there was far more blood on his dagger, which he held at the ready in one hand, his pistol in the other.

"Aniri!" he said harshly. "Are you all right?"

"Yes." Her voice was mostly a gasp.

"The First Son?" Janak asked, scanning him for injuries.

Pavan released her and quickly said, "I'm fine." Then he stumbled toward the last train car. Janak caught him at the edge of the platform steps, gripping his arm and holding him back.

"Wait." Janak's even voice contradicted the tension in his body.

Pavan grabbed his arm. "Let me go to her!"

"Wait." Janak's gaze was locked on the rear car.

Aniri arrived next to them, heart pounding. "For what?"

"They're clearing the car."

Her gaze darted between Janak's steely focus on the train car, Pavan's panic-stricken face, and the train car itself, which was surrounded with dead raksaka, swords, and tossed aside pistols. The car shook slightly with the activity inside, but there was no sound.

After a moment, she realized no more shots had been fired. The crowd on the platform had long fled, into the building, down the tracks, along the path into the town. They weren't waiting to see if any more shooting was going to occur, but that was exactly what Aniri was straining to hear. Or cries of pain.

The air was breathless around them, the only sound a creaking hiss of the train cars settling into place. Her chest felt like it might cave under the pressure. Finally, one of the Queen's raksaka emerged from the last train car and gave the same closed-fisted signal as the others.

"Now," Janak said quietly, and all three of them dashed toward the train car.

Aniri prayed it held her sister. And that she was still alive.

Chapter Ten

PAVAN REACHED the final train car first, but only because Janak let him. Aniri's raksaka kept pace with her slightly slower strides. She was only a heartbeat behind Pavan until they reached the two metal-grated steps up into the car. Then he leapt past the steps and flung himself through the open doorway, while Aniri hesitated at the sight of the fallen raksaka outside. They had given their lives, on both sides, in this war that was only getting started. More bloodshed that could have been avoided. Should have, if only Natesh weren't orchestrating all of this for his own gain.

An anguished cry from within the train car seized her heart and wrenched her forward. The scene inside was no less bloody, and for a terrifying moment, Aniri couldn't make sense of what she was seeing. Then it came into focus.

Two Samirian royal guards lay dead. Three live raksaka, the Queen's protectors, stood at each of the doors to the train car, two on the side and one between the train cars. Two of the raksaka had bloodied faces, but they were impassive, just like Janak at her back. Pavan stood in the center, his back to Aniri, gripping hard onto the shoulders of a disheveled figure she couldn't quite see—Pavan was blocking her view.

"Where is she?" Pavan demanded, practically shouting in the person's face—it clearly wasn't Seledri. Did they somehow have the wrong train? Aniri's gaze swept the train car again and again, but her sister definitely wasn't here.

"She's all right, Pavan, I swear it."

That voice.

"Why… she was supposed to… I don't understand." Pavan's words were punched with holes of desperation.

Aniri stumbled forward, her heart beating its way ahead of her, pulled by a frantic hope that she wasn't hearing things… wasn't imagining…

"We will go back for her, I promise."

Aniri edged around Pavan to see who he was

holding onto. "Ash?" Her eyes went wide and blinked rapidly, as if he was some kind of mirage standing before her.

Ash's head whipped toward her, his face lit with surprise. *"Aniri?"*

Pavan released him, turning away, his fist pressed to his mouth.

Aniri was still frozen in place, not breathing, afraid to move in case Ash might disappear.

He limped toward her, a strange clanking sound coming from the floor with him. The chains that bound his ankles together seized her attention, and for a moment, she couldn't look away. Then, as he shuffled across the wooden floor, she took in the rest: he had the same adventuring clothes he wore in Bhakti, only now they were filthy and torn. The gashes weren't just in the clothes, but marks on his body as well, revealed with each lumbering movement. When her gaze reached his face, she saw only the bruised cheeks, the blackened eyes, and the swollen eyelid where it was cut across the brow.

She closed the remaining space between them. Her hands flew to his face, her fingertips gentle on it. Gasps that were more like sobs shuddered out of her. "Ash... Oh gods, Ash... they *hurt* you..." Her hands trembled as they floated over his injuries.

His slipped his arms around her and held her gently. There was wonder in his eyes. "Aniri… how is it possible that you're here?"

She swallowed back a sob. "How could I be anywhere else?" Then she threw her arms around his neck and held him so tightly she was afraid she might be hurting him—with all of his injuries, all of his pain at the hands of Natesh—but she had to hold on. Because she was shaking so hard, she might fall to pieces if she let go.

"Aniri, my love, my love." Ash was whispering into her hair and running his hands along her back to soothe her, as if she were the injured one, the one in need of comforting. "It's all right, my love. It's going to be all right."

Her body shook once more, then calmed… as if her body believed his touch even more than his words. She held him a moment longer, then forced her arms to slowly release their lock on him. She let enough space creep in between them that she could see his face, but no more.

"Tell me you're all right." Her voice was still trembling.

"I'm all right." His hands found her face, touching her like he wasn't quite sure she was real, either. There was a frown for the scratches he found there, but he simply said, "I feared I would never see you again."

Pavan's panicked voice broke into the tight space between Ash and Aniri. "She was on this train!" They both twisted to see his reddened face nose to nose with Janak. "You have to search the other cars again!"

"I assure you, the Second Daughter isn't here." Janak's steely voice only ratcheted up Pavan's distress. He turned away from her raksaka, hands fisted against his forehead as he cast around the small train car again, as if he hoped to find her sister hidden in some corner.

Aniri turned back to Ash. "Do you know what happened to Seledri?"

"Yes," Ash said, one hand coming back to rest on her cheek. "She was alive and well when I last saw her."

Ash's words grabbed Pavan's attention, so Ash released her enough to include Pavan in his explanation. But he kept one hand firmly in Aniri's, holding her by his side. "I saw Seledri just before Natesh put me on the train."

Pavan's shoulders dropped. Indeed his whole body seemed to sag with Ash's assurance that Seledri was alive.

Ash continued, "She convinced one of her guards to let her visit me before I left. She wanted to get my…" He seemed to choke up. "She wanted to get my final words to give to my wife."

His wife. Her heart skipped a beat, then swelled that he thought of her so. But she couldn't speak to that, not with so many eyes watching. Instead, she asked, "Your final words? I don't understand. I thought Natesh was sending Seledri back to the capital."

Janak spoke up again, his voice still measured. "This was clearly a trap for the First Son, one he didn't expect Prince Malik to survive as well. Natesh knew you wouldn't be able to resist the lure of a relatively unprotected train carrying your wife. He was expecting your attempt to take the train and sent his own raksaka to lay in wait."

Aniri nodded. "Only he didn't know Pavan would bring a dozen Dharian raksaka with him."

Pavan's frantic looks calmed into something darker. He turned to Ash. "My brother sent you to die."

Ash's battered face twisted with disgust. "He meant the same for you, Pavan." He gave a tight nod to Janak and small smile for Aniri. "Natesh is making a habit of underestimating you, my love. I can only imagine his fury when he finds out Pavan and I are both still alive."

Pavan stepped forward and put a hand on Ash's shoulder. "We came for Seledri, but we were planning on traveling back to Natesh's hideaway to retrieve you as well, Ash."

"Your priority was here first, Pavan. Believe me, I understand completely." Ash glanced at Aniri. "But now, we really do need to make haste to return to the airharbor before word of this reaches Natesh. He's been keeping Seledri in relative comfort, not the filthy box he had me locked in. He wants to appear innocent of her death, whenever that occurs, so he's taking care not to ill-treat her. If Pavan had been killed today, Natesh's path would be cleared, and Seledri would have no longer mattered. But he's drunk on power, Pavan, and I fear for what he might do to her now. She still presents a danger to him. And he knows that you know that. He will be expecting you to come for her. We must act quickly."

Pavan nodded through all of Ash's speech. He turned to Janak. "Have we secured the train?"

Another one of Janak's raksaka had been quietly updating him by the door. "We can leave at any time, your majesty. But no matter how swift the train, I'm not sure we can beat the news of this event back to the Second Son. This small mining town may be backward, but they're still in possession of a wire for news. And we've given them rather a lot of news to report today."

Pavan took a breath. "He might know we're coming. But we're limited on options."

"Agreed. I'll get us underway." Janak turned and left the train car with light footfalls, his fellow raksaka a shadow behind him.

"Let's get you out of those chains," Pavan said with a nod to Ash.

Chapter Eleven

THE TRAIN RIDE WAS LONG, hot with the afternoon sun, and painfully tense.

Riva gave instructions to a couple of Pavan's guards on how to keep the train engine running as they drove the train backwards along the tracks, then she joined the rest of the planning crew in the last passenger car. The bodies of Natesh's slain guards had been cleared out, but their blood stains were wet reminders of the costs that lay ahead. Natesh's dead raksaka had likewise been left at the station, but Janak's three slain raksaka rode in the train with them, laid out in the forward passenger car. Aniri might not have been able to arrange proper burials, much less send their bodies back to Dharia, but at least the Queen's raksaka could be accorded the respect they were due for the time being. The remaining nine raksaka quartered for now in the second passenger car with Pavan's guards, all of whom had survived the fight, given the raksaka had targeted their own kind as the greatest threat.

That left the crowded and uncomfortable last passenger car, which was really just a hollowed out prisoner transport, for everyone else: Aniri, Ash, Janak, Pavan and his lead guard, and the trio of Riva, Devesh, and Akash. Each had a part to play in the upcoming assault on the hidden skyship fleet, but that didn't make the car any larger or the tension between them any lower.

Janak hovered with the ring of spies, tinkers, and royalty over a map made from one of the pulled-down curtains and a chunk of coal borrowed from the tender car up front. Ash had helped him draw the airharbor from his memories of his internment, and Devesh helped fill in the pathway to get there. Ash and Devesh hadn't spoken a word during that time, but the exchanged looks between them were part of what heated the air. Or maybe it was only Aniri's face that was on fire throughout.

"There were four of Natesh's raksaka involved in the attack on the Jungali capital," Janak said. "I killed one, and there were only three in today's assault. Is it possible that's all the raksaka Natesh has in his employ?"

Pavan shook his head. "I can't say for sure. Part of the handicap I've been laboring under is the question of the raksaka allegiance."

Janak nodded. "And a split in the royal family could do the same for the raksaka, at least until a normal ascension order is solidified again. But to commit an act against a member of the crown?" Janak gripped the coal chunk in his hand, and small bits of dust fell from it. "Even with turbulence in the royal household, I cannot imagine any but the most partisan raksaka would raise a hand to slay a member of the royal family. Our code requires us to act in a defensive capacity only in such situations."

"The raksaka who attacked today," Akash spoke up, and all heads turned to him. "They were young, were they not? Perhaps they had special ties to the Second Son. Or their political leanings caused them to buy into the nationalism that is sweeping Samir at the moment, especially among the younger populace."

"They would be the raksaka for whom war is something from the distant past," Janak reluctantly agreed. "And who are young and undisciplined enough that they still itch to show the world their Samirian prowess."

"Or they're simply dim and bored," Riva said.

That pulled a chuckle out of most of the group, with the notable exception of Janak. But Aniri knew any of those things made a potent and dangerous mixture, and not just in raksaka. How much of the Samirian population supported Natesh's lust for Samirian glory, even if it cost a war, rather than Pavan's more gentle approach... and his Dharian wife?

"I didn't see any raksaka at the airharbor," Ash said, bringing them back on point. "Just Natesh's guard. But I spent most of my time in a very small box."

Janak stroked his chin. "We'll have to assume there could be more. And it's possible they will be assigned to the Second Daughter, assuming Natesh is on guard for a rescue attempt."

Pavan nodded. "Retrieving my wife is our top priority."

"Agreed," Janak said. "However, we'll have one chance at this, and we shouldn't neglect the opportunity to attack the skyships themselves. Besides, an attempt to sabotage the ships will provide a useful distraction."

"Even more useful, if they're actually success-ful," Akash added.

Aniri had held back from the discussion, still in a haze, grappling with the events of the day. But now she stepped forward and knelt by Ash's side, joining the ring gathered around the map. In all her time spent with Captain Tarak, learning the operations of the *Prosperity*, it had never occurred to her to learn how to intentionally disable a skyship. But she was fairly certain it could be done.

"You can't simply fire a bunch of pistols at the gasbags," Aniri said, "or climb it and attack it with sabers. You'll only vent the air that's in the outer chambers. You might let loose some of the navia, but you won't permanently disable the ships."

Riva dipped her head in agreement. "Yer majesty is right on that. Far as I can tell, the gasbag has a bit of defenses built into it. On the other hand, if ye mess with the controls, ye can right ruin almost any good ship. It won't matter how much navia ye have, if ye can't steer the boat."

"You can switch off the controls?" Aniri asked, wondering exactly how that would work.

"Or lock them down and run it hot," Riva replied. "We could send those ships straight up into the sky, and with no controls and burning all their fuel, they'd lift and lift…"

"…and only have one way to come down," Aniri finished for her.

Riva nodded solemnly. "By venting their navia until they no longer had enough float."

Aniri swallowed. "By falling."

It was a rather complete way of destroying a skyship. And all the crew left on board.

A hush had fallen over the group. Aniri stared at the sketched out ships on the curtain-map and wondered how many more people would have to die before this war was over.

"Could you accomplish this and still exit the ship before it lifts off?" Janak's cool voice sent a shiver through Aniri.

"Aye," Riva said. "At least, I can give it a go. Will need a bit of assistance, though, to get to engines and do my work unmolested. And for getting off the skip as well."

"It appears we have two missions and two teams, your majesty," Janak said to Pavan.

Aniri narrowed her eyes and examined Janak's expressionless face. She didn't have to wonder which mission he would be on: Janak would be wherever Natesh was.

"One team to liberate Seledri." Pavan nodded his agreement. "The other to sabotage the *Dagger*."

Janak turned to Ash. "Prince Malik, could you tell if more than one ship was operational? Or is the *Dagger* their only flightworthy vessel?"

"I didn't really get a good look at them," Ash replied. "There are four ships, as you said before that you suspected. And I'd say they're at least partially operational. They had semi-inflated gasbags."

"But not enough navia to lift," Riva guessed.

Ash shrugged. "Perhaps."

Janak gave a short nod to Riva. "We'll focus on the *Dagger*. Eliminate the known threat and deal with the others should we have the opportunity. I can give you a small team of raksaka and perhaps some of the First Son's men as well. I'll be with the team to recover the Second Daughter, along with the remaining raksaka and guard. If that is acceptable, your majesty." He was speaking to Pavan now.

Pavan nodded and looked to Ash. "It would be helpful to have you along on my team. You're the most familiar with the airharbor."

Ash nodded, but a wave of protest surged up in Aniri's chest. She didn't want to give Natesh another chance at killing Ash. He'd already sent him to die once.

Before she could get the words out, Akash said to his prince, "By your leave, I'll be going wherever you are, your majesty."

Ash gave him a small, grateful smile, but Aniri threw Akash a hot stare for not helping.

Riva spoke up. "I could use the Third Daughter on engines with me. She knows her stuff. Might be helpful in a pinch."

Aniri doubted how helpful she would be, but before she could turn the conversation back to Ash going on the mission, he threw a hand out to Riva.

"No!" he said harshly. "Aniri needs to stay far from all of this. Natesh will kill her outright if he so much as sees her."

Riva pulled back and bit her lip, glancing up at Aniri. But that concerned her far less than Ash's words.

"*Me?*" Aniri protested, even though he was probably right. Natesh had already tried to shoot her once. "*You're* the one he just used as elaborate bait with the intention of killing both you *and* Pavan."

Ash gave her a look like she had just stabbed him in the heart. Which made her mouth drop open, and her fists curl up. How could he be so blind to the danger he was in?

"Aniri's right," Janak said coolly. "No royals should be involved in either mission."

"I am not staying back while we rescue Seledri," Pavan said deadly calm.

Janak's cool broke a little. "With the exception of the First Son."

"You could use my help," Ash said to Pavan. "I know where she's being held, and none of the rest of you have set foot in the airharbor."

He was determined to go.

Frustration propelled Aniri to her feet. She turned and marched to the door between the train cars, unable to stand this mission planning that could send the man she loved right back into Natesh's grasp.

"Aniri, wait!"

Ash's voice didn't slow her down, but a stubborn Samirian door did. She banged and rattled it, wondering if it was locked and if she should just vent all her frustration on it regardless, when it finally sprung free. The noise of the clacking train wheels surged up with a blast of heated, coal-smoke-laden air rolling along the backs of the train cars ahead of her. She stumbled across the short walkway between cars, holding onto the side rail so she didn't lose her footing in her anger, and was stymied once again by the next door. This time she suspected it was locked.

"Aniri." Ash's voice was close behind her, carrying over the train noise. "Come back inside."

Aniri banged on the window of the train car door. It promptly opened. One of Janak's raksaka stood just inside, one hand on the door. He was one of the bloodied ones who had been the first inside the train car to rescue Ash. His face had been cleaned, but there was still a slash through his eyebrow, a fresh cut from the fight. She noticed it because he lifted that one eyebrow at her sudden appearance, which she supposed was all the surprise she would ever get from a raksaka. She glared at him, daring him to stop her.

He dipped his head, a sort of half bow, and stepped aside to let her pass.

She strode past him into the car, only to realize that it was *filled* with raksaka and guards. There was no privacy here, nowhere to go to pound on a wall and vent her anger. She heard Ash's boots on the wood floor behind her, so she straightened, held her head high, and marched forward to the next train car, as if that had been her intention all along.

A guard ahead of her scrambled to unlock the door and slide it open. She held out a hand for the key, an elaborate clockwork Samirian one, and he hastened to hand it over. She strode into the blanket of train noise outside once again. The heated air buffeted her hair into a sheet behind her as she crossed the walkway to the next car.

She slipped the key in, hastily turning it, even though she could feel Ash at her back, catching up to her. She slid the door open. This was the most forward passenger car. The one where they had laid out the raksaka.

The car of the dead.

She strode inside and waited. It only took a moment, but Ash followed and closed the door behind him. A muffle fell on the world. The silence of death. The raksaka were covered with curtains taken from the windows, and the sway of the train car gave a small motion to their forms. That was all the movement they would ever have again.

She felt Ash at her back and whirled on him. "How dare you!" Angry tears leapt to her eyes. "How dare you go back there again! I just got you back—" She cut herself off, because the rest of it was far too painful to say. And they were the words he had already said to her. *I feared I would never see you again.*

Ash pulled her into his chest, wrapping his arms around her and holding her tight. She sobbed into his dirty adventuring clothes, gripping them with both hands and burying her face in them, not caring. He simply held her, not speaking, stroking her back like he did before. Her body eased into him, and his arms curled even closer around her.

They stood that way for a while.

Eventually, the storm inside her quieted. She pulled away enough to peer up into his face. It was bruised—beaten by this war that was battering her heart—and furrowed with worry. She didn't bother to wipe away her tears. Her heart was already laid bare before him.

"I can't lose you again." She said it simply, because it was a plain truth. It needed no elaboration, no adornment. No proclamation could hold more of her heart in it.

His nod was small, a tiny motion meant mostly for himself. "I wasn't afraid to die. I knew what Natesh had planned for me, but that wasn't what struck fear in my heart. The only thing I feared was that I would never finish what we had started."

She smiled through her tears. "I may have

skipped a step. I've been calling you my husband ever since…" Her smile faded away.

His hands glided up her back and found her cheeks. He leaned close and whispered, "In my mind, I've married you a dozen times already."

He bent to kiss her, and what started soft, his lips sweeping across hers, a gentle caress of love, quickly fanned into a hungry need, a consumption of each other that went deeper and more urgent. His hands slipped down to grip her back again, holding her tight against him. She clutched at his shoulders, then dug her fingers through his hair, climbing on her toes to reach him better, to lose herself more completely in his embrace. She gasped between kisses, breathing in the very air that he breathed, joining together in the only way they could with no time, no place, no room for the love they were desperate to share.

Ash still held her tight even as their passion cooled to small touches of lips and soft sweeps of fingertips on faces. They were quiet through it all, except for the sound of their breathing, which had quickened, and now evened out to a steady rhythm to match their heartbeats.

"I keep thinking…" His voice was so soft she wouldn't have heard it if his lips weren't nestled close to her ear. "…that each time I kiss you I can't possibly love you any more than I already do. And yet, the next time, I still do."

Her heart was full to brimming. "I never want to be apart. Ever again. Promise me, Ash."

He pulled back enough to look deep into her eyes. "You're right. Whatever we do, we need to do it together."

Her small rapid nods weren't enough: she had to put it into words. "Together."

He ducked his head to sweep his lips to her ear again. "Together," he whispered.

They needed to return to the planning room. To plan and to risk and to hope. They needed to find a way to rescue her sister, stop Natesh, and prevent a war.

But not just yet.

Chapter Twelve

AFTER TWO TRAIN RIDES, several hours, and a climb through a winding mountain ravine on foot, Aniri's band of raksaka, spies, and royals arrived at the airharbor. Or more accurately, they snuck up the side of a mountain to have a strategic view of the airharbor they planned to soon invade.

Aniri lay flat against the rocky lip of the canyon, peering over the edge with a small, collapsible aetherscope she had borrowed from one of Janak's raksaka. The summer sun had set late, well into the eve before it dipped below the mountains, but its light kept the sky blue. Only one of the moons, Raka, had risen. Its slim crescent didn't give much light, but Aniri could still see the outline of the four ships, including the *Dagger*. It differed from its harbor-mates by the full, red gasbag that billowed above it. The other three ships were similar in design and size, but their dark red balloons were mostly deflated, sitting like squashed and bloody mushrooms atop of the hulls of their ships. Two of the three were nearly flat, while the third appeared half full. The steady breeze through the narrow canyon ruffled their sides, but it would take a substantial amount of navia to fill them like the *Dagger*. Three deflated skyships was the best thing she had seen in a while, with the exception of unexpectedly finding her husband-to-be in a Samirian train car.

In addition to the ships, two on each side of the canyon, there was a cluster of rugged, wood-sided buildings in the center. A set of train tracks drew a straight line away from the buildings and toward a village several miles down the mountain. Ash said the buildings were workshops and barracks for Samirian sailors and tinkers. His time had been spent in a tiny room inside that grouping, less a cell and more a closet. A larger, stone building sat separate from the workers' quarters and built into the canyon wall: Natesh's miniature estate. Ash said that was where Natesh kept Seledri. A softer cage of comfort than Ash's closet, but still a prison. Farther up the canyon, spanning the narrow end was an elaborate mining operation. Train tracks, carts, cranes, and a massive stone-and-metal façade building which must contain steamworks, as it chugged soot and steam from twin chimneys that reached above the top of the ravine. A smoky haze slowly drifted down and dissipated throughout the canyon.

If they weren't after the *Dagger*, that would have made a fine target for sabotage as well.

Riva would lead the team to take the skyship, but Aniri and Ash would be joining her along with Akash, five of the remaining raksaka, and a half dozen of Pavan's guards. Janak fought hard to keep Aniri and Ash out of the missions altogether, but they were both unwilling to sit by while everyone else risked their lives. Not when they could help. Their only stipulation was that they remain together. Janak eventually relented. And while he wanted them on the team he was leading to rescue Seledri—so he could personally guard all four royals—he allowed that an assault on a skyship filled with sailors was somewhat less dangerous than an attack on a fortified granite bunker possibly guarded by raksaka.

Aniri suspected the real reason he acquiesced was even simpler: he was after Natesh, and with Aniri not accompanying him, he would be freer to run a blade through the Second Son. After seeing what Natesh had done to Ash, Aniri didn't have even the smallest protest.

"Are ye ready, my lady?" Riva's voice came from a few feet behind her.

Aniri collapsed the aetheroscope and climbed to her feet. "As ready as I'm going to be, Mistress Tinker."

Riva grinned, and Aniri followed her down to their awaiting team. She picked her steps carefully, as the waning sun was quickly drawing down the light. The cover of darkness would serve them well, as long as she didn't stumble through it.

Aniri stood by Ash while Janak gave out final instructions.

"We'll meet back here when your mission is complete," he said to the two gathered teams. "Hopefully, you won't bring any raksaka or royal guards with you. If you're being pursued, there are some old mining tunnels halfway up. I'll show you where they are on the way down. Remember it. You can take refuge there, at least until we can all coordinate once more."

The raksaka were silent, as always, but even the rest of the teams' members were quiet. The guards took their cue from the raksaka and maintained a stoic face. Devesh stood on Pavan's right, pledging to help on that team, but he looked agitated, and kept sending furtive looks to Aniri's team. She tried not to notice, but she prayed he wouldn't do anything to give Janak pause—she had a feeling her raksaka would have little patience for it during the mission. Pavan's steely looks past the edge of the canyon said he was ready to get on with it.

"What if we're unable to rendezvous?" Akash asked. He had switched to Riva's group of raksaka and royal guards when Ash did, and he seemed the most at ease of all of them. His hand rested casually on his pistol, and he chewed the end of some native plant dangling, straw-like, from his lips. Riva gave an appreciative nod to Akash's question, and he smiled warmly for her. Aniri suspected he wasn't on her team simply because of his allegiance to Prince Malik.

"Make every attempt to reconvene here," Janak said gravely. "But if that proves impossible, then our final resort is to meet at the Free Tinker warehouse headquarters in Mahatvak."

"That's half way across Samir," Akash noted with humor in his voice.

"Which is why you should endeavor not to be late," Janak replied. "However, it is likely that, even if we manage to reconvene as a group, we will have to break up and travel in pairs, or no more than groups of three, when we return to the capital."

"Because Natesh's men will be hunting us." This time Akash's voice was dead flat.

"Precisely." Janak turned to give a nod to the entire assemblage. "Gods be with you."

As the teams readied for the hike down the hill, Aniri caught Janak's elbow.

She kept her voice low. "Your mission is to rescue the Second Daughter."

He narrowed his eyes at her. "I hardly need a reminder of that, your most royal eminence."

His arched tone made her smile. "I'm simply reminding you of your *primary* mission. Please make sure my sister is safe before you engage in any secondary activities."

His skeptical look settled into an anger as cold as his blade would be on Natesh's neck. "Understood."

Janak signaled his men, and they went first down the mountain. Devesh looked like he wanted to say something to Aniri before they left, but changed his mind as Ash rejoined her. Ash seemed to notice it as well. He kept his gaze straight ahead as Riva waved for them to follow Janak's group down the hill.

"I wouldn't want to be your ex-courtesan," Ash said lightly. There was humor in his voice, not jealousy, which settled the tension the momentary exchange had conjured in Aniri's chest.

"Facing a possible legion of raksaka to rescue his lord's lady? There are worse things Dev could be doing with his time."

"He does seem rather urgent in his desire to redeem himself." He threw her a sideways look, the humor reduced by half. "He's clearly still in love with you."

"That's his problem, not mine."

Ash smirked. "I see."

She looked at him full-on, hoping not to stumble on the rocky dirt path they were descending. "I hope you do, Ash."

He nodded, the smirk gone. "I'm the one by your side, Aniri. I know that."

She slipped her hand into his, and the warmth

of it batted away, at least for the moment, the raw tension that floated over all of them about the mission.

The darkness fell deeper as they worked their way down the mountain. When they reached the bottom of the canyon, even Aniri was having trouble telling the intruder teams from the shadows. A narrow dirt road skirted the edge of the canyon to the airharbor encampment, and the raksaka following along it were only visible when they stepped into a wan patch of Raka's moonlight.

Janak's team stole ahead, finding shadows in which to creep around the edges of the central buildings and heading for Natesh's pretentious castle-like building on the hill. Aniri watched them go until she couldn't discern them anymore, except for a brief flicker of shadow that could have easily been the trees swaying in the gentle breeze.

Riva's group likewise broke apart and disappeared like spooks into the shadows, only these ghosts were headed for the *Dagger*. It loomed over them, the pitch-black of the ship like an inky well that the Samirian-red gasbag dipped into with its multiple tethers. Two guards manned the end of the main walkplank, and there was some movement on deck, but otherwise, the giant skyship was as still as a grave. Up close, Aniri could tell it was substantially larger than the *Prosperity*. The Samirians no doubt designed it to be able to reach her home in Kartavya—that was the only way it would be an effective warship.

Muffled laughter rose up, but it seemed to come from the central buildings, not the ship. By prior agreement with Janak, Aniri and Ash held back in the shadows, while Akash and Riva stepped out into the moonlight and strolled toward the ship. The guards were leaned against the sturdy posts that marked the airship dock, their boots making small shuffling sounds as they sought a comfortable position in which to pass the hours. Their small talk didn't carry more than a whisper to Aniri's ears, but there was no particular sense of tension in their tone.

Until they noticed Akash and Riva.

Both guards came to attention. Their blunderbusses glinted silver in the moonlight as they were raised.

"What's your business?" the taller of the guards asked.

"I've some work to do on engines." Riva's voice was confident enough, but as they closed the distance, the guards peered suspiciously at her and Akash.

"All the *Dagger's* tinkers are done for the day," the shorter one said. "And I know them all. You're not one of them."

"Go back to your other ship, tinker," the taller one sneered. "You'll not make a name for yourself on the *Dagger*."

Akash pulled the weed out of his mouth and gestured to the guards. "I told you they wouldn't go for it," he said to Riva. "They're too sharp for that."

The guards exchanged a quick look.

Riva let out an elaborate sigh, then lifted her chin to the guards. "I just want a peek, aye? We're having trouble with our starboard boiler and some lot has messed with the trim on the settings. I just need a moment with yer controls panel, and we'll be on our way."

"That's not our worry," the taller one said.

"No, it's not," Akash said lightly. "But they are."

Two raksaka had melted from the shadows and materialized behind the guards. The skyship guards didn't have time to react before a flurry of strikes sent them slumping to the ground. The raksaka caught the blunderbusses before they could fall. The other three raksaka on their team were already half way down the walkplank, and six of Pavan's guards emerged from the shadows and boarded the ship as well. Akash and Riva waited until Ash and Aniri caught up with them to follow the rest.

They were onboard the *Dagger*.

Chapter Thirteen

Ash led the way toward engines—Riva may know how to run the steamworks, but she hadn't been on a ship before. Her eyes were wide and adoring. Akash was likewise impressed, although he still seemed slightly amused by the whole adventure. For Aniri, it was like walking over a grave: she couldn't keep the image of the *Dagger's* shadow floating over Bhakti out of her head, dropping bomb after bomb on her beloved city. She shuddered as they worked their way down to the lower levels of the ship. The layout was basically the same as the *Prosperity*, only the stairs kept going past the engine level… that was probably where they kept the armaments.

Their team glided through the ship undisturbed, although occasional muscular grunts and thuds of falling bodies could be heard reverberating throughout the ship as the raksaka and guard sought out the nighttime crew. When the four of them reached the engine room, there were only two sailors keeping stations, one at the controls, the other feeding coal into the boiler engine. Akash and Ash drew their pistols without a word, and the sailors' hands went up. Ash marched them at gunpoint out into the corridor, where Akash lashed them to one of the handholds along the wall with a coiled rope he'd snagged along the way. Aniri didn't want the sailors watching while Riva sabotaged the ship—they might figure out a way to fix it before the ship was destroyed altogether. Riva went immediately to the control panel, both wide-eyed with wonder and biting her lip, like she couldn't quite decipher the readings.

"Can you work it, Riva?" Aniri asked.

"Aye," Riva said, a single finger on each hand lightly skimming the dials as she read them. She glanced to the back where the twin massive boilers fed the steam turbines that turned the giant propellers outside the ship. "But we've a bit of a hitch here." She shook her head. "Shoulda thought of that. 'Course they're not going to keep her spin-nin' all the time."

"What is it?" Aniri's voice hiked up. Ash and Akash had returned from tying up the two engine-room sailors, but she wasn't sure how it was going with the rest of the ship. Nor how much time they had to complete their sabotage before reinforcements arrived from the camp.

Riva didn't answer, just skittered across the controls, cycling several switches, scanning readings, and finally halting in front of a large toggle switch. She grabbed it with both hands and pulled it down. It thunked with a deep mechanical sound, and something to the back of the engine room echoed it back with a clunking of its own.

The tinker's face lit up. "I think that's got it."

"Riva," Aniri said, her patience wearing thin as she kept one eye on the doorway to the engine room. "Tell me what you're doing."

Riva dusted her hands and stepped back, hands on her hips, to survey the needle gauges. Even Aniri could see they were starting to move.

"No lack of fuel in the harbor, so they keep the boiler primed," Riva said in a light way. "Which makes a spot of sense, as it can take an hour or so to get those things a hummin'. But there's no sense in spinning the turbine while yer docked, so they shut her down."

Ash remained by the door, but Akash edged up to Riva's side, his face alight with curiosity. "So you had to turn it on?"

"Aye," Riva answered with a smile. "But ye have to take it slow. The steam heats those turbine blades right hot, and ye don't want them spinning up too fast. Might throw one or two. Would make for some grand sabotage actually, but our objective here is to take her up, not break her parts."

"How long will it take?" Aniri exchanged a glance with Ash. He was listening in, but keeping his eyes on the door and the prisoners outside.

Riva frowned. "Well… not sure exactly. Haven't worked on engines this big before." She tapped a dial. The needle was slowly rising. "Seems to be heating up right quick, though. The next trick will be routing the steam to the gasbag. Need to get that good and hot as well before we lock her down."

"And you know how to do all this, right?" Aniri asked, an edge in her voice.

"Aye." But Riva was still scanning the controls, so Aniri was a bit less confident.

"We haven't got all day, Riva."

"I know, I know." She found a row of smaller switches, flipped them back and forth, watched some dials for a moment, then nodded to herself and flipped them all to the *up* position. "That oughta do it." She turned back to Aniri. "Now, yer going to have to get us unlashed for this to work. All but one or two tethers. We'll have to cut those on the way out."

Aniri nodded. "The guards should be working on that as soon as they secure the ship."

When Riva went back to the control panel, Akash turned to Aniri. "Should I check on our status, my lady?"

"No, Janak tasked one of the raksaka with checking in once everything was set." Aniri frowned at the door. "However…"

"We'll give them a minute, yes?" Akash said. "Then I'll see what the trouble is."

Aniri nodded her agreement, then turned back to watch Riva skim across the controls, gazing at every gauge as if it were a treasured jewel.

"Such a shame to be breakin' all yer parts, Miss Dagger," she said softly.

"Riva," Aniri said, a warning in her voice.

Riva glanced back with a sheepish look. "Don't mind me, my lady. Just thinkin' out loud." Then she dove into a satchel of tinker tools and pulled out a wrench. The large toggle switch she used before to start the turbines was her first target. She quickly liberated the bolts holding it in place and removed the switch. Behind it was a nest of gears and clockwork that must be the true mechanism behind the simple switch.

"Yer weapon, please, Mr. Akash." Riva held out her hand.

He give her a concerned look, but handed over his pistol.

Riva aimed it at the gears buried inside the control panel and fired. Everyone ducked, flinching far too late. Smoke trailed from the tip of Riva's gun, and she peered at the gears which now had a twisted hole through the set, snarling the carefully aligned wheels.

"Queen's breath!" Aniri said when she straightened. "Riva, you can't fire a weapon in here!"

Riva shrugged. "Did make a right mess of that switch, though. Doubt they'll be able to fix that anytime soon."

Akash was working hard to hold back his laughter.

Riva handed him back the pistol. "Ye might want to reload, Mr. Akash. I've got one more key bit to destroy."

He took it, chuckling while he fished out the supplies to reload his pistol.

Ash had a slightly more shocked look on his face. "I'd like to get out of this without getting hit by a stray bullet, Mistress Tinker."

"Aye, yer majesty." She was already tackling a new set of smaller switches, using the wrench to twist off the bolts of the cover plate, one by one. "That's a fine goal for the lot of us."

Aniri just shook her head and looked to the door again. The guards and raksaka were taking far longer than she expected to secure the ship. Akash was grinning as he reloaded. As soon as he was finished—

A series of pops that were alarmingly like gunshots sounded in the distance. Akash's eyes went wide, and he fumbled to reload faster. Riva's wrench screeched metal protests from the control panel as she worked the bolts off fast and faster.

"Ash!" Aniri called to him. "Shut the door!"

He dashed behind the industrial sized bulkhead door to close it, but before he could get the heavy door shut, two dark figures arrived on the other side to block it. The two of them shoved hard, flinging the door back with more force that Aniri would have guessed possible, and Ash lost his footing on the polished floor. Aniri raised her weapon to the figures and fired. One black-robed figure stumbled backward, going down across the threshold. The other reached Ash before he could get his weapon raised and knocked Ash's pistol from his hand. In a blur, his attacker slammed him face-down into the floor. Ash grunted as the raksaka held him down with a foot to the middle of his back and wrenched Ash's arm into an unnatural position.

Aniri swung her pistol around. "Let him go!" Only then did she realize she'd already fired her gun and didn't have another shot.

A loud metal clanging drew their attention to the control panels. Riva had worked the bolts free, and she was slamming her wrench into the clock-works behind the switches. The Samirian raksaka quickly drew a pistol out from his black-wrapped clothing and pointed it at Riva.

"No!" Akash shouted, moving in front of Riva, blocking her with his body.

The raksaka fired. Riva screamed and dropped her wrench.

But it was Akash who staggered to the floor, holding his arm. His half-loaded pistol tumbled away as his hand went slack.

Aniri was still in shock at Akash being shot when Natesh walked through the door. He carefully stepped over his fallen raksaka, as if concerned he might get blood on his shoes. Ash struggled against the second raksaka holding him down, but that got him nowhere. His gun was still far out of his reach. And out of Aniri's. And she was guessing Akash's wasn't fully loaded or he would have used it.

The Second Son surveyed the scene, his gaze quickly landing on Aniri. His dark look for her had a hint of pleasure in it, like he wasn't altogether displeased to find her in his engine room. "Third Daughter of Dharia, is your own skyship so broken that you must have one of mine?"

Aniri just stared at him, desperately trying to think of some way out of this. Why was Natesh *here*, with his raksaka no less, and not in his miniature mountain palace? She prayed Janak was stealing away with her sister as they occupied Natesh's attention. Maybe they wouldn't make it out of this, but Aniri could at least buy them some time.

"I'm afraid your skyship is far too ugly for Jungali to covet." Aniri held her head high.

Natesh shook his head. "Witty to the end, Aniri. It's really a shame we're not on the same side. I find more to admire in you than in any royal I've known in a while."

"That's funny," she said, her calm voice belying

the pounding of her heart. "I find more to despise in you than in any royal I've ever met."

He chuckled, then took a closer look at the destruction of the control panels behind her. Riva had dropped to Akash's side. He was gritting his teeth through the pain and clenching his arm with one hand, but that just told Aniri he was alive. At least for the moment.

She wasn't sure how long any of them had to live.

Natesh pulled a pistol from behind his back and pointed it at Aniri. "I tried to kill you once, Third Daughter." He looked thoughtful for a moment. "Actually twice, if you count the fire."

Ash struggled again under the raksaka. "Aniri, don't let him—" His words were cut off by a groan as the raksaka twisted his arm even harder. Aniri bit her lip hard to keep from crying out, uselessly, for him to stop. She had assumed Jungali General Garesh was behind the original attempt on her life, firebombing her bed in Ash's palace, but apparently Natesh had been behind the scenes on that. As well as taking a literal shot at her in a shopkeeper's store in Mahatvak. Not that any of that mattered now.

Natesh glanced at Ash under his raksaka's foot.

"You and your barbarian lover are proving a bit more difficult to kill than his brother was."

Aniri's heart wrenched, and Ash twisted a murderous glare in Natesh's direction.

Natesh looked unimpressed. He turned to Aniri and waved his gun at the open control panel. "How about you tell me exactly what you've done to my skyship? That way I can fix whatever inconvenience you've wrought before it does any more damage."

Aniri wasn't sure how far Riva had gotten. The engine room seemed to be heating up, but that could just be the tension. Then again, a quick peek at the control panel Riva had shot showed several gauges edging into the red-colored zone. That couldn't be good.

For Natesh.

Regardless, she wouldn't be telling him anything. She straightened and stared defiantly into the eyes.

He gave her a bored look, then signaled to his raksaka to let Ash up from the floor. Aniri watched wide-eyed as the raksaka scooped up Ash's gun, hauled him to his feet, and held Ash's own gun to his head.

"No." Aniri hadn't meant for the word to slip out, but Natesh heard it all the same.

"Oh, yes," Natesh said, the pleasure in full-force on his face now. "You see, I've figured you out, Third Daughter of Dharia. I've found your weakness. You are far too attached to those around you, even the sisters you compete with for the crown. And that's a weakness a real leader cannot afford to—"

A sudden hiss from the engines interrupted him. A small billow of steam leaked from one side of the boiler, and a metallic creaking sounded of something under greater strain than normal. Aniri's heart pounded even harder in response. The engines were running too hot. Any moment, they could throw a blade or whatever Riva said before. If she had routed that heated gas through the navia bag, it would destroy that, too. But had she had managed to lock down the controls, so that it couldn't be stopped?

Natesh's smirk had fled, replace by a cold fury focused on Aniri. "What have you done?" When she didn't answer, he turned to his raksaka. "Where is the engine crew?"

"Out in the hall, my lord."

Aniri looked to Riva. She was bent over Akash, trying to apply pressure to his wound. If she had locked the controls before Natesh arrived, they wouldn't have to get aloft like they planned—they could wreck the engines, and even the gas bag, right here on the ground. But when Aniri caught her eye, she slowly shook her head, *no*.

So the controls *weren't* locked down.

Aniri's chest squeezed. If they wanted to destroy the *Dagger*, they had to keep that knowledge out of Natesh's hands… until it was too late to stop. Until the ship had burned too hot, too long, and had either burnt out the engines or the gasbag or both.

He pointed the gun back to Aniri's head. "Go out in the hall, Third Daughter, and release my men. If you take too long, I'll put a bullet in your lover's head."

"Call one of your men to do it." Anything to delay him.

He narrowed his eyes at her. "You're stalling." He stalked toward her until the business end of his gun was only a couple of feet from her head. "*Why?*"

Aniri tried not to stare at the barrel and just hold Natesh's gaze. But she said nothing.

He growled his anger and gestured his raksaka to bring Ash over to him. Aniri blinked rapidly as Ash stumbled, his arm twisted behind him, the gun at his head. When Ash reached Natesh's side, the

Second Son pressed the tip of his gun to Ash's head as well, so hard that it bent over.

"I *will* kill him, Third Daughter," he said, anger making his breaths short. "Now tell me: *what have you done to my ship?*"

"Don't tell him anything, Aniri." Ash's gaze held hers, imploring.

She knew what he wanted. She knew he'd rather die that let Natesh take the *Dagger* on another bombing run to kill who knew how many innocent people. *I wasn't afraid to die,* he told her. He was brave and selfless and noble… and she couldn't do it. She couldn't let Natesh put a bullet in the man she loved. It was too much to ask. The price of nobility was too high… or at least, it was too high for her.

"Wait." Aniri put up her hands, and Ash closed his eyes, defeated. "I'll tell you."

Natesh lowered his gun, triumph burning in his eyes. He waited.

"We shot out the controls for the turbine. The engine's running too hot, but you can still stop it before it burns out the gas bag." She pointed to the controls that Riva hadn't been able to destroy in time. "It's those ones." Aniri avoided the look of disappointment in Riva's eyes.

Natesh's grin grew as she spoke. He waved his gun at her. "Go untie my tinkers and bring them here."

With slow, leaden steps, Aniri did as he said. Tears gathered in her eyes, but she held them back. Once the tinkers were free, they scurried back into the engine room. She watched as they flitted across the control panels, checking what damage Riva had wrought. Aniri's heart sank to her stomach as she watched them work. They may not have watched her do it, but they were figuring out what was wrong quickly enough.

"Can you fix it?" Natesh asked them as they scurried around the control panels, flipping switches.

"Aye, your majesty," said one. "We can temporarily re-route the exhaust gases away from the gas bag while we try to cool the engines."

"We're going to be running hot for a while, though," the other said. "Have to find a way around these disabled controls. Might be able to do it from the override on the bridge."

"Then do it!" Natesh said. "I want us in the air as soon as possible."

Both tinkers stopped what they were doing, looked at Natesh and then each other.

"You can still make it fly, right?" he said between gritted teeth.

"Aye, sir," they both said and hurried about their work.

Natesh examined his four prisoners in turn. Aniri standing, shoulders drooped, holding the ropes that had bound the tinkers. Riva and Akash on the floor. Ash under the hold of Natesh's raksaka.

Natesh lifted his chin, gesturing to the bulkhead door. "Lock them up somewhere they can't make any more trouble."

Chapter Fourteen

Natesh's raksaka marched the four of them—Aniri, Ash, Akash, and Riva—at gunpoint out of the engine room. Shouts and activity came from the floor above them, and sailors hurried down, passing them and heading to the engine room. The raksaka ushered them back up the stairs to the main level, where it became clear why Pavan's guards and loyal raksaka had never sent the signal that they had taken the ship. Natesh's sailors and raksaka were everywhere, far outnumbering the five raksaka and six guards who had been on Riva's team. Aniri's chest grew tight as she watched the limp bodies of the guards and raksaka being carried off the ship.

Ash's hand found hers, but even that couldn't ward off the chill. She thought they might be next in being carried out, but Natesh's raksaka simply took them up another level to the crew quarters. Perhaps he would lock them away, as Aniri had been imprisoned on the *Prosperity?* But as they reached the corridor, another raksaka stood guard. Judging by all the raksaka onboard, the three who were killed at the train hijacking clearly weren't the only ones working for Natesh.

The raksaka guarding the hall held up a hand, looking over their entourage. "Hold up. You can't bring them here. No prisoners allowed on this deck."

Which seemed a strange thing to say, given there was a whole host of guards escorting another prisoner in a long, dark cloak into the captain's quarters. The prisoner turned for a second to look down the hall, just before disappearing through the threshold.

Aniri sucked in a breath. *It was Seledri.*

Her sister was gone before Aniri could see if she recognized them.

The raksaka guarding the hall scowled. "Take them below. There's a brig of sorts down there. The rest are being left behind. Too much weight."

Natesh's raksaka didn't reply, just pointed the gun in their faces and forced them back down the stairs. The "brig" turned out to be a cage on the lowest deck of the *Dagger*. The iron-barred prison was only ten foot by ten, and may have once been meant for food, but now it housed Aniri, Ash, Riva, and a bleeding Akash. Once they were locked in, Natesh's raksaka returned to help the others in their hasty preparations for the ship to lift off.

As soon as they were alone, Aniri said to Ash, "Did you see her?"

"Your sister." Ash nodded solemnly. They didn't discuss it. They didn't need to. If Seledri was *here*, on board the *Dagger* with Natesh, then Pavan's mission to rescue her had failed. Aniri couldn't stomach the idea of what that might mean: Pavan, Janak, Devesh, and everyone on their team might be bodies lying on the floor of Natesh's miniature castle, just like the bodies of their team being off-loaded from the skyship right now.

They had failed utterly.

There were no windows in their deck level, but Aniri knew just when the *Dagger* lifted off. Her stomach sunk even lower and turned slightly nauseous as they lifted into the heavens. They had lost by every measure, and much of the blame lay squarely at her feet.

She had let Natesh win this round. He had his

skyship *and* Seledri, and now they were aloft, headed for who knew where. The horror of her decision had yet to come into full relief. Ash hadn't said a word about it, but he didn't have to: she knew he loathed that she spared him and allowed Natesh to keep his instrument of war. There was part of her that loathed it herself, but she simply couldn't be the cause of Ash's death, any more than she could stand to be what brought him down in his own country, with her mistakes and her fecklessness. She knew the choice would have a horrible result… but in the heat of the moment, that consequence was an ill-defined evil. Whatever Natesh might perpetrate in the future with the skyship she refused to destroy couldn't compare with Ash dying now by his hand.

But Akash was already paying the price. Riva tended to Ash's Jungali spy, and it appeared his wound wasn't life-threatening. But it still left him with a sheen of sweat on his color-drained face. Ash helped Riva bind the gunshot wound tightly with a torn piece of shirt. The bleeding slowed, but still seeped a spreading blotch of red across his sleeve. Aniri kept staring at it, watching it grow, until she forced herself to look away.

Shudders tormented her body as she thought of

what lay ahead. She could barely look Ash and Riva and Akash in the eye. Instead, she sat in a corner of the cage by herself, staring at her hands and ardently wishing there was a possibility of escape. Maybe she could yet undo this disaster if she could just get them free.

The only problem: that looked fairly impossible.

The cage bars were incredibly sturdy—a shashee couldn't bend them, even with the beast's great strength. The door was constructed of an inch-thick sheet of steel and was locked with elaborate clockwork: more Samirian technology that was beyond anything Dharians or Jungali possessed. The lowest deck housed more than their cage, but nothing that might spring them from it. A wide assortment of armaments sat nearby, no doubt similar to the bombs the *Dagger* dropped on Bhakti. A stack of the sleek, bullet-nosed bombs was tantalizingly close. Aniri could almost reach them, if she strained her arm through the gap between the narrow iron bars. But what would she do with them, if she could?

The *Dagger* hadn't been in the air for long when a cohort of Samirian sailors trotted into the room. Next to the bombs was a hatch in the floor with a clockwork lock and crank, which they swiftly opened. After a flurry of commands and arguments, they pushed several of the bombs out, one by one. Aniri and Ash had risen to watch them, while Riva stayed with Akash on the floor. It was dark out, and hard to see what possible purpose the sailors could have. Had the *Dagger* even left the harbor? Were they bombing their own skyships? It seemed insane. But then Natesh was driven by passions she didn't understand.

After three bombs were rolled out, the Samirians stood back to watch. Through the open hatch, Aniri could see the flashes of the explosions light up Natesh's stone estate. It was a fortress built into the canyon wall, so she imagined the damage wouldn't be too severe, but the fact that he was bombing his own castle at all perplexed her.

Apparently, the sailors were equally concerned, because they quickly closed the hatch and withdrew. They had ignored Aniri and her entourage completely. The hatch was large enough that they could just as easily have pushed their entire cage out the bottom of the skyship. But they hadn't. Natesh was keeping them alive, and that was also a mystery to her.

Ash let loose a long sigh and turned to Riva. "Any thoughts, Mistress Tinker?"

"Other than the right mess we're in?" She had finally risen from tending Akash and stood on the opposite side of the cage, examining the spare contents of the deck. Aniri glanced at Akash, but his eyes were closed as he sat resting his back against the bars.

"Yes, other than that," Ash replied.

"Not as yet."

Ash nodded, then swept his gaze to Aniri. She ducked away, staring at the dusty floor with a sudden great interest. She returned to her corner, sitting in the dust and keeping her head down, as if that could hide her responsibility for being in this mess. Her obvious attempts to avoid him in the tiny cage were apparently lost on him, as he came over and took a seat next to her anyway.

She gathered her courage and turned to face him. His light amber eyes were pinched with concern. It nearly undid her. Her shoulders flinched together, as if they were trying to hide by caving in.

"Ash, I'm sorry," she said in a rush. "I just... couldn't." Then she ducked her head away again, feeling the heat of his stare and having nowhere to go to escape it.

He didn't say anything, but his hand gently brushed back her hair where it had fallen forward.

He tucked it behind her ear, then traced the edges of it along her face. His touch was so gentle, so tender, her heart constricted with it. Even in this, he would forgive her, she could feel it. And then she would loathe herself even more.

"If it were me in your place," he whispered in her ear, speaking just for her in this tiny, crowded cell, "I wouldn't have been so calm. If Natesh had put a gun to your head, I wouldn't have been able to control myself. We would likely all be dead because my hands would have found his throat before I could think about what I was doing."

Aniri slowly turned to face him, disbelieving. "I thought you would… I didn't want… Ash, he'll destroy everything you've worked for."

He cupped her cheeks. "And what would it be worth, if I lost you?"

She blinked back tears, breath held. "The price would be too high."

"Only a monster would force such a choice." Ash ran a thumb across her cheek. "We'll find another way to defeat him, Aniri."

She let out her breath, daring to believe he truly meant it. "Together."

He flashed a grin. "Together."

It was like a crushing load lifted from her heart.

Ash would have done the same in her position—of course. She couldn't imagine anything different, yet she hadn't managed to see it that way. He might be willing to sacrifice his own life, but he would never allow anyone he loved to come to harm. Which was exactly how she felt. Why she could hardly stand every moment of duty that kept her from finding him. Aniri slipped her arms around his neck and held him tight, hiding her face, until she could compose it again. After a moment, when she could, she pulled back and gave him a small smile.

Ash trailed a finger along her hair again, pain returning to his eyes. "I have to believe someone like Natesh can't carry the day. He's mad with power, bent on claiming the throne at any cost. That's not the kind of leader Samir wants." He glanced at Riva, who was paying attention to their conversation, now that it wasn't so closely held. "At least, I don't think *all* Samirians would want that kind of King, if they knew his true temper."

"The Second Son's temper isn't such a secret," Riva said. "For those who pay attention, that is."

Akash drew in a long breath, as if rousing from a deep sleep. He squinted open his eyes and peered at them. "There are plenty of Samirians who like Natesh's particular brand of hatred. The docks are rife with people who despise all things not Samirian. The capital city as well."

"True enough," Riva said. "And the Guild is a rotted corpse of jealousy and greed that takes advantage of it all."

Akash raised his eyebrows, humor returning to his washed-out face. "Spoken like a true Free Tinker."

Red ran up Riva's cheeks. "Just sayin' like I see it. But I believe yer young prince here is right." She tilted her head to Ash. "Most folk don't brag so loud and so awful about how they can't stand Dharians, much less Jungali. They just want to feed their families and live their lives."

"I believe she's right, your majesty," Akash said. "I would guess most Samirians want the stability that peace brings."

Ash nodded. "Which is why Pavan needs to wear the crown. He's the kind of leader Samir needs. It's very unfortunate that Natesh still has his wife." He turned back to Aniri, his face remaining close where they sat cuddled in the corner of the cage. "As long as Natesh has her, Pavan is as much a prisoner as she is. We can only pray to the gods that, whatever happened when they tried to rescue Seledri, Pavan actually survived. And escaped."

Aniri nodded. "And we have to find a way to free my sister."

"Agreed." He sighed and looked around their cage. "Although at the moment, I'm not sure precisely how that's going to happen."

Aniri frowned. "The thing I can't figure is why *we're* still alive."

Akash sat up a little, wincing as he leaned away from the bars. "I've been wondering the same thing, my lady. The Second Son may be many things, but he is not a fool. Either he still fears retribution from Jungali, or perhaps Dharia, if he were to actually take your lives… or there's something else at play."

Riva gripped the bars of their cage. "Would help if we knew where we're going."

"He could be headed anywhere," Aniri said. "Maybe Dharia? But could he reach it from here? If the *Dagger* has to stop somewhere for fuel, that could give us an opportunity to escape."

"Perhaps," Ash said. "But I think Kartavya is within range. When the *Dagger* struck Bhakti, it had to fly across half of Samir, the ocean, and a pretty vast stretch of Jungali mountain territory to get there."

"And return," Riva added. "It's a larger ship than the *Prosperity* and can carry more fuel. If it can reach Bhakti, that about puts Kartavya in its range as well."

Aniri worked her way up to standing and took another look around the deck. "There are plenty of munitions here, if he was of a mind to attack. But why would he strike the capital of Dharia now? Or Jungali for that matter? He has us both in his brig. He could continue to hold our countries hostage with it."

"We've found his airharbor," Ash said, standing as well. "And we know the *Dagger's* his only ship. Maybe he's set out to strike first, before the *Prosperity* can attack his secret airharbor."

"He sure was all fired to get in the air," Riva said, eyes narrowed. "He wanted to go somewhere in a hurry."

Akash groaned a bit as he struggled up from the floor. "Perhaps it's more important who he *doesn't* have in the brig."

Aniri frowned at Akash, then looked to Ash. "Pavan."

Ash nodded. "If Natesh had just defeated Pavan's rescue attempt, you wouldn't think he would leave him behind. Dead or alive."

"And yet he has Pavan's wife." Akash braced his good hand against the iron bars. "Who he brought to the *Dagger*, and then hastily commanded we go aloft. Not the behavior of a man who just won a fight."

"You think Natesh was *fleeing* Pavan?" Aniri asked. She liked that possibility a whole lot better than Pavan lying dead in the airharbor.

"Natesh is power-hungry," Ash said, "but he's also a braggart and a coward. It wouldn't surprise me if, once he saw the rescue-in-progress, he grabbed Seledri and fled for his ship."

"Maybe that's why Natesh bombed his own estate on the way out," Aniri added. "He was trying to kill his brother."

"And he may have succeeded," Akash said. "But if Pavan's alive... what would you do, if your power-mad brother just took off with your wife in a skyship?"

Aniri frowned. "Chase after it?"

"And try to beat it back to the one person who could possibly stop Natesh from killing her."

Aniri's eyes went wide. "The Queen Mother in Mahatvak."

"Which is precisely where Natesh would go as well," Ash said. "Because he can't afford for Pavan to get there first."

"So… you think we're headed to Mahatvak?" Aniri asked.

"I sincerely hope so." Ash smiled at his Jungali spy, who ducked his head with a humility Aniri suspected he didn't actually possess.

And Aniri hoped so, too. Because if Natesh had decided to keep them alive, and he was heading back to the capital, there might be hope for them all yet.

Chapter Fifteen

Natesh's sailors were none-too-gentle when they came to haul Aniri, Ash, Riva, and Akash out of the brig. The sailors had donned royal guard coats over their uniforms, and Natesh's raksaka were apparently occupied elsewhere. The six sailors-turned-guards clasped chains on all of their wrists, as if they might contemplate a run. Akash had to muffle his groan when they yanked his injured arm forward in order to shackle it. Aniri didn't object, knowing it was useless. Or worse, it might bring further harm to Ash's spy.

She was simply glad they were all being kept together.

The *Dagger* had landed just a few minutes prior, if the sinking feeling of descent in their stomachs was any indication, but Natesh hadn't wasted any time calling for them. The trip had taken a few hours, and while it had felt interminable in their tiny cage, Aniri felt sure it hadn't been enough time to travel across the sea. Her hope that they had landed in Mahatvak was realized once they stepped from the depths of the skyship onto the darkened walkplank outside. It was still night, but she recognized the fortified apartments of the palace, that solitary wing that looked to be carved out of the mountainside of the Samarian capital. The twin moons, Raka and Indu had almost set again, and while the morning sun hadn't yet broke, it wasn't far from it, either.

The contingent of six guards held them on the balcony in the chilly early morning breeze, waiting for something. She thought they might bring Seledri to join them, but her sister was nowhere to be seen. The palace was lit sporadically, its sharpened towers mostly dark except for the occasional lord or lady who was up early. Or perhaps the lights were the keepers of the palace already at their work. The deep-red gasbag of the *Dagger* billowed above them, made even more gruesome in color by the silvered light of the moons. The city lay below, gaslamps marking the streets like strings of pearls laid out with fastidious straightness. The shops hadn't yet opened for the morning, but when dawn came, and the shopkeepers emerged from their businesses, they'd see the *Dagger* in her glory at the palace. And probably wonder what new day was upon them.

Finally, Natesh emerged from the skyship, dressed in royal attire, as if about to attend a high tea. His stride was hurried, as if he hadn't a moment to lose, and he brushed past them without a look. But his guards shoved them along to follow. Aniri was tempted to drag her heels, causing any delay she could in Natesh's plans, whatever they were, but Ash shook his head and urged her forward. They kept their silence, but Aniri was on high alert for any chance to break free and turn this stop to their advantage.

Natesh marched them through the outer embroidered stone wall of the palace, through a labyrinth of hallways and stairs, until they landed in a well-appointed receiving room. An unoccupied throne sat at one end, which seemed to instantly infuriate Natesh.

He whirled to his nearest guard, the burly one who was keeping close escort on Ash. "I was told my mother was awake. Why is she not here?"

The guard's eyes went wide. "Would you like me to inquire, my lord?"

"Yes." Natesh's impatience seethed under his words. "I would like you to inquire."

The man glanced to his fellow sailor-turned-jailor, jerked his head to have the man take his place guarding Ash, then scurried from the room. Natesh stalked to the throne at the far end and stared at it, his hands working into fists and opening again. Finally he took a seat, casually draping one leg over the arm while drumming his fingers on the other.

Aniri snuck a glance at Ash, but his glower was focused on Natesh, watching him like one would watch a snake that had entered the room, casually winding its way across the floor. Several minutes passed without a return of Natesh's guard, and the Second Son's agitation just seemed to grow. He shifted right and left on the throne, as if there weren't a sufficiently comfortable spot in which to lounge like an insolent child.

Perhaps because it doesn't belong to you. If Aniri's thoughts had power, Natesh would find himself thrown from the embroidered granite and lush red cushions of the chair... directly into the dungeon. Unfortunately, she suspected that was more likely her own destination.

Riva stood stiffly by her guard, but her cheeks were growing redder by the moment. Aniri could only guess what being caught with the Jungali prince, his spy, and his Dharian wife-to-be would mean for the Samirian tinker. Akash seemed concerned about that as well, with the way he hovered near her, giving steely looks to the Samirian sailor-turned-guard who stood next to her. Akash was broad shouldered, tall, and muscular from his work on the docks. Even with his injured arm, he could present an imposing figure when he wanted… and he very much seemed to want to intimidate the guard, whose looks of disgust rained down on Riva. Unfortunately, the four of them were in chains while guards possessed pistols. And a fortress castle they were deep inside.

After a long stretch of minutes, during which Natesh continued his silent war for comfort on the throne and everyone else shifted nervously, a figure emerged from a darkened alcove behind the throne. Aniri saw him before Natesh: his attire was from the royal guard, but he wore ink-black wrapped leggings, his movements were smooth, and his black boots made no sound as he approached the throne from behind. Aniri would be shocked if he wasn't raksaka.

"Your majesty," the man said, his voice quiet but carrying enough power to jerk Natesh upright and out of his mother's chair.

"Gods, Tajet!" Natesh exclaimed, hastily wiping his hands on his pants as if to wipe away the evidence that he had just been sitting on the throne. "Must you slink around like a shadow *all* the time?"

Tajet breezed past that as if Natesh hadn't spoken. "Your mother is glad you've finally returned to Mahatvak." He cast a glance toward their group of prisoners and guards, but didn't linger.

"Where is my mother?" Natesh asked in practically a growl. "When I messaged ahead, I was told she was already awake."

"Yes, her majesty has had some difficulty in her sleep lately," Tajet answered coolly. "I can't imagine why that would be."

"You and your snide little comments can be excessively tedious, Tajet." But Natesh's voice was regaining some of its cool as well. "And I asked about my mother's whereabouts. It's most urgent that I speak with her."

"That's unfortunate," said Tajet, in a voice that implied he was quite pleased to have the opportunity to delay Natesh in obtaining what he wished.

"Your mother is occupied at the moment with another visitor."

Natesh took a moment to respond. He glanced back at his prisoners, and it seemed some of the color and all of the swagger had drained from his face. When he turned back to Tajet, he said calmly, "Has my brother returned to the palace already?"

"Unfortunately, no," Tajet said, his voice flat.

The relief in Natesh's shoulders was clear from across the room.

"And neither has Princess Seledri, about which the Queen is most concerned."

Aniri's tired body perked to attention. Given that Seledri was being held on the *Dagger* at the moment, this Tajet person, clearly a raksaka for the crown, must not be fully aware of what was happening. Perhaps that meant he was allied with Pavan. Or at least *not* with Natesh.

"That is indeed alarming." Natesh's voice had cooled ten degrees. "And Seledri's safety, among other things, is precisely what I need to discuss with the Queen. It turns out my concerns were very well placed, something you would have seen much more clearly, Tajet, if you left the confines of the palace on occasion."

Tajet's face went impassive, a look Aniri recognized from Janak's stoic demeanor all too often. Raksaka would defend the lives of royals with their very own. But they weren't always fond of their charges.

"The Queen requests my presence nearby at all times," Tajet said stiffly.

"A situation I hope will change in several ways. Soon."

Tajet barely kept his glare under control, but then he frowned and glanced again at their group of guards and prisoners. The exchange between the Second Son and the Queen's raksaka had every-one's rapt attention. Aniri's entire body was tense. What was Natesh up to? She dashed a look to Ash, but he was still boring a glare at Natesh, watching his every move.

"So, you're not here to…" Tajet's gaze locked with Aniri's and his eyebrows lifted. "Who *are* these prisoners you've brought to the Queen?"

"*These…*" Natesh threw out his hand to indict their group. "These are the spies I caught attempting to sabotage my skyship."

Tajet's eyes went wide, and a triumphant smile lit Natesh's face.

"Perhaps next time," Natesh said, "you could argue for the Queen to heed my counsel, instead of trying to thwart my every move. I would like to see my mother. *Now.*"

Tajet nodded slowly, then scrutinized their group once more. "The Queen is awake, but the night has been hard on her. She has received her guest in her bedchambers—"

"Then I will see her there as well."

Natesh's sharp tone brought Tajet back to face him. "Yes, your majesty," he said with a slight bow, hands pressed together. "I will accompany you there."

Chapter Sixteen

THE QUEEN of Samir's bedchamber was surely not meant to hold four prisoners in chains and a half dozen Samirian sailors in guard uniforms. Aniri stayed close to Ash, while Riva braced Akash's good arm as they were herded into the softly lit room.

Dozens of paintings covered every inch of the walls, transforming the room into a museum of Samirian landscapes. One wall held four contiguous paintings of the Samirian coast, with the naval piers and proud Samirian frigates crowding the far end. Another was a rolling mountainscape complete with mining operations and rock climbers, while the third held a portrait in miniature of the capital city, lit at night, like they had just seen when they debarked from the skyship. The last wall appeared to be countryside, with tall grasses and wildflowers like Aniri had seen outside the capital when they fled. But half of the wall was obscured by live blooms in a dozen vases and the rest by an enormous four-poster bed, which was draped in nettings so thick they would block all the light of day—and which kept the prisoners from seeing the Queen within.

Tajet signaled Natesh to wait before approaching the bed, then he disappeared around the corner. Whispered voices carried through the netting, but so soft-spoken that Aniri couldn't tell if they were male or female. A handmaiden scurried from a corner of the room to the side of the bed they couldn't see, beckoned by someone. The four prisoners and six guards shifted their weight, holding their position, but cramped in the corner to which they had been relegated.

The handmaiden reappeared and came around to the near side. She slowly lifted the netting, rolling it upwards to finally tuck it above the railings strung between the posts. As she edged along, she revealed the Queen sitting in her bed. Aniri could immediately see the Queen was not well. It caught her breath, and flashed back an image of Aniri's own Queen Mother, stricken in her bedroom in Dharia.

Only Aniri's mother was recovering from a Samirian raksaka's bullet.

She gritted her teeth and watched as the hand-maiden worked her way around the bed. The Samirian Queen Mother was sallow-cheeked, her gray hair loose around her, and she still wore her red silk bedclothes. Several pillows propped her up, and she was surrounded by a voluminous gathering of comforters. The Queen was nearly lost inside them, she was so thin. Her bone-like fingers lay in her lap, and her face had a gauntness borne of an illness that was eating away at her from the inside.

Tajet reappeared around the netting, which still obscured half the bed and whoever the Queen's visitor was, and he waved Natesh to approach. The Second Son skirted the bed, but pulled up short when he saw the visitor.

He put a smile on his face and his hands together to bow. "First Daughter Nahali," he said in a sweet voice. "What an unexpected pleasure."

Nahali?

Ash gave her a wide-eyed look, but Aniri just shook her head in disbelief… until the handmaiden rolled up the last of the netting to reveal her sister standing by the Queen's bedside. Attired in a corset and full skirts in muted greens and golds, with a sweep of glittering fabric over her shoulder, she was the picture of Dharian royalty. Including the bump of the future Queen of Dharia she was carrying. And she was standing in the bedchambers of the Queen of Samir.

Nahali pressed her hands together and held them high in front of her, the greatest sign of respect. "It's a pleasure to be in the great country of Samir," she said with a small bow to Natesh.

His smile slid onto his face, and he returned the gesture of respect. "Welcome to our great country."

Aniri's heart thudded in her chest. Then it froze as Nahali caught sight of her. Her sister's eyes flashed momentarily, then her look hardened, and she turned back to Natesh. "I was just discussing with your mother some of our mutual concerns."

"Were you, now?" His voice took on some edge.

"Natu," the Queen chastised gently. It was obviously her nickname for Natesh, but the soft way she used it, like Natesh was her favorite person in the entire Queendom, make the hairs on the back of Aniri's neck stand up. "The First Daughter is here simply to check on Pavan and Seledri. And to discuss a few diplomatic matters along the way."

Natesh eyed Nahali, then turned to his mother.

"How are you faring today, Mother? I'm sorry to disturb you at such an early hour."

"The hour doesn't seem to matter much these days." Her voice was very weak, with a whisper of death at the edges. No wonder the Sons were fighting for her crown. Aniri's mother might yet recover her health—it was only a bullet that stole it—but the Queen of Samir seemed much closer to death and much less likely to evade it. It was a wonder no news of this had leaked out of the royal household, but then Aniri knew there were many royal secrets the household took pride in holding close. And a monarch on the verge of death was one that would shake the country. That the Queen allowed Nahali to visit was shocking in itself.

Unless… the Queen was even closer to death than she appeared. *Some of our mutual concerns,* Nahali had said. Was the Queen forging peace with Dharia before she died? And at what price?

"I wouldn't disturb you at all, Mother, but I'm afraid I have some rather unsettling news." Natesh glanced at Nahali.

The Queen finally noticed the crowd in the corner, but Aniri wasn't sure how well her filmed-over eyes could see them. Especially in the low, predawn light of the flickering gaslamps.

"Have you brought an entire legion of guards to watch over me, Natesh?" she asked, her voice attempting sternness, but simply sounding like a mockery of it. "I'm not sure they will be able to forestall the inevitable."

Natesh eased onto the bed and took his mother's hand. "Mother, please. I don't want to hear that kind of talk."

"Well, it will happen, regardless of whether we discuss it."

Natesh gave an elaborate sigh. "Can you forgive your son for wanting to pretend, just a little longer?" The concern was so sweet in his voice, Aniri almost believed it herself.

By the Queen's smile, she was certainly taken by it.

She patted his hand. "I know, Natu. But as the young First Daughter of Dharia has reminded me, the matters of state will not wait for an old woman's death to resolve them."

Natesh glared at Nahali. "I would take care with any words the First Daughter has for you, Mother. With the exception of our lovely Seledri, the Daughters of Dharia are not so trustworthy as you might think."

The Queen adjusted her pillow so she was

sitting upright a little more. "What do you mean, Natu? Please speak plainly."

Natesh gestured to the guards. Two of them took Aniri and Ash by the arm and hauled them to the Queen's bedside. Their chains rattled along the way, causing the Queen to frown at them. She seemed to struggle to understand who they were.

"Mother, this is the Jungali prince I've been telling you about," Natesh said. "As well as his lover and fellow spy, the Third Daughter of Dharia. I caught them both trying to destroy our skyship. It was only by great good luck that I was able to stop them in time."

The Queen scowled.

Aniri's heart sunk. "Your majesty, don't listen to—"

"Be quiet!" Natesh said harshly. "The Queen does not want to hear your lies and justifications."

The guard's hold on Aniri's arm tightened until it was painful. She was tempted to blurt the truth, but she wasn't sure how far she would get. She needed just the right words... Ash's hand found hers, reassuring her. *Together.* They would find a way out of this.

The Queen turned to her son. "The skyship? I don't understand."

"It's like I told you, Mother. They're afraid of our technology. They're threatened by us as we grow stronger." He looked up at Nahali, whose expression was as inscrutable as any Janak ever had. "Your majesty, we truly need to discuss this in private."

The Queen sighed and scrutinized Nahali hovering behind Natesh. "First Daughter of Dharia, do you have any explanation for what my son claims? Why is your younger sister on my son's skyship?"

"Your majesty, I have no idea."

Nahali's voice was so cold it sent a shiver through Aniri.

"You may not have noticed from your sickbed," she continued, "but the Third Daughter of Dharia has, shall we say, a history of reckless behavior. When she panicked before and whisked Seledri away, that was not sanctioned in any way by the crown of Dharia. Whatever she is doing here in Samir, I promise you, it is nothing that the Queen approves of. If she has performed some kind of sabotage—"

"*If?*" Natesh cut her off. "Mother, I caught her and the Jungali prince and their tinker spy literally destroying the controls of the ship with their bare hands. I was shocked to find the airharbor had been discovered, and that someone had found a way to attack us, but I can't say I was terribly surprised at who was, in fact, responsible."

"Like I said," Nahali said stiffly, once he had finished, "if the Third Daughter is responsible for some kind of sabotage, she bears that responsibility herself. The crown was in no way involved, and I can assure you that Dharia respects Samir's right to prosecute her for her crimes. The goodwill between our countries is too important to be squandered by one wayward Daughter with ideas of her own about stirring up war."

Nahali's words sliced through Aniri's heart: her sister was disavowing her *completely*. Whatever arrangements Nahali was brokering with the Queen of Samir, she was utterly willing to sacrifice Aniri to them. It left her speechless, and even Ash's gentle squeeze on her hand couldn't bring her to say anything in response.

"Do you see, Mother?" Natesh said. "Even the First Daughter thinks the Third is dangerous. And as much as I respect the First Daughter's attempts to mend the relations between our countries, we need to discuss these matters in private."

The Queen Mother took a deep breath and

waved her hand weakly to her raksaka. He appeared by her side. "Will you please escort the First Daughter out and provide her with some tea and refreshments?"

"Arama, your majesty," Nahali said, pressing her hands together and giving a small bow. "I completely understand the need to discuss matters privately with your Second Son. Hopefully we can resume our discussion when you are finished."

The Queen's raksaka guided Nahali toward the door. Her silk skirts whispered against each other, the only sound in the hushed silence that awaited her departure. Nahali didn't look at her, but Aniri couldn't keep her eyes off the stiff-backed retreat of her sister from the room. When she reached Akash and Riva in chains by the door, she gave them a quick look-over, as if disgusted by the lot Aniri had fallen in with. Akash, for once, had no humor in his face. He mirrored her look of disgust, which simply made Nahali exit the room more quickly. Riva bit her lip and looked to Aniri as if she wanted to say something. Or possibly hear some consoling words from her. But she had nothing to offer.

The Queen's raksaka quickly returned to the foot of her bed.

As soon as the door closed, Natesh turned to the

Queen and said, "Mother, you can't believe anything she is saying. I just caught them sabotaging our ship. The Dharians mean to destroy us."

"Your majesty!" Aniri broke in. "You have to know your sons are fighting for your crown!"

Natesh fixed his gaze on Aniri and smoothly glided to standing from his place on the bed. "Mother, even her sister doesn't trust her to speak the truth." He stalked around the bed toward Aniri, who was trapped in her chains and the close custody of the guard who still held her tight. "She's a traitor and a spy. I think summary execution is in order."

"Natesh." The Queen's voice had a momentarily stronger tone.

It was enough to check Natesh's purposeful stride toward Aniri, but not enough to erase the deadly intent in his eyes.

"Third Daughter, I don't know what you mean by coming her and interfering with my Queendom. My *family.*"

"Seledri is *my* family, too!" Aniri was becoming shrill with her desperation. "Your Second Son—"

"Do not presume to lecture me in my own bedroom." The Queen Mother cut her off with a royal reserve that sounded much more like the monarch Aniri remembered from Seledri's wedding, a scant two years ago, rather than the dying woman before her now. "I may be frail, but I am not stupid."

"But Natesh is the assassin behind the attempts on Seledri's life!" *There.* She got it out. And the words had the force of truth behind them. The Queen had to hear them.

Natesh's light laughter mocked her. "At least come up with a *plausible* lie, Aniri."

Aniri ignored him and kept her gaze on the Queen, but she just shook her head sadly. Aniri's shoulders dropped. She didn't know why she dared to hope her words would make a difference.

"It's true, your majesty," Ash said softly. "Seledri herself will confirm it. In fact, she's on Natesh's skyship at the moment. Ask her yourself."

Natesh's face fell serious, his glare for Ash this time.

"Is that true, Natu?" his mother asked. "Have you brought my Seledri home to me?"

"No, mother, it's all lies." Natesh gave an elaborate sigh, as if he was attempting to be patient with them. "As I told you before, the safest place for Seledri is my mountain estate, where she remains at the moment."

"But Tajet said she would be returning by train to the capital soon."

Natesh turned his glare on Tajet. "I warned Tajet that transporting the princess was risky, especially when it was still unclear as to who made the assassination attempt in the first place. So it's fortunate I took the precaution of sending a decoy train first."

Tajet frowned. "A decoy?"

"I couldn't take the chance of anything happening to her," Natesh continued. "And it's quite fortunate that I sent a decoy in her place, as the train was attacked, and even the three raksaka I sent to protect it are now dead. Seledri clearly has a bitter enemy targeting her." The gloat in Natesh's voice made Aniri's fists curl up. But then he turned to give a pointed look to Aniri. "For all we know, the Third Daughter is involved in that, too."

"*I* was the one who rescued her from Samir in the first place!" Aniri burst out.

But apparently, that was the utterly wrong thing to say, because Natesh just chuckled. "Do you see, Mother? It's just as I told you."

"*You* were behind that?" the Queen asked Aniri. "Pavan said he sent her away for her own protection, but it was *you* who stole my future grandchild from me?"

"No, it *was* Pavan." Aniri cringed as she heard the weakness in her own voice. "I mean, he agreed to it—"

The Queen held up a shaking hand. "I've heard enough. The poor Queen of Dharia must be heart-broken by the infighting of her daughters. My boys may fight, as boys often do, but they do not kidnap one another. Or worse." She dropped her hand and sighed the long, drawn-out breath of a woman who may not have too many left.

It was obvious to Aniri their cause was lost. The Queen was sequestered away, too heavily influenced by her Second Son, secluded and lied to. This must be how Natesh had gained as much power as he had. The Queen was being manipulated by her Second Son, and nothing Aniri could say would convince her otherwise.

She gritted her teeth in frustration and tried to pull away from the guard whose hand gripped her, but it was no use.

Natesh came around to sit with his ailing mother again. "My sources tell me Dharia means to attack us at any moment, Mother. This tactic with the First Daughter is just stalling on their part. They are preparing armaments in their naval yards. They've even begun building a skyship fleet of their own. We cannot let them have the advantage. With their burning glass, it would mean devastating destruction for Samir. We need to strike now, by air and by sea, while we have all the Daughters here in Samir. It's the perfect opportunity. The Dharian Queen will be very reluctant to retaliate."

Aniri bit back the raging protests in her head, knowing they were pointless. And might even work against them somehow. Her words had done nothing but snarl their situation further.

But the Queen only shook her head sadly. "I know you're just thinking of Samir, Natu, but I gave the Queen of Dharia my word that her First Daughter would not be harmed in coming here on her diplomatic mission. Even though tensions were running high between our countries. I must honor that promise."

Natesh gritted his teeth, but then he used that sweet voice again. "I know what your word means to you, Mother. I respect that. But what of the Third Daughter? Surely, it has to matter that she's a saboteur in our midst."

The Queen sighed and looked to Aniri. "You're a

Daughter of Dharia, Aniri. You should know better than to play these games. My Second Son loves Samir so much, it pains him terribly to see anyone work against it. But I know the Queen of Dharia, and I know she will deal fairly with you, as a Daughter, when you return. For now, you will be confined to your room, until Natesh can make arrangements for you to return to home. As for your friends…" She looked them over with her squinted, watery eyes. "They will pay the price for your folly. Prince Malik, you should have known coming into my country for this act of sabotage was, in fact, an act of war."

Aniri's mouth dropped open. Natesh had kidnapped Ash, held him captive, and tortured him. How secluded from the realities of her country was the Samirian Queen, if she did not know even *that* much?

"I wanted to trust we had made a good alliance with the Jungali," the Queen continued, "but apparently, I was naïve about that. You've committed an act of war against Samir, Prince Malik. And that I cannot forgive."

Then it seemed all the air slowly went out of the Queen. Her shoulders caved, and she slumped where she sat. "I am fatigued, Natesh. Will you please see that the proper judgments are rendered for those involved?"

"Of course, Mother," Natesh said with a sickening smile that made Aniri's stomach turn. He gave his mother a quick kiss on the head as she leaned back into her nest of pillows. "Rest now. Don't worry about a thing. I will take care of it all."

She reached up to lightly pat his cheek. "Thank you, Natu." With that she closed her eyes.

Aniri wanted to close her eyes as well, to block out the horror of what she'd just seen: the Queen abdicating all responsibility for them to Natesh. But the guards were shoving them back toward the door. Riva's eyes were wide and round with the same horror that had gripped Aniri. Akash and Ash exchanged a look, but with the rattling of chains and hasty exit, Aniri couldn't parse what it meant. She glanced back, one last look, but the Queen was asleep before they had even left the room.

Chapter Seventeen

NATESH MARCHED the four of them—Aniri, Ash, Riva, and Akash—back through the winding palace halls. The estate was starting to stir, curious keepers of the royal household watching them in their solemn parade through the early morning light. The sky was the grayish pink of predawn. They were herded out onto the balcony of fortified apartments where the *Dagger* was docked. Aniri thought, for a moment, Natesh might return them to their cage, possibly drop them out the hatch after all, but then they stopped in front of one of the stone-doored rooms.

The apartments were jails after all. Or at least Natesh was putting them to that use.

The guards shuffled them inside, one at a time,

and removed their wrist chains. The smallish room was carved from the gray rock of the mountain: the walls were left rough-cut, but the floor at least had been smoothed well enough that they didn't trip over the uneven surface. Or possibly it had been worn flat by the pacing of its inmates. An iron-barred wall split the room in two: the front half was empty of furniture, and the back held two cots that were barely more than a thin straw mattress and an even thinner gray wool blanket. A tiny square window in the door was all the light they had.

Natesh took a key from inside his properly royal attire and unlocked the clockwork mechanism that held the cage closed. They filed inside, and Natesh locked them in, an irrepressible smirk on his face. The guards retreated from the front half of the room, leaving the stone door just barely open behind them. Maybe they would be returning to their jobs as sailors now that the saboteurs were safely behind bars? Despair settled into her bones so heavily she could hardly spare a thought as to whether the guards would remain posted outside their prison cell or not.

Natesh paused at the door, then turned to admire them in their cage.

"Your friends will hang, Aniri." His voice was

light with the coup he had just accomplished. He lifted his eyebrows in a faux show of regret. "Which, I'll grant you, ought to be punishment enough for your interference. As I said before, it's been truly entertaining, watching you and your antics. But now it's time to put the games away and definitively show the world that Samir is no longer a second-class nation in any way. And you're far too much trouble to keep around for that." The humor fled his face. "Don't worry about outliving your friends long enough to regret your decisions. I can't promise it will be painless, but I'll see if I can't manage something swift for you."

He tipped his head, giving her a mocking two-fingered salute, and pushed open the heavy stone door. It closed behind him with the sound of a stone sarcophagus sliding shut.

"I really don't like that guy." Akash's bravado was undermined by the grayish pallor in his face.

"Aye," Riva said. "But yer going to have to stand in line, if ye want a crack at him." She was still steadying Akash with a hand on his good arm, which made Aniri think he was growing worse with his injury, not better. Riva urged him toward one of the cots, and when he reached it, he moved with great slowness as he eased down into it. He winced with the pain, and the deep red splotch had grown to cover a good fraction of his arm. Ash could tear a bit more from his shirt for a fresh bandage, but it wasn't a good sign that the blood had continued to flow. Akash closed his eyes as he relaxed into the mattress, taking deep, measured breaths, she imagined to counter the pain.

Riva stood, and her dark-brown eyes held a deep torrent of emotion: anger, fear, a kind of pain as if Akash's injury was hurting her as well. She didn't say anything with that accent that reminded Aniri so much of Karan. But she looked to Aniri as if she expected something from her. A plan. Some hope.

"We'll find a way out of this," Aniri said, but her voice was hollow. It was what she was expected to say, but there was no weight to it. In all likelihood, Natesh would have his way in killing them all.

Ash's arm slid around her shoulder, but she could hardly take any comfort from it. She turned away from him and went to the cage bars, clinging on to them as if she could wrench herself free. Through the small square window in the door, she could see the edge of the blood-red gasbag of the *Dagger*, billowing slightly in the breeze. A shadow passed across it, a quick flurry of people again, past her window. She thought for a moment the guards had come back, but then she saw a hood in their midst: a dark hood like her sister had been wearing before being locked away on the skyship.

Natesh was sneaking her off the skyship. To secret her away somewhere until he could plot a good time for her to die as well.

Consequences. She and Seledri were both here because Aniri let Natesh have his skyship back. Ash was alive, but not for much longer. Riva and Akash would die for their trouble as well. Her hands gripped the bars harder. Small bits of rust ground under her palms, broke free, and fell in tiny scattered bits to the dust covered floor. The air in the room was stale, like not even rats had lived long within its cold granite walls.

Ash came up beside her and leaned his back against the bars, peering at her face.

She refused to meet his gaze. "They're moving Seledri."

He glanced to the door, nodded, then looked back to her.

"Natesh is going to kill her, too." Aniri gripped the bars tighter.

"You have to make it home, Aniri," he said softly.

She frowned and turned sharply to him. "Natesh isn't going to let me live any more than the rest of you." It came out harsher than she wanted, but she couldn't stand the thought of him believing she would outlive him. That she would let him go to the gallows while she went home to a palace in Dharia. "We're in this together, remember?"

"Not when together means you dying when you don't have to."

Aniri sighed and stared at the pulsing gasbag of the *Dagger* again. "I'm going to get all of us out of this," she said, not looking at him. "Or none of us."

"Aniri," he said in that soft voice again such that she had to look at him. "Promise me you'll keep yourself alive. Do what it takes to evade Natesh and *go home.*" His light amber eyes were filled with such tenderness, she could feel her heart melting. "It will be easier for me to do this, if I know you'll—"

The static of stone sliding on stone interrupted him.

The guards had secreted Seledri out of the skyship just moments ago, and already they were back? But it wasn't the guards this time, but Natesh. And he wasn't alone: he held open the door for a woman in broad green-and-gold silk skirts. Aniri saw the dress, and the tightly bound corset, before she saw Nahali's face. Did she see her own sister whisked away a moment ago? Nahali had abandoned Aniri, disowned her completely, without a look back—was she abandoning Seledri, too?

Aniri composed her face into an inscrutable look that would have made Janak proud. If Nahali was coming to chastise Aniri for her "foolishness" once more, Aniri wouldn't give her the pleasure of watching her squirm.

Nahali strode in ahead of Natesh. He lingered by the door, leaning against the wall next to it and casually crossing his arms and legs to watch them. Aniri supposed this would be entertainment for him. All the more reason not to let Nahali get a rise out of her.

"I see you once again have embarrassed the crown," Nahali offered as she arrived just in front of Aniri at the bars.

"I suppose that's a matter of perspective," Aniri replied coolly. "Have you only given away your sisters' lives to appease the Samirians? Or is there something more I should know about?"

Nahali's stone-cold face didn't flinch. "Mother will deal with you when you return, Aniri. I'm just here to verify that you're alive and well." She cast a slow look back to Natesh, then returned to facing the cage they were boxed in. "In the meantime, I'll see if I can't arrange a decent room for you. Possibly something presentable to wear. And a bath."

Natesh chuckled under his breath.

But while this was no doubt amusing to him, and Aniri didn't want to give him any more satisfaction, this short visit was, in all likelihood, the last time she would see her sister. Aniri greatly doubted she would make it back to Dharia alive, no matter what Ash wished or how much she tried.

"Nahali," Aniri started, but didn't know what to say after that.

Her sister waited, her face impassive.

Aniri took a breath and nodded. "Please tell our mother I'm sorry I failed her." That should cover it well enough. Certainly her mother would know what she meant by it. Nahali knew what her mission was, even if she didn't approve, and clearly was willing to disavow it completely. Even if, in the face of the complete failure of it, Nahali was left to pick up the pieces.

Her sister opened her mouth to say something, then seemed to think better of it. She closed it and pressed her lips together. She turned to Natesh. "Perhaps you could give us a moment alone?"

Natesh grinned. "Nahali, you have a sense of humor. I wouldn't have thought it possible." His grin twisted into a smirk, and he folded his arms, but he made no move to leave the room.

Nahali turned back to her. "I will let Mother know you have some measure of remorse for what you've done. Perhaps she will go easier on you because of it. Although I wouldn't get your hopes up, Aniri. Things rarely seem to go as you expect. You may have to shift your plans for the future."

Aniri frowned. What did Nahali mean by that? Other than the obvious that Aniri hadn't managed to stop Natesh—his skyship was docked right outside her jail cell—nor had she managed to destabilize the Samirian government or rescue their sister Seledri. Ash stood behind her, having traded one jail cell for another, only this one came with a hangman's noose.

But there was something off about Nahali's approbation. As if she was telling Aniri something in code that she couldn't quite understand.

Battle has a way of shifting plans, Janak had said, back in Jungali, when speaking of the attack of the Samirians on the capital. The one that had gone awry and required them to change their strategy mid-battle. *Nahali is using Janak's words.*

Somehow, some way… Janak had communicated with Nahali. And told her their plans had shifted. Aniri tried to steel her face to show no reaction to that thought, just as she could see now that Nahali was carefully controlling hers.

"I will try not to get into any more trouble until I see you again." Aniri hoped that Nahali would take took her meaning: *I will wait until I hear the revised plans.* Not that she had anywhere she could go, or much she could do, regardless.

Nahali gave her a short nod. *Message received.*

Aniri held her breath while Nahali swept from the room, her head held imperiously high. Her skirts brushed Natesh on her way out the heavy stone door. Natesh's satisfied smirk told Aniri that he, at least, had read nothing into their exchange. Aniri only hoped that she wasn't imagining there was more to Nahali's words than there appeared.

The tomb-like door slid shut, the stone-grinding sound reverberating throughout their cell. As the echoes died away, Aniri turned to Ash. He still had a sorrowful look on his face, but it didn't tear at her like it did before. Hope was burning bright in her chest now.

"Aniri," he started up again, "please promise me

you'll try. I need to know that you, at least, are going to make it out of this alive."

"We're *all* going to make it out of here, Ash."

He frowned at her confident tone, confused, but Riva edged forward, a new eagerness on her face. "My lady? Do you have a plan?"

"Plans have a way of shifting in battle, Riva," Aniri said. "A wise man told me that once. A man I should have known wouldn't be so easily defeated by the likes of Natesh."

Ash's eyebrows flew up, and he glanced at the now-closed door, as if just realizing he had missed something. "Janak is here?"

Akash's rhythmic breathing caught, and he raised his head, peering at them.

"I'm not sure," Aniri said. "But my sister Nahali is sharper than most Queens could ever want to be. She's not leaving us here to rot. I don't know what she has planned, but whatever it is…"

"… we'll be ready for it, my lady," Riva said.

The hope on her face brought a smile to Aniri's.

Chapter Eighteen

MINUTES STRETCHED INTO HOURS. The sun rose, turning Aniri's jail cell a reddish hue with the reflection from the *Dagger's* gasbag. As the afternoon wore on, the red light turned to shadow, the great skyship blocking most of the sun's rays. The coolness of the rock caused a constant chill in the air, which slowly seeped into their skin. Along with the shadows falling through the window in the door, it gave their cell a feeling of perpetual twilight. A timelessness that was much worse than the slow ticking of hours as the sun moved across the sky.

Twice, meals had been brought, then taken away. Natesh wasn't going to starve them to death, but that didn't mean he intended them to live much longer.

Akash had a place on the cot which he occupied. Most of the time, he lay prone while doing his breathing exercises, but occasionally, he would sit up to give room to Riva to join him. Aniri and Ash shared the other thin-mattressed cot, using it as a bench for the most part. Once or twice, they cuddled so close in their whispered conversation that it became like a lover's couch—an intimate retreat from the world even though that world was currently comprised of a simple twenty-foot cell carved from the mountain. But in those moments, Riva and Akash gave them their privacy, for which Aniri was vastly grateful.

"How many children would you wish for?" Ash asked in one of those close-held slivers of time. Her hand rested on his chest, and the gentle rumbling of his voice tickled her fingers.

She snuggled closer into the crook of his neck, her lips speaking soft breaths across his skin. "You mean how many Daughters or how many Sons?"

"Do you get to pick?" Ash asked. She could feel his smile as his face brushed into her hair. He seemed to like the feel of it, because his hands, and now face, often found their way into it. "Dharian technology must be more advanced than I realized."

She lightly thumped his chest for his insolent answer, then brought her hand back to lightly trace the buttons on his shirt. This ability to touch him in such an intimate way was new, and even their morbid situation couldn't steal the pleasure of it.

He waited for her to answer, seemingly content with their many small touches as well.

She drew in a breath. "I would have only one Daughter. So that Jungali could have a Queen, but I wouldn't have to worry about arranging a marriage for her. No Second or Third Daughters to concern me. My First Daughter would find a dashing Jungali lord to marry and have many beautiful children herself."

"She would choose him because he was dashing?"

"She would choose him because his heart was pure," she said with a grin that he couldn't see. "And because he loved her with all of it."

"If she's anything like her mother, that Jungali lord will have no chance whatsoever."

She pulled back to scowl at him. "What exactly does that mean?"

He grinned and touched the tip of his nose to hers, a tiny act that completely disarmed her. She would have kissed him right then if they had been truly alone.

"It means that our Daughter would be both beautiful and relentlessly charming, not to mention brave and selfless," he said. "What man could possibly resist that?"

"I see." She lifted one eyebrow, teasing him with her skeptical look.

He pulled her close, gently kissing the top of her head. "I hope you do, Third Daughter of Dharia."

She sighed into him, snuggling again. If they weren't in Natesh's cell, this would be the kind of perfect moment she dreamed of having with the man she loved. Once upon a time, that was Devesh. But now she realized he was just a placeholder, a man who seemed to fit into her life in precisely the right way at the exact right moment. That was Devesh's skill, knowing how to be what someone wanted or perhaps needed. But Ash didn't fit at all into her life—he was precisely the wrong man at the wrong moment. And yet… he was everything that was truly missing from her life. Things she didn't even realize weren't there. Purpose. Meaning. A nobility in spirit, not just in bloodline. And a wholehearted and open way of loving, of not holding back, of trusting completely in the goodness of the other person. It took her a while to trust her own heart, but Ash had somehow seen it in her from the very start. Even when she thought she was lying to him, spying on him, tricking him into revealing his secrets... from the beginning, he had seen right to the heart of her and loved her in spite of all of it.

She used to think she wasn't worthy of a man like that. But loving him had helped her see just how much she had to give. No matter what happened going forward, that was something that had forever and completely won her heart.

They slipped, unspeaking, into a cozy nether-time. All their cuddling seemed to force Akash and Riva into close company as well. Aniri would have felt more concern for the awkwardness of a Jungali spy and a Samirian tinker having to pass time in a Samirian cell, if their conversations didn't seem already so comfortable. Maybe it was Akash's natural ease or Riva's plain spokenness. But it was as if they were already allies and had discovered they might be friends as well. During the lull in Aniri and Ash's whispered discussions, she couldn't help but overhear some of theirs.

"So yer cover work was in the naval yards?"

Riva asked. She had turned the cot so that the head of it was braced against the wall. Akash sat at that end, his back leaned against the rock. The arrangement allowed Riva to sit at the opposite end, facing Akash to keep him company, while also keeping her back to Aniri and Ash, giving them privacy. It was one of the many small, and not so small, gestures Riva made that had Aniri hoping they would be friends as well. If they ever managed to get out of this cell.

Akash nodded in response to Riva's question. "Worked the docks, unloading and reloading cargo. Hard work, but lots of idle talk. Great for spies."

"Sailors are big talkers, are they?" Her tone was teasing.

"You'd be surprised what comes out after a bottle or two of ale."

She laughed lightly. "Actually, no, I don't think I would."

Akash pulled in a breath as he adjusted his shoulder, seeking comfort he wouldn't likely find in the cell. "What about you? A Free Tinker in Mahatvak. That must be a difficult secret to keep. Are you sure you're not part spy?"

Riva picked at the loose strings on the blanket

between them. "Well, there's not much secret to how I feel about the Guild."

"Why is that? I sense there's a deliciously dramatic story behind it."

"Aye," she said, not looking up. "But not one I'll be tellin'."

"Oh!" Akash feigned a strike to the face that sent his head back into the rock behind him. "Trapped in a cell, sentenced to die, and you're depriving me of my one last entertainment. You're a cruel, cruel woman, Mistress Tinker."

Riva shook her head, but Aniri thought she heard a soft laugh under it. "Ye smooth talkin' spies always expect to get what ye want, don't ye?"

"Now I'm truly wounded."

"I doubt that very much."

"No truly." His voice went earnest. "I was shot. Didn't you notice?"

She laughed a true chuckle this time. "Aye, I noticed. Noticed ye bleeding all over everything. A right mess ye are."

He gave a long sigh. "Don't I know it."

With that, Riva crawled forward on the cot. As she got closer, Akash looked her up and down, with open curiosity as to what she had planned. Riva went up on her knees to free her hands to check his bandage. Aniri noticed that he was looking far more at Riva, up close, than the wound she was tending.

"Seems the bleeding has stopped," Riva said.

"Because I have an excellent healer," Akash said softly. There was definitely something there, in his voice, and Aniri looked away, affording them some privacy in case something came of the soft looks Akash was giving Riva.

But Riva just laughed, and the creak of the steel frame of the cot said she was returning to her end again. "What ye have is a prince who knows how to tie a bandage." The laugh was still in her voice. "If it were left to me, ye would have bled out long before now. I'm decent with the mechanical things, not so much the livin' ones."

"And a fine tinker you are. At least tell me how *that* came to be." Akash's undertone of disappointment told Aniri she wasn't the only one who thought the two of them might have need of some privacy.

"Well, that's simple enough," Riva said. "My mother and father were both tinkers. I come by it natural."

"Any brothers or sisters?"

"No." But her voice was tight. "Well, not anymore."

Akash was silent a moment. "I'm sorry, Riva, I didn't mean to—"

"Not your worry," she said. "Besides, it was a while ago. My parents are gone, too, so now it's just me and my shop. And the laboratory. My father built that for my mother, although I suspect it was a present for the both of them. I practically grew up there."

"Which explains your fine talent for building things," Akash said.

"As well as destroying them, apparently." She was referring to the *Dagger* and her near-success in disabling it. But that brought a hush back to their conversation, and they lapsed into not speaking again for a while.

Time seemed to slow during the conversations, but it suspended altogether during the silent stretches. However, it must have marched on, because eventually Aniri realized the twilight of their cell was turning to actual darkness. Her eyes had slowly adjusted, and only when Akash's dark-stained wound was indistinguishable from the wall behind him, did she realize they were losing the light.

She roused herself from Ash's warm embrace and

went to stand at the steel-barred door. The skyship's gasbag blocked anything else she might see outside. It had turned as dark as Akash's blood-stained shirt with the night. Small ripples shed silvery light every once in a while. The breeze and the moons worked together to bring tiny, occasional illuminations. But not enough to light the cell in any substantial way.

As the prospect of an entirely-dark night stretched ahead of her, worry began to nibble at the edges of her mind. What if she misunderstood her sister? What if there was no rescue party coming arranged by her raksaka? What would happen to Seledri, if there was nothing but the gallows for Ash and Riva and Akash... and some other form of death-in-transit for her?

The joints of the cot she shared with Ash creaked as he rose from it.

He joined her at the door of their jail. "What are your thoughts, Aniri?"

"I'm wishing Janak would hurry with his shift in plans." She didn't want to worry the others with her fears, so she tried to keep it light.

"I'm sure his plans will take time. If Janak and Pavan are coming, they would have to make their way back to the capital by train or something even slower. They haven't the luxury of flying here from the airharbor by skyship."

"True, but if they've already messaged Nahali, then there could be something started here in Mahatvak already. At least, I hope that's what's happening." She bit her lip, not wanting to share her fears, yet they were eating away at her.

"What is it?" Ash asked, leaning on the bars next to her.

She sighed. "What if I misunderstood all of it, Ash? It's not as if Nahali has ever been… well, on my side of anything before. It could have been wishful thinking on my part that she wasn't truly going to abandon me to the Samirians."

"She's your sister, Aniri."

"She's the First Daughter." Aniri gripped the cage's bars. "She's always been that more than my sister. And now, with my mother injured, she finally has her chance." She looked to Ash in the waning light, his bronzed skin more silvery with the occasional reflections of moonlight off the skyship. "What if she actually believes Natesh? What if she thinks she'll just deal with her troublesome youngest sister when I return to Dharia?"

"And she would let her sister's husband simply hang in the interim?" Ash said it like it was unreasonable to think Nahali would sacrifice him. But he didn't know her like Aniri did.

She turned to stare at the tiny window in the stone door. "She would say we're not married yet. And she's not quite in love with Jungali the way I am." Then she turned back to him and frowned. "I just don't know, Ash."

A soft scraping sound floated into the cell. Aniri turned back to the stone door, thinking maybe it was one of the sailors on the skyship again—every once in a while the sound of a crate being loaded, or pamgari full of coal, or a rustling of lines would drift into their prison—but this was a steady sound. Footsteps. Boots, lots of them, by the heavy scuff-scuff sound. A dancing light proceeded them, so by the time they arrived, shadows waltzed crazily around the cell. One soldier held the gaslamp in front of the prison door, while another bent to insert a key into it.

Aniri held her breath while the heavy stone door swung open and the soldiers marched in. The one with the lamp came first, throwing sudden illumination throughout their cell. Aniri had to blink her eyes to have them adjust, but she and Ash both backed away from the iron-barred door of their cell. Akash and Riva stood up from their cot and likewise edged away from the door.

There were six, maybe seven, of them. Soldiers, not guards, wearing the sharp black uniform of the Samirian military. Aniri scanned their faces, her heart racing, but she recognized none of them. These were not Janak's raksaka in disguise. They weren't Pavan's soldiers come undercover to rescue them.

They were the official soldiers of the Samirian military.

The one with the lamp stood by while the one with the key approached the cell. Ash grasped hold of her hand, and she squeezed it in return, but he wasn't holding it to reassure her. He tugged her behind him, placing himself between the coming guards and her.

Two soldiers entered the cell with a third trailing behind them with wrist chains.

But they weren't coming for her.

"No!" Aniri cried out when she saw they planned to put them on Ash.

He put out a hand to hold them off a moment longer, then turned to Aniri and pulled her close with the clasped hand between them. He kissed her, hard and fast, then he was ripped away. The two soldiers had yanked him back by the shoulders and spun him around. Ash didn't struggle, but he didn't help them either. They clamped the handcuffs on his wrists.

"Let him go!" Aniri couldn't help reaching for him, grasping for his shirt or any way to hold on to him. But one of the soldiers met her surge forward with a full-arm block that sent her reeling back. Akash caught her with one arm, steadying her, but also holding her back from lunging for Ash again. The soldier who had blocked her raised his hand, in case she broke free.

"Stop!" Ash roared. Then in a quieter but no less harsh voice, "I'll go with you."

His back was to her, but she could see the defeat in his slumped shoulders, his hanging head. His chest was heaving. The two soldiers who stood on either side of him locked their hands onto Ash's arms and shoulders. They turned him sideways as they marched him through the iron-barred door.

Ash glanced back to her, his eyes wide. "Go home," he whispered, just loud enough for her to hear over the shuffling of boots on the granite floor. The soldiers shoved him forward again.

Before Aniri could fight through the fist-sized lump in her throat to say something in return, the soldiers had pushed Ash out the stone door of their prison. The light went with them, the heavy door thudding shut and cutting off the steady scrape of their receding boots. Akash slowly released his hold on her, as if he wasn't sure she could stand on her own.

She stood alone. In the dark.

They were going to kill her husband.

Chapter Nineteen

THE SOLDIERS CAME BACK.

It wasn't long, maybe ten or fifteen minutes. They took Akash. He didn't resist, but they wrenched his shoulder anyway, so the last thing Aniri saw of him was his handsome face twisted in pain.

Aniri hugged Riva until they came for her, too. Aniri let go only because she was afraid they would hurt the tinker if she didn't. Riva held her head high, giving the soldiers looks of disgust. They returned her snarls with a special ferocity, apparently reserved for the Samirian they thought had betrayed them. Aniri was afraid the tinker might provoke them, but she simply squared her shoulders and strode ahead, going off to the gallows with a wake of soldiers trying to keep pace with her.

When the darkness fell around Aniri this time, it was utter and complete. It filled her heart and mind as well as her eyes. She broke down in ugly sobs, curling over and sinking to the floor. Her tears watered the cold granite floor, each sob turning her inside out. The contents of her heart spilled onto the floor with them.

There was only a blank nothingness for her eyes to see, blurred by waves of tears, so she kept them shut. When there was nothing left to cry, she simply stayed bent over, curled on the floor, hands wrapped around her stomach, holding what little she had left together.

They wouldn't come for her. She knew this now. Her sister hadn't been sending her coded messages. She was preparing her for the simple reality that her life, as she had known it, was now over. Natesh might find a way to end it before too long, but he'd already cut all the good out of it.

Natesh. His smirking face filled her mind along with a burning desire to run a blade through him. Obviously Janak hadn't accomplished it, and Aniri was more likely to be the one dying in such an attempt. But if there was any chance, any slim hope that she might work her way free to hunt down the Second Son of Samir, she was taking it.

Aniri slowly uncurled her fists, which were clenched tight against her body. Her hands ached, echoes of the gut wrenching agony from before. Then she unfolded the rest—her arms wrapped around her stomach, her legs tucked underneath, her back bent forward until her forehead almost touched the floor—until she was able to crawl on protesting hands and knees, through the darkness, to the bars of her cell. Grasping hold of them to steady her shaky legs, she pulled herself to standing. She waited until the dizziness faded, then opened her eyes.

A faint square of moonlight fell through the door's window. One or both of the moons must have risen, providing a ghostly light that gave a dim glow to the empty room. She pulled in deep draughts of the cool night air, thinking how Akash breathed through the pain, tamed it, and carried on. She had no laughter in her soul, like his had seemed to perpetually carry. But she would follow his example and focus her mind on the singular task of finding Natesh and ending his life.

The square moved. She watched it until her eyes blurred, then blinked to clear them again.

Eventually they would have to come for her. Maybe tonight… but it had already been too long since they had taken Riva. They would have returned already. So, in the morning, then. Or the next day. Or the day after that.

Eventually.

And when they came, she needed to be ready for any chance to escape. Any opportunity to slip away and find Natesh. Which meant she needed to rest—to somehow gain the sleep she would need to be her sharpest.

She looked back to the cot shrouded in the blackness of the cell. The outline of it was a deep, iron gray against the endless dark of the walls. Ash had spent hours with her there: cuddling, talking, touching. It was the closest they would ever have to a marriage bed. She shuffled on leaden feet toward it, by feel as much as by sight, finding it with her knees and her outstretched hands. The straw mattress was musty and cold—there was no residual sign of Ash's time there. She crawled into it, curling up as she had been on the floor. She pressed her hands and face flat on the thin mattress, conjuring that time with Ash in her mind and holding fast to it like a physical thing.

She would dream of Ash. And when she woke, she would be ready for his killer.

IF ANIRI HAD ACTUALLY SLEPT, it had been an empty thing, devoid of dreams or hope. Cold like her cell and frozen like her heart. But she must have been unconscious for part of the night because a sudden shift in awareness made her think it was morning even before she opened her eyes. The air was warmer. Light pushed at her closed eyelids. And the light scuffing sound of boots, *many* boots, maybe ten or twenty, sounded from outside.

That jolted her awake.

She rolled up quickly on her mat, yanked open her eyes, then squinted in the sun. It wasn't really bright—still the early morning gray of pre-dawn—but it was far more than the blackness of the night before. She forced her body to standing before it was ready, teetering but determined to be ready. It only took three heartbeats more before they arrived at her cell door.

There were six or seven of them, but this time, they weren't the black-clad soldiers of the Samirian military. They were royal guards, unlocking her door and filing into her rock prison. She studied them, one by one, while the lead guard used his clockwork key to open the iron-barred door of her cell. They weren't going to take her for execution. Or Natesh sent guards because he wanted to give the appearance she was being treated differently than the others—spared because she was a royal, sent back home like a spoiled child caught out after curfew. It was a pretense. She was sure he would arrange her death along the way home. But for now, the slightly more lax security could present an opportunity.

Just as her cell door swung open, her gaze fell on the last of the guards: *she knew him.*

She tried not to react, simply swinging her gaze to the guard with the key, but her heart lurched inside her chest as she tried to remember... was he a Samirian she had met before? Maybe a Free Tinker? *No.* Maybe he was simply familiar from her time in the palace, possibly the guard who had escorted them to the Queen? *No.* In fact, the difference was subtle, but he didn't look Samirian at all, more... *Dharian.* She flicked a look to him again and saw plain as day the still-healing slash across his eyebrow: *he was one of Janak's raksaka.*

She nearly choked with surprise, then coughed to cover it, pressing the back of her hand to her mouth and looking away. But she was certain: it was the raksaka from the train, the one who let her pass as she stormed away from Ash in a fit of anger that now felt like bitter poison in her veins. But: *one of Janak's raksaka was here.* He hadn't been with her on the *Dagger*—she would have remembered—so he must have been on Janak's team at the airharbor. A surge of hope pricked her eyes and would have brought fresh tears if she had any left in her. Instead, she held her head high and marched out of the cell, playing the part of the haughty princess while trying hard not to look at the raksaka again. Every muscle in her body tensed, ready for whatever he might have planned.

Nothing happened as the guards surrounded her and ushered her from her prison. The early sun hadn't warmed the air yet, and a chill swept across Aniri as they strode past the *Dagger* docked alongside the balcony, its gas bag rippling slightly in the breeze. But her mind was spinning a thousand thoughts a second. If Janak's raksaka was here, then what of Janak? Was he here in Mahatvak. If so, why send his raksaka rather than come himself to rescue her? It seemed very unlike Janak… unless he hadn't survived.

Aniri swallowed, then refused to let herself think that for even a moment. More likely this was the most prudent choice, for some reason unknown to her, but clear to Janak. She would have faith in his judgment, even in his absence. Besides, she didn't have much time to think of all the possibilities. Her guard escort quickly ushered her to the palace proper and through the two-door entranceway. When Janak's raksaka finally made his move, Aniri needn't have worried about being prepared—before she realized what had happened, the six Samirian royal guards were laid out on the floor, none having even had time to draw his weapon.

"My lady," her raksaka liberator said quietly, "we must make haste."

She didn't reply, just nodded and followed him. It was early, so the corridors of the palace were relatively empty, but it wouldn't take long for Natesh's people to find the disabled guards and coming looking for her. She tried to match the raksaka's stealthy footfalls, but her boots insisted on making noise. Still, they only attracted the attention of one handmaiden, who scurried back into her room, wide-eyed. Aniri didn't recognize much of the palace until they arrived at a room that, astonishingly, the raksaka had a key for: her sister Seledri's bedroom.

Aniri held her breath, half hoping Seledri would be inside… and there *was* a dark-cloaked and hooded figure, but the frame was far too large and sturdy to be her delicately beautiful sister.

He turned around.

"Pavan!" Her voice rasped from the crying and the lack of use. She rushed to him and threw her arms around his shoulders. He held her in a brotherly hug, and it nearly undid her with relief. If Pavan was here... surely they would be able to rescue everyone now.

She pulled back, and her words spilled out fast. "We have to find Ash and Akash and Riva. Oh gods! What if we're too late—"

He gently squeezed her shoulders to slow her down. "We will, Aniri, I promise. My spies tell me Natesh was waiting until dawn for a public display, and he wanted you brought from the stone cells to witness it. That's why I sent Vivek in to rescue you first. I prayed you would all be there, but you have to tell me: is Seledri all right? Have you seen her?"

Aniri pulled in a breath, trying to keep her wits. "Yes, yes. Natesh brought her on the skyship with us. But he moved her last night. I... I don't know where she is now."

That news rippled pain across Pavan's face.

"I think she's alive, Pavan, I do," she rushed out. "I'm sure he's holding onto her in case you came back. Or until he has need of her in some way."

He was nodding and pulling in his own calming breaths.

"Pavan, what happened at the air harbor?" She belatedly glanced around the room, but there was only the First Son and the lone raksaka. The hidden door to the tunnel she knew lay under the palace, the one she had used to escape with Pavan before, was closed. "Where is Janak? And the rest of your guard? Were they... did you..." She couldn't get the words out. If Janak was dead...

"No, Aniri, Janak's alive." Pavan released her shoulders and ran a hand through his hair, which was dusty and unkempt from the travels and the trauma. "But he could only spare one raksaka for me to come after Seledri. The rest he needed at the air harbor. Even Devesh stayed."

"For what?" Aniri couldn't imagine Janak letting another raksaka take his place in guarding royalty unless there was some higher purpose involved. "What exactly happened with your team?"

"We attacked Natesh's estate, as planned, but even though we overwhelmed the guard, Natesh had more raksaka at his disposal than we suspected. Somehow, while we were fighting through them, Natesh managed to slip our grasp and take Seledri with him." Pavan looked like he was ready to kill his brother with his own bare hands. "By the time we realized he had roused the rest of his guard and raksaka and boarded the *Dagger*—and apparently foiled your attempts at sabotage—it was too late. The *Dagger* was aloft."

She nodded. "Then the *Dagger* came back around to bomb the estate."

"Thankfully, we saw you coming and managed to get clear of the bombing. But with Natesh sailing away in the *Dagger,* taking most of his crew and guards with him, and us having already defeated most of the rest…"

Aniri's eyebrows lifted. "There was no one left at the harbor to fight you."

"Precisely," Pavan said. "Janak was able to secure the other buildings with the few men we had left. With Natesh sailing away, we had lost our chance to take him on the ground. But Janak was convinced we could get the skyship with the half-filled balloon operational."

Her eyes were wide by now. "You were going to go after him in the air?" If Janak could manage it… that would change everything.

"I told him I thought it was impossible," Pavan said. "If Natesh couldn't get a second ship off the ground in time to attack Jungali, I didn't see how we were going to. Not in time to save Seledri, in any case."

"So you came after her yourself." Aniri was nodding. "I understand. Completely, Pavan."

"You said Seledri was taken from the skyship. When? And by whom?"

"I don't know." Aniri's hands wrung one another as she tried to think of some clue. "It wasn't long after we were docked. Natesh probably had to move her before the sun fully rose, before anyone could see… it wasn't until that night that he sent the Samirian soldiers for Ash and Akash and Riva. But it could have been the soldiers who took Seledri as well. I'm sorry, Pavan, I'm just not sure."

"Soldiers, you say." Pavan frowned. "There was an elite corps of Samirian soldiers guarding the secret dungeon where he held your father and

Devesh. It's where he keeps prisoners without the Queen's knowledge."

Aniri gripped his arm that still held her shoulder. "Do you know where it is?"

"Yes."

"Well, let's go!" she cried. "Who knows how long before Natesh discovers I've been freed. Then he'll come for Ash and the others."

Pavan nodded. "Yes. All right." He was hesitating, like he wasn't quite sure this was the best plan.

"What is it, Pavan?" Her voice hiked up.

His voice was strained. "It's still early. Natesh may not have risen yet. Which… complicates things."

"Why does that even matter?" Her voice was shrill. He must have a good reason for hesitating, but her patience had been destroyed by everything that had transpired. And her need to free Ash and the others gnawed at her like a wild beast trapped inside her.

Just when she thought she might explode with it, Pavan's brow furrowed with determination. "No, you're right. My brother has had every chance to avoid the tip of my blade in his back. If I have to kill him, I will."

Aniri shook her head slightly, not entirely

understanding. Although she was sympathetic to the murderous impulse—she had it herself—she didn't quite connect it to their plans.

At her puzzled look, Pavan elaborated, "The entrance to the prison is through a secret door—in Natesh's bedroom."

Chapter Twenty

PAVAN'S HOOD WAS UP, and Vivek, Janak's raksaka-on-loan, was dressed like a royal Samirian guard, but Aniri didn't think they were fooling anyone. She had likewise obtained a hooded cloak from her sister's bedroom, but the three of them looked like spies and assassins as they hurried through the corridors of the palace toward Natesh's bedroom. It was a good thing the morning was still new, and the hallways were still relatively empty. The household staff who were awake seemed used to clandestine operations within the palace: they scurried off to their duties without a glance back.

"Do you think he'll be in his room?" Aniri asked as they ascended another set of stairs. The Samirian palace was extremely vertical in its layout

—it was built into the mountain and seemed to endlessly climb with it.

"I hope so." Pavan rested his hand on a blade he had hidden under his cloak. He had a small arsenal with him, and even after sharing a dagger and a pistol with Aniri, he still had two of his own —of each—plus the saber.

Would Pavan truly kill his brother, if they encountered him? She understood the sentiment and checked the position of her own pistol tucked into the waistband of her pants. If Pavan couldn't bring himself to, Aniri wouldn't hesitate.

"Will there be guards?" she asked quietly.

"Not normally," Pavan said just as softly. "Today, however, I'm uncertain we'll even make it there."

Aniri took that as a hint to keep quiet. They stole up the stairs to the next floor and peeked around the corner. The corridor was empty. As they strode down it, Pavan pointed to a doorway up ahead. It must have been Natesh's room, because he put a finger to his lips to keep her from asking. Just as they reached the door, Vivek stepped in front of them. He leaned back, preparing to kick the door in, when it suddenly opened.

One of the household staff stood in the doorway, one hand full of sheets, the other on the door-knob. She drew in a breath of surprise, but before she could make a noise, Vivek swooped in and covered her gaping mouth with his hand. She struggled as he dragged her inside the room. Aniri and Pavan quickly followed and closed the door behind them.

"Vivek!" Aniri chastised him when he didn't immediately let the woman go. She was a grandmother, if she was a day, and sturdy in the way housekeepers were, but no threat to them whatsoever.

He still held onto her, and the maid's eyes grew wider the longer he restrained her.

"It's all right," Pavan said, holding out his hands and approaching her. He threw back his hood. "It's just me, the First Son."

He nodded to Vivek, who slowly released her and set her up on her shaky-kneed legs. She gasped for breath and darted looks all around the room, like she might run away and hide under the bed.

"You're not in trouble, and we're not going to hurt you." Pavan's voice was soothing. "Do you believe me?"

The maid was quaking with fear, but she nodded rapidly.

"Now, I'm trying to find the princess, my wife," Pavan said. "I believe she's being held captive in the palace, and I mean to free her."

These words seemed to calm the maid more than anything else. She finally found her voice. "The princess is *here?*"

The tension in Aniri's body drained out. She should have known that even her sister's name would have this effect. Anyone who actually spent time around Seledri loved her.

"Yes." Pavan smiled. "At least, I think so. But if I've any hope of getting her out alive, I need your help."

"Anything, your majesty." She did a small curtesy that brought a smile to Aniri's face.

"Can you keep watch for us?" Pavan pointed to the door. "And lock this door, so that no one may enter while we're gone."

The maid glanced at Aniri and Vivek, then her gaze traveled back to Pavan, but it held nothing but confusion. "My lord, but… where are you going? There's no other exit from the prince's room."

"Trust me," Pavan said with a small smile.

She dipped her head, then scurried to the door. Taking out a key on a long necklace, she locked it, then turned her back to it and gave Pavan another nod.

He returned the nod and hurried to the far side of the room. As Aniri might have expected from Natesh's personal living quarters, it was opulent beyond belief, draped in curtains and paintings, with a mountain of silk pillows on the bed and on the floor for sitting. Pavan shoved aside a thick tapestry on the far wall and pressed the wall in exactly the right way to spring open a secret door… just like in Seledri's room.

"How did you know?" Aniri asked.

He simply gestured her and Vivek to follow him into the dark corridor beyond. Once they were inside, torches lit, door shut behind them, and descending the stone steps, Pavan spoke in a hushed voice, "Much of the staff is loyal to one brother or the other, but they won't often speak of it. However, when Natesh started bringing prisoners into his room… who never left… word leaked about a secret prison. I finally found someone who was willing to talk. That's how I broke out your father and Devesh to begin with."

"Is there another entrance?" Aniri asked. "Or is this the only one, like the tunnel beneath Seledri's room?"

"There is only one way in or out—but there's a myriad of catacombs down below. I only hope we can find Seledri and the others before whoever is guarding them finds us." Pavan lifted his chin to Vivek. "Your priority is the princess's safety. But we want to bring everyone out."

Vivek nodded his understanding and took the lead in their descent down the spiraling stone staircase. The air grew thicker, and the walls became moist with trickles of underground water. It was dank and fetid and just as Aniri imagined the worst of dungeons would be. When they reached the bottom, the stairs opened into a corridor that branched three ways.

By mutual understanding, they didn't speak, but Aniri gestured her confusion as to which way to go. Pavan shrugged and cocked an ear to listen. A slight echo could be heard—not a voice, or even the whisper of a voice, more the leftover remnant of a conversation muffled by a thousand tons of rock and still air. Pavan tipped his head to the left and headed down that carved-out corridor. Aniri and Vivek walked slowly and took care not to scuff their boots along the dusty rock-hewn floor, but it seemed to Aniri they were a herd of shashee lumbering through the tunnels, making as much shuffling noise as the giants beasts would make in the narrow halls. But as they turned corner after corner, the voices they were following grew sharper, a beacon more clear than their amorphous footfalls, which could have been the rocks sighing for all the guards ahead could tell. She hoped.

One more turn in the tunnel, and the rock walls were lit far *ahead* of the circle cast by their torches. Vivek threw up a hand, bringing them to a halt. They doused their torches and fell into a twilight darkness. The beacon ahead was now one of light as well as sound.

As they crept closer in the dimness, the voices became more clear.

"Oh, go on."

"No, seriously. You haven't seen color until you've been to a Jungali meadow in high spring."

"We've meadow flowers in Samir."

"It's not just the flowers. It's the sky."

"We've that here as well."

"You're missing my point."

"Yer point seems to be to bore me to death before the noose rescues me."

"*Boring* you—"

"Shut it already." That was a gruffer voice. The others were clearly Riva and Akash. Aniri prayed Ash and Seledri were there, too, only silent as they awaited the gallows, rather than gallantly distracting Riva, as Akash was attempting. Aniri, Pavan, and Vivek were close enough now that they could see the wrought-iron bars driven into rock that comprised the prisoners' cages. Aniri couldn't see the prisoners themselves, as the rest of the cages were tucked around the corner, along with the guard to whom the rougher voice must belong.

Pavan drew his pistol and his saber, one in each hand, and Aniri did the same only with her dagger instead. Vivek was unarmed, but a gun would only slow him down. The raksaka held them at the corner, listening. There was silence now, and he seemed to be waiting for some hidden signal. Aniri tensed, ready to spring at any moment.

"Have I told you about the dance festivals, especially the Festival of—"

The gruff voice cut him off. "Oh for the love of—"

A scuffle of boots and a clang on the iron bars was apparently the signal. Vivek sprang around the corner, and Pavan and Aniri rushed to join him. By the time she skirted the rock-hewn edge, pistol and dagger forward and ready, Vivek had one soldier unconscious on the floor and was beating a second in submission.

Only there were *four.*

Gunshots rang out. Aniri fired, praying her shot would find a soldier and not a wall where it could dangerously ricochet. One of the two soldiers went down. Aniri charged forward, but Pavan beat her there with his saber, running it through the last soldier, who then slumped to the floor, a shocked and stricken look on his face. Aniri tossed her spent weapon to the ground and rushed the cages. Seledri was in her own cell, separate from Ash, Akash, and Riva: *but they were all alive.*

Relief made her knees weak. She clung to the bars, Ash meeting her on the other side.

"Gods, Ash, I thought you were dead." Her voice cracked, and she glanced to Akash and Riva behind her. "I thought you all were." She reached through the bars to grab onto him, like he might be a ghost, and if so, she would will him into being by the strength of her hold alone.

Ash likewise held her face across the barrier of bars between them. "I can't believe you're here."

"Aniri, unlock the cells," Pavan said hoarsely. Instead of unlocking the cells, he was bent over Vivek. *Oh no.* The raksaka's wound must be grave, because he appeared barely conscious. Pavan had his hands full, helping the raksaka to his feet.

Aniri dashed to one of the slain soldiers and quickly dug through his black, tightly-buttoned uniform, finally finding the key to the cell buried deep underneath, on a chain around his neck. She leapt up and unlocked Ash's cell first, then hurried to her sister's.

"Seledri!" she exclaimed as she hastily worked the key in the door. "You cannot know how glad I am to see you."

Her sister didn't respond, too busy holding her husband through the bars. They were touching each other as Ash and Aniri had, whispering words of love that swelled Aniri's heart, seeing them together again. She focused on unlocking the door, so they could reunite for real. And so she could embrace Ash who had come to hover protectively right behind her. As the door swung open, Seledri broke away from her husband and met Aniri at the threshold.

Then caught her in a hug. "Aniri, we were so worried."

"Worried for me?" Aniri pulled back and gave her a disbelieving look. After all, she wasn't scheduled for execution at the dawn's first light. "I was the last one you should have worried for."

Seledri glanced at Ash behind her. "We all knew Natesh was cruel. And had a special hatred for you."

"Yes, well… I'm none too fond of him either."

A small smile broke out on her sister's face. "But we should have known you would slip his grasp. You do seem to evade trouble far more often than is reasonable. I, on the other hand, have the talent for being at the wrong place at the exact wrong time."

Aniri stepped out of the way so Pavan could take his wife in his arms.

"You're safe now, my love," he whispered.

Tears threatened Aniri's eyes. She turned to Ash and knew exactly how Pavan felt. She slipped her arms around Ash's neck and bunched his jacket in her hands, allowing herself a tiny moment to truly *feel* him alive in her arms again.

She must have been shaking, because Ash gently held the back of her head and whispered, "It's okay, my love." Then he kissed her, fierce and quick, and pulled back. "But we really must go."

Aniri nodded and turned to Vivek. He had to braced himself against the cell bars to stand, but he was upright.

"Can you walk?" she asked.

He gave a nod but didn't speak.

She quickly scanned Akash and Riva, standing together outside the cell, holding hands. "Let us go, then." Aniri squeezed Ash's hand, as much to reassure herself that he was indeed alive as to tug him toward the hallway. The entourage followed them, their pace set by the hobbling raksaka. Akash and Riva both were assisting him, one on each side. No one bothered to keep their steps quiet.

"Natesh could well be waiting for us at the top," Aniri said to Ash, their hands still clasped as they hurried. "Our raksaka made quick work of his guards. If Natesh finds us… it will not go well."

"I didn't dare to hope you would escape." His voice was thick. He threaded his fingers with hers. "All night, I kept thinking of what Natesh might do to you. At least the three of us had each other for consolation. It was killing me to know you were spending the night alone."

Aniri glanced at Riva and Akash, and as horrible as her night had been, she could tell the night had treated them worse. Akash's pale face sent a stab of pain through Aniri's chest, but it was the bruises on Riva's face that welled up a murderous rage in her heart. The guards must have given her special mistreatment because they thought she was a traitor. When in fact she was the finest of Samirian patriots, fighting to save her country from war and a power-mad prince. Whatever else happened, Aniri was still bent on killing Natesh—or at the very least, removing him from power. But she much preferred that he die.

"I must confess," she said to Ash, "I have every intention of running a blade through Natesh the next time I see him."

"Not if I get to him first." He smirked and released her. They had reached the stairs, and it quickly became clear they would be a challenge for Vivek. Pavan and Ash took the place of Akash and Riva in helping the injured raksaka ascend as quickly as possible. They were cautious at the top, but there was only the maid to greet them. Her eyes went wide when she saw Seledri, but the maid quickly shuffled back to allow their entourage into the room.

"No one has been to the room, my lord," she said to Pavan. "But I've heard stirrings in the hallway."

"Thank you for your help," Pavan said, still laboring to keep his raksaka upright.

They paused by the door, with Aniri checking

the hall. It was clear, but who knew for how long. They ran though the marbled hallways and stair-wells of the Samirian palace, Seledri leading the way as they raced toward her room and their escape. When they turned to the corner to reach it, they found two palace guards had been newly stationed there: certainly they hadn't been there when Vivek had brought Aniri there the first time. The guards drew their swords, but seemed confused by what was happening. The appearance of Princess Seledri seemed to throw them, especially given she was leading such an injured and unkempt lot.

"My lady?" asked one, eyebrows raised.

Aniri drew her dagger, and Pavan drew his remaining pistol.

"Stand aside!" he ordered, edging in front of Seledri, who was unarmed.

The guards frowned and looked at one another. "The prince ordered us to keep watch, but—"

"I am the First Son, and I'm ordering you to stand aside."

They hesitated, then shuffled to the side. Seledri took the key from Vivek and opened the door to her bedroom.

As she did so, Aniri whispered to Pavan, "We

can't leave them here." The guards would tell Natesh they had slipped into the tunnel below, and he might catch up with them before they could make their escape.

Pavan nodded, then caught Ash's eye. Together, they helped Vivek limp toward the bedroom, then broke at the last second to grapple with the two guards. Vivek heaved himself toward Pavan and his guard first, delivering a blow that sent the guard slumping to the ground. Ash kept his at bay long enough for the raksaka to knock him out as well. Then they dragged the bodies into Seledri's bedroom with them and locked the door behind.

"Well done, Mr. Vivek," Aniri said, amazed.

He didn't respond, but the raksaka seemed to have gained back a little steam. He lumbered toward the hidden door. Beyond it, the stone staircase spiraled into the depths of the Samirian palace, but it was empty of any more guards. Once inside, with the door closing them into darkness, Riva lit torches to lead the way.

They were alive, all of them... *and escaping.*

A hysterical giggle bubbled up in Aniri's chest and slipped out in small gulps of air. No one spoke as they pounded down the stairs. Once they reached the tunnel, their group flowed out into it, their many boots splashing through the small trickling stream down the center.

"What are our plans from here?" Aniri asked Pavan. They were speeding through the tunnel, but that would only put them in the heart of Mahatvak. What would they do from there?

"We will meet up with Free Tinkers in Mahatvak," Pavan replied, "and make plans from there."

She nodded and once again examined their group as they fled the palace. It was comprised of an injured raksaka, a handful of royals, a tinker, and a spy. It didn't seem much against the entire Samirian military, a skyship, and her sister Nahali determined to make a pact with a prince bent on war. But with Pavan and her sister free, it seemed… *possible*. Perhaps it was just the thrill of miraculously being spared and reunited—not only with Ash, but Akash and Riva, and Seledri and Pavan—when Aniri thought certain she would have to carry out her vengeance all on her own. It was as though the gods were smiling on them now. A sudden hope existed where it had not before.

Whatever the source of their turn in luck, she was determined, this time, to actually stop Natesh and the war he was intent upon.

Chapter Twenty-One

It took some time, weaving through the heavy traffic of the streets of Mahatvak, but they eventually made it to the cavernous warehouse in the industrial sector which served as headquarters for the Free Tinkers. As they stumbled in, Aniri was amazed by the bustle of activity within the nondescript building. By her reckoning, nearly a hundred people filled the main area: tinkers and citizens, royal guard and raksaka. Where had they all come from? They were pulling weapons out of wooden crates, wheeling pamgari across the floor, and gathering in furtively whispering groups. In the center, hovering over a table with an enormous map, were her father... *and Nahali.*

Aniri broke away from her entourage and

hurried toward them. Did he not know of his daughter's treachery with the Queen? That she was responsible for their incarceration in the first place? As Aniri stormed up, all the pain and anguish of the previous night boiled like black tar inside her, and she was more than ready to spill it on the head of the future Queen of Dharia. Her father may not realize Nahali had made some kind of deal with Natesh, but that would change soon enough.

The First Daughter watched her approach with a cool look. "I'm glad to see you——"

"Don't!" Aniri thrust a finger in her sister's face, which shocked Nahali into momentary silence. "Don't give me your lies! I saw what you did."

Nahali drew herself up taller. "I did what I had to do." Only then did Aniri notice that her sister was no longer dressed in her royal finery. In fact, the bump that was her baby was nearly concealed by the heavy leather jacket, loose vest, and adventuring clothes she wore now.

The rest of the Aniri's group finally arrived at the mapping table. Pavan took a stand next to Nahali and her father. Seledri hurried up to give Nahali a hug. They shared a wordless moment that flummoxed Aniri. A hand came to rest at the small of her back, and Aniri felt Ash's presence even before she turned to look up into his pale, amber eyes. They were marked with concern. Akash and Riva were holding back. They looked uncertain about finding Nahali here as well.

Aniri turned back to Pavan, her sisters, and her father. They all looked apologetic toward Aniri and completely unsuspecting of Nahali. The anger inside Aniri fizzled like a flame running out of fuel… she had missed something.

"What are you doing here?" Aniri asked Nahali.

"Here in Samir?" her sister asked coolly. "Or here in the underground headquarters of the Free Tinker-Loyalist alliance?"

Heat rose in Aniri's face. "What are you trying to accomplish here in Samir?"

Nahali sighed and pushed back from the map table. "I set out to come here on a diplomatic mission soon after you left. Janak informed me that you had found Pavan alive, and while you had another mission of urgency, that he thought a diplomatic mission from Dharia might be necessary to bolster Pavan's efforts to regain the Queen's favor."

"You've been in contact with Janak?" Aniri asked incredulously. "All along?"

"He is the Queen's raksaka," she said stiffly. "He wanted assurances about her health. I needed to know about your movements in Samir. Under the circumstances, it seemed prudent to keep open a line of communication. He agreed."

Aniri shook her head, disbelieving. Why didn't Janak tell her? Probably because he thought she would object in some way.

"You knew we were meeting mother's raksaka in Mahatvak," Aniri said, mostly to herself, sorting it out.

"I was the one who suggested it." Nahali's imperious tone was starting to come back. "I stayed at the ports in Dharia until I was assured that Mr. Karan could ably oversee our operations there. But when you and Janak left the capital on your mission to retrieve Seledri…" She gave a nod to their sister, who just smiled in response. "…well, Karan and Janak were both in agreement that I should come to Samir. As well as bring more of the Queen's raksaka. In case there were greater measures that needed to be taken."

"In case we needed rescuing." Aniri stared gap-mouthed at her sister. "You were *worried* about us."

Nahali's imperiousness faded, replaced by something that sounded almost broken. She blinked. "Is it so hard to believe that I might care if my sisters lived or died?"

Aniri lurched toward Nahali and wrapped her in an impetuous hug that took them both by surprise. Her sister was stiff and uncomfortable in her arms, but Aniri didn't let go. If she wasn't wrung out from tears the night before, they would have crested her squeezed-shut eyes.

"No," Aniri whispered, low so only Nahali would hear her. "It's not so hard to believe."

When she finally pulled back, Nahali's face was blotched with discomfort and some kind of expression she was trying to mask. Seledri beamed by their side. Aniri cleared her throat and released Nahali completely.

"It was a ruse from the start," Aniri said, confirming what was finally becoming clear to her. Nahali had come for *them,* not to broker some peace arrangement with a half-mad prince and a dying Queen. Aniri had been right the first time. "You were trying to tell me that in the prison cell."

Nahali straightened her clothes, slightly mussed from Aniri's hug. "Yes," she said. "I had to visit you to verify that Natesh hadn't *already* murdered you. And to put him on his guard to not do so before I could arrange for your escape."

"You arranged the escape."

"With some help." Nahali gave a quick nod to

Pavan, who returned it. "Through Janak, we knew Natesh had whisked Seledri away in the *Dagger* and that he likely had you as well."

"So you've heard from Janak recently," Aniri said. "Has he had any success with the other skyship?"

"Last we heard, no." Nahali looked grim. "But at least he has secured the airharbor, which should prevent Natesh from being able to use it, either. Meanwhile, we knew Pavan was returning to the capital, but until he arrived, it was unclear exactly how a rescue would be accomplished. I was coordinating with the Free Tinkers remaining in Mahatvak to arrange some kind of assault, but that seemed a far-fetched plan. We were entertaining several even less probable plans when the First Son returned to the city with knowledge of how to get into the palace. And a plan to at least liberate you."

Aniri smiled. She could count on one hand the number of times her sister had admitted she was unable to solve a problem by herself.

"We would have found a solution," her father said softly from behind Nahali. Her sister turned her head to give him a small nod of acknowledgment. "We wouldn't have let Natesh hurt you,

Aniri." Her father's voice was soft, but it riveted her. "Not without a fight."

A strange flush ran through Aniri—Nahali had reunited with their father, and they had been working together to rescue her, all while Aniri had thought she was betrayed, alone, and forgotten. The warmth that spread through her was a kind of happy guilt at being completely wrong about all of that. About all of *them*.

Nahali simply nodded in agreement with their father's words and turned back to face Aniri. "When I first arrived in Mahatvak," she continued calmly, as if there hadn't just passed a moment of tenderness between all three of them, "I had every intention of brokering peace through diplomatic means, if that was possible. But you saw the Queen, Aniri."

Aniri took a breath and nodded. "She's completely under Natesh's control."

"Agreed," Nahali said. "And far too close to passing that control completely over to Natesh. Which makes our next moves clear."

It does? It wasn't clear to her, but she was still recovering from the trauma of the day and the sudden escape from prison. Not to mention realizing that her sister had not in fact betrayed her, and even her father had been working to win her release.

Ash touched her shoulder. He seemed worried, but touching her appeared to calm him. His touch certainly had that effect on her. Pavan likewise stood next to his wife, his hand resting at her waist and gently holding their unborn child. Nahali stood in the middle, one hand at her side, the other resting on her child-to-be as well.

It was the future of the three countries lined up around the mapping table.

Aniri and Ash, the future Queen and King of Jungali; Seledri and Pavan, the rightful heirs to the Samirian crown; and Nahali, a Queen-in-waiting, but likely with the full powers of the crown during their mother's recovery. It was a future she wanted desperately to come true.

"What's our plan?" Aniri asked.

Nahali gave her a small nod. "With Natesh in possession of the *Dagger*, and the Queen under his control, our options are limited." She pointed to the map. Dead in the center of Samir was Mahatvak, but she wasn't pointing there—her slim finger circled the sea port on the coast, where Aniri and Janak had first arrived and met Akash. Ash's spy had shuffled over to lean against the mapping table, and Riva with her bruised face was still by his side. A couple of Pavan's loyal guards and several raksaka, even their injured one, Vivek, also joined them around the table, until it was full.

"I've messaged Karan," Nahali continued, "and he is standing by. Now that we've secured all the Daughters of Dharia, we need to prevent an attack on our homeland. That will be Natesh's next logical move, indeed, the one he's been planning all along."

Aniri frowned, and the hard look on Pavan's face said he hadn't been privy to this part of the plan.

Nahali turned to him. "We will only be targeting ships, Pavan, I promise. You can evacuate the crews."

"While you destroy our navy." His cold voice sent a shiver down Aniri's back. Seledri's mouth hung open, as aghast at their sister's suggestion as Aniri was.

"It will be a *warning*," Nahali said. "One that hopefully will stop Natesh from daring to attack. We are unlikely to be able to stop the *Dagger*—the ship has a longer range than the *Prosperity*, and is already armed."

"What makes you think he won't simply retaliate?" Pavan demanded.

Nahali leaned back. "We will tell him the next target is Mahatvak."

"What?" Pavan stepped back. The raksaka and guards tensed, but didn't move, watching the royals and their fight. "You're insane if you think I'm going to agree to this."

"Nahali," Seledri said, wringing her hands and staring at the map. "This is crazy. You can't hope to win peace by bombing the shipyards."

"No, I'm winning peace by preventing war." Nahali's voice had gone cold again.

"But we can avoid this!" Seledri patted the space above the mapping table with her open hands as if to contain the battlefield with the power of her will. "I'm here in the capital now. And *free.* I can go to the Queen. Explain to her that Natesh has been behind the assassinations. You have to give Pavan a chance to take the crown peacefully!"

Aniri bit her lip. "I hate to say this, Seledri, but I'm not sure if even your word will matter to the Queen now."

Ash gestured to Nahali. "After you left the room, Aniri tried to tell the Queen. She was too far under Natesh's influence to listen."

"She's very ill," Aniri said to her sister. "Did you know?"

"I haven't seen her for some time." Seledri frowned. "But *you* aren't carrying her grandchild. I'm sure she will at least hear me out."

"By then it may be too late," Nahali said. "The *Dagger* can move at any time. And as soon as Natesh realizes that Seledri has escaped… not to mention the rest of you…"

Aniri's heart stuttered a little. "You think that will tip off…" She couldn't even say it. Would breaking all of them out of prison set off the war? Natesh was intent on it anyway, she knew that much. But would it hasten an attack on Dharia just that much sooner?

"I think we have to strike before he does." Nahali's command voice was coming back, and Aniri was afraid her sister would follow through on that intention no matter what. And if she attacked the docks, Aniri knew it wouldn't stop Natesh—it would only enrage him. And the people of Samir. Natesh would win their support in a heartbeat. And then more people would die. She had to find another way out. Aniri pressed the heels of both hands to her eyes, pushing away the fear and the worry.

Think.

What would stop Natesh from striking? How could they convince the Queen to rein in her own son when she was on her deathbed? What would convince the people themselves that Pavan was their rightful king?

Aniri dropped her hands. "Seledri—you have to speak to the people."

Her sister frowned. "What do you mean?"

All eyes around the table were on Aniri. "The people haven't seen you since the assassination attempt. Go before them, outside the palace. Speak directly to them. Tell them that you're *alive,* and that no assassin will keep you from being their Queen." Aniri gestured around the room to the many Free Tinkers and raksaka and royal guard who had paused in their activities to listened. "Bring your loyalists. Fill the crowd and gather more. Take this directly to the people. While you're gathering support in front of the palace, Natesh won't be able to move against you. And with the people's support, you can go to the Queen herself."

"But what will I tell them?" Seledri frowned.

"Tell them you love Pavan." Aniri glanced at the First Son, who was now beaming as he stood next to his wife. "Tell them that love is stronger than war."

Seledri blinked rapidly. "I can do that."

Aniri grinned.

But Nahali's face was still taken over by a scowl. "What if Natesh decides to bring his raksaka and guard to this gathering?"

Aniri shook her head. "He relishes power. But he's also a coward who's always worked behind the scenes."

Pavan nodded, his arm now around his wife's shoulders. "It's true. Natesh would murder Seledri in private, but in public he won't move against her. She's too popular with the people."

"Only *some* of the people." The voice was frail, but it stopped the conversation cold. Akash added, "I'm sorry, my lady, but I fear there are many in the capital who will not want to hear your message of peace."

"He's right, my lady," Riva said, a hand bracing Akash as he leaned on the table. "There'll be more than cheering in the streets. This will stir up some unrest as well."

Seledri squared her shoulders. "Whether they want to hear it or not, it's the truth."

Riva nodded.

Vivek spoke for the first time. "Then we'd best be prepared if they don't like the message."

That got solemn nods all around. Vivek and the other raksaka and guards listening in around the table slipped away to make arrangements. Aniri watched them gather the weapons they had unpacked, silently making ready.

Either they would bring peace with this declaration… or they would tip off the civil war she came to Samir to start in the first place.

Chapter Twenty-Two

ANIRI HADN'T ENTERED the Samirian palace through the front door since Seledri's wedding—the last couple of times she had arrived via skyship, occasionally in chains, and exited through secret tunnels. Not that she was going inside now, but she was hoping their entourage would at least make it to the front steps.

They steadily trudged through the streets of Mahatvak like a mob gathering speed. Seledri and Pavan were in the lead, with Aniri and Ash close behind. Farther back was Riva leading her Free Tinkers, Pavan's guards, and several of the raksaka Nahali had brought from Dharia. Together, they comprised almost the entire loyalist movement. Vivek and Akash had stayed behind with Aniri's father to get properly stitched up by a healer. As their entourage filled the street, pushing forward like a wave, pamgari skittered out of the way and pedestrians kept to the sidewalks. Slowly, their group grew. Not so much in the industrial district, but as they reached the common businesses and dwellings of the city, people began to drift from the storefronts to join them. Whispers rose up behind them, then raced ahead. People left their shops, sometimes following, sometimes running up to the edges of their group.

They asked, *Is that Princess Seledri? Where is she going?*

She's to make a speech at the palace. Come join us, the word spread back. And they did. Every time Aniri glanced back, the crowd had grown. She could see the faces in the street ahead turned toward them in anticipation. There were so many people flowing from the buildings that they narrowed the opening in the street. Their collection of citizens and raksaka, royals and tinkers, continued to press through and eventually reached the open square at the foot of the heavily-spired and mountain-backed palace of the Samirian crown.

It was still early in the morning, but the bright sunshine made the dark gray steel and granite of the palace sparkle. Even the cobbled streets had a certain shine, as if greeting them with joy at finally having their princess return to her rightful place at the palace. The guards at the massive steel doors of the palace entrance were dumbfounded as Seledri and Pavan approached. They seemed frozen, uncertain whether they should be bowing to the First Son and his wife and opening the door, or possibly arresting them. Instead, they did nothing as Pavan and Seledri stood in front of the closed door and turned to face the crowd.

The steps up to the palace door gave them a platform from which to speak, but the open courtyard was massive. Aniri wondered if the people could possibly hear Seledri's normally soft and lilting voice over the murmurings that rose and fell like the chatter of a hundred birds disturbed on their perches. Aniri stood next to her sister, visually trying to show that Seledri was the bridge between Samir and Dharia, even though Aniri felt more Jungali than ever with Ash by her side. She was a bridge of sorts, too. The kind of bridge that would be bombed to extinction if Natesh had his way. They had only a couple of raksaka flanking them, the rest mingling into the crowd.

Aniri's gaze lifted for a moment to the billowing

red balloon of the *Dagger* docked next to the palace and the balcony of prison cells next to it. A few sailors traveled back and forth between the palace and the skyship, most likely resupplying it with fuel or other goods, but Aniri couldn't discern them well enough to tell if Natesh was among them. If he wasn't watching them already, she was certain word would soon spread about the gathering in the court-yard. Not to mention Aniri's obvious escape, along with Ash and the others.

And Pavan and Seledri at his doorstep.

It was a dangerous move. Aniri already knew this, but she felt it more keenly as they were exposed to the crowd. Nahali was among them, hidden in her adventuring clothes. Aniri searched the faces of the people for her, but it still took a long stretch of seconds before she recognized her sister—her long hair was plaited and hidden underneath the hood of a heavy leather cloak. Nahali's loose-fitting shirt disguised that she was with child, and a brown kerchief drawn across her face made her all but unrecognizable. The sturdy boots and pistols strapped to her sides completed her mercenary look, and the raksaka on either side of her played the part of her henchmen well. The entire effect would have been amusing had their situation not been so dire. And the unspoken agreement between Aniri and Nahali—that should this speech of Seledri's not go well, Nahali would slip away to order a first strike on Samir's naval ports—hung like a pall over Aniri's heart.

Seledri's voice drew back her attention. "My lovely people of Mahatvak. My sisters and brothers of Samir." Her sister's arms were raised, her hands outstretched as if she could hug the entire assemblage. The crowd answered with a quieting of voices and an uplift of chins to see her better. Small children were hoisted onto their father's shoulders, shoppers still carried their goods in their arms, and the collection of packages and shining faces and children clutching toys added small bits of color to the normally colorless streets of the capital. It was the natural warmth of humanity, and it made the gathering a visual sign of affection for their princess. For all the differences between the countries—the boisterous color of Jungali, the cool steel of Samir, the gentle detachment of Dharia—underneath the surface layers, they were all filled with children to be fed and shopping to be done and business to be conducted. They were all *people...* and they all deserved peace. Aniri had never felt this more profoundly as she did at that moment.

Seledri waited until the quiet fell more completely before continuing. "Since the attempt on my life, I have been running. I have been afraid. I have let those who care for me secret me away, all to protect me from those who would rather see me dead than have a Dharian on the throne of Samir."

A murmur went up through the crowd, and Aniri could feel some of the warmth dissipating. She glanced at her sister, but Seledri's face shone with the love Aniri had always seen there—the deep caring that had always set her sister apart and drawn people to her, more so than her physical beauty or her humor. But her words seemed to fall hard on the people's ears.

Seledri lowered her arms. "I am done with running."

Her words rang through the sudden silence of the crowd.

"I am done with letting my enemies define who I am, where I will sleep, who I will fear." Her voice grew stronger with each word. "I am here, because *here...*" She gestured to the palace behind her. "...is where I belong." She paused, and Aniri scanned the crowd. There were some nods of agreement, but there was much grumbling as well. Seledri waited until they quieted again. With less passion, but more resolve, she continued, "I know that some of you may dislike, or even outright *hate*, my home country of Dharia. I know some of you believe it was a mistake for the First Son to break with tradition and ask for my hand in marriage. You believe the Dharians look down upon you and do not treat you fairly. That they think they are better than you, simply because they are richer and more prosperous, because they are the largest country with all the land and food and resources they could possibly want." She paused and seemed to be letting the grumbles grow.

Aniri flicked another nervous look to Seledri, then back to the crowd to find Nahali. She could feel her sister's hard stare across the heads of the people filling the courtyard, and it made every muscle in her body tense.

"I'm here to tell you that all of it is true."

Aniri sucked in a breath, and the crowd's grumbles broke into audible mumblings. Aniri tried to catch Seledri's eye, but her attention was fixed on the crowd. Even Pavan looked slightly surprised, but he made no move to stop his wife.

What was she doing?

"It made absolutely no sense for Prince Pavan to ask for my hand in marriage. None at all." Seledri gave her husband a secret smile, and that one small look seemed to enrapture the crowd. They fell silent as she turned back to them. "There was only one reason Pavan wanted to make me his wife: *he loved me.*"

Were they in Jungali, Aniri would have expected the soft sounds that escaped the mouths of the people in the courtyard. But in Samir? She wouldn't have been surprised if there were angry shouts about breaking with tradition. But the Samirian people must have softer hearts than she knew. They were holding their breath, waiting for Seledri to continue.

"Love is a very foolish thing." Seledri seemed to tear up for a moment, and Aniri worked hard to keep her mouth from falling open. "It loves blindly. It hopes when there is no hope. It presses on anyway…" She glanced to Pavan, and Aniri could clearly see the tears in her sister's eyes now. "… even when that love is not returned."

Now even Aniri was holding her breath.

Seledri faced the crowd again. "But a love like that is a powerful thing. It can win hearts. It can *change* tradition. It took time and patience, but a love like that could make a spoiled Dharian princess love the people of Samir with all her heart. A love like that can build impossible bridges, like the unprece-dented connection between our countries that a Dharian-born Queen would represent. And I *want* to be your Queen someday, my beloved sisters and brothers of Samir. Not because I am Dharian. Not because I want to wear the crown of Samir. But because I love the man who should be your King more than I love any country."

The cheer started as a sob, then an audible agreement, and then it grew to an exclamation. But when Pavan slipped his arm around his beaming wife and pulled her into a kiss so passionate that it put Aniri and Ash's balcony kisses to shame, the crowd erupted with joy.

Aniri herself couldn't keep from laughing. She grinned at Ash, whose face was likewise full of an exuberant smile, then she sought out Nahali's face in the crowd. For a tense moment, she couldn't find her sister and her raksaka at all, but when she did, her heart stopped altogether.

A legion of black-clad Samirian military were carving a path through the crowd. They were only a dozen or so strong, but they were backed by an angry mob of plainly dressed Samirians, and together they were parting the sea of citizens in the courtyard.

And Nahali was directly in their path.

"Ash!" Aniri grasped onto his hand to warn him, but he had already seen. When she looked back to the crowd, it was shrinking farther from the intruding soldiers. Aniri breathed a sigh of relief when she saw Nahali had disappeared into the crowd.

Then she realized the soldiers were driving toward the palace steps. They were coming for *them*. The crowd seemed to realize it at the same moment she did. They started to push back against the soldiers, crowding the way. Angry shouts rose up, both on the sides of the people in the courtyard and the mob infiltrating them behind the soldiers.

Aniri grasped hold of Seledri's arm. "You must go inside!" Aniri said, but already one of the guards at the door had blocked the entrance with his body, while two others had grabbed Pavan, one on each side.

"By what right do you dare lay hands on the prince?" Seledri was demanding of their impassive faces. But it was immediately clear that they were holding him not to keep him from entering the palace, but for the soldiers heading their way. The only reason they hadn't yet arrived was because the crowd had roused to block their path. At the back of the courtyard, where the mob and the crowd were most intermingled, fists were already beginning to fly.

The two raksaka on the steps with them flew into action and disabled the guards restraining Pavan. They managed this without a shot being fired, but as soon as they moved, the other raksaka and guards within the crowd must have taken that as some kind of cue… because the courtyard instantly turned into a melee.

Aniri watched in horror as parents with children and women hugging their baskets fled for the edges of the courtyard. The raksaka targeted the soldiers first. They weren't prepared for an assault so quick and deadly from the crowd, but a few managed to get off shots from their pistols before being taken down. Screams went up, and the fleeing took on more urgency.

"My lady, we must move off the steps." It was a raksaka at her side, one hand on her elbow, the other clasped on Ash's shoulder. The other raksaka had liberated a key from one of the guards and was opening the palace door. Pavan hovered over Seledri, placing his body between her and the crowd, protecting his wife and unborn baby.

Aniri allowed the raksaka to shuffle them

towards the door, but she looked back to the courtyard one last time. Several raksaka lay unmoving on the cobbled street of the courtyard alongside the fallen black-uniformed Samirian soldiers. The rest of the loyalist guards were engaged in hand-to-hand combat with the Samirian mob. The courtyard was quickly emptying out, when a large, slow-moving shadow passed over the fight like a dark omen.

Aniri looked up.

The *Dagger* had left its dock and was sailing away from the palace.

Toward Dharia.

Chapter Twenty-Three

THE TWO RAKSAKA on the palace steps had successfully unlocked the giant, steel doors of the Samirian palace and forced the four of them—Aniri, Ash, Seledri, and Pavan—inside. The raksaka with the key locked the doors shut again, but Aniri protested against moving any farther from the door.

"My lady." The tall, bearded raksaka at her side was dressed like a merchant, but hidden under his plain clothes were the lumps of two pistols. "You cannot remain here." He eyed the servants within the palace who were hanging back from the royals and peeking out the windows that gave them a view of the melee outside. "If we regain control of the courtyard—"

"The courtyard no longer matters." The stridency of her voice pulled the attention of Seledri, Pavan, and Ash to her.

Aniri stabbed a finger to the sky above the palace. "Natesh is *leaving* the capital. In the *Dagger.*"

Pavan rubbed his hand over his face, and Seledri looked pale.

But only Ash seemed to grasp what that meant completely. "He's going to attack Dharia." His face had lost color.

"And my sister is headed right now to give the command to attack the Samirian ports." Aniri's fists were balled up. Just when it seemed like Seledri had won over the people, everything had quickly gone wrong. And now it was spinning out of control. "We need to reach Nahali. We need to… *stop* her before she makes this worse."

Ash took a breath and gave a side look to Pavan. "I don't want the *Prosperity* to attack the Samirian ports, Aniri, you know that. But how else can we stop Natesh? What else can we do?"

"There may be an alternative," Pavan said gravely, Seledri's hand clasped in his. "You know the last thing I want is for Natesh to attack Dharia. And I believe we have support among the people to take the crown…" He held Seledri close to his side. "Even more now. But we need to pull that support together, here on the ground, and fight the war *here.* Maybe if Natesh hears that he is losing the ground war, he will be forced to turn back—"

"Or he will simply bomb everything in Dharia that he can," Aniri said. "Because he has nothing left to lose."

"Either way," said Pavan, "Destroying the Samirian navy will only turn the ground war decidedly against making peace with Dharia. No matter how much the people love my wife."

"Agreed." Aniri threw her hands out in frustration. "Which is why we need to find Nahali and stop her."

"All right," Ash said. "But how do we do that? Do you think she's returning to the Free Tinkers headquarters? That's all the way into the industrial district."

"No." Aniri glanced around the palace. Her sister was in a foreign country, with a civil war breaking out around her, and only two raksaka for aid. She would need to get a message to Karan, then find a way out of the country as war broke loose. "Nahali would assume that Seledri and I would be safe, or at least as safe as possible, now that we've managed to gain entrance to the palace. But she would try to return to Dharia as quickly as possible." Aniri paused, thinking it through. "Where is the Dharian embassy?"

"Just on the other side of the courtyard," Seledri said.

Aniri rubbed her temples, an ache sprouting there as she tried to get hold of the situation. "Nahali said she was the one who sent the raksaka to the embassy. She was already communicating through them." She turned to the bearded raksaka. "Is there an aetheroceiver at the embassy that connects with someone in Dharia?"

"Yes, my lady."

Aniri nodded quickly. "She must be planning to send word there. And I'm sure they would have a way to secret her out of the country. She must be heading to the embassy."

Pavan turned to the raksaka. "Take us there."

"No!" Aniri held a hand out to them. "You and Seledri need to stay here. You have a civil war starting outside, Pavan." Aniri turned to her sister. "You need to go to the Queen and tell her what you told the people. Tell her Natesh is headed to Dharia. See what you can do. She may yet have some influence with the people in the Samirian court in his absence. Maybe you can find a way to call him back or stop him."

Seledri nodded. "She's right, Pavan. We need to stay here. Trust Aniri to do whatever she can to forestall the attack on the docks while we work to stop Natesh from here."

Pavan looked uncertainly at Aniri, but then said, "Gods be with you, Aniri. Please do what you can." Then he clasped Seledri's hand tighter. "The Queen will listen to you, my love. I'm certain of it. Come with me." He tugged his wife away from the door, hurrying past the startled-looking keepers of the estate and toward the sweeping staircase at the heart of the palace.

Aniri turned to the tall, bearded raksaka at her side. "Stay with them. Keep them safe like the fate of Dharia depends on it. Which it very well may."

He nodded sharply and dashed after Pavan and Seledri. He would only be one raksaka against the entire royal guard, but that was less concerning than if any of Natesh's raksaka remained in the palace. Aniri took a breath and forced herself to turn away from their fleeing backs. There was nothing more she could do to help them.

She turned to the one remaining Dharian raksaka by her side. "You need to get us to the embassy."

Fallen bodies remained in the courtyard, but the

fight had moved down the street toward the heart of Mahatvak. Aniri had lost sight of Riva and the rest of their guards, but she didn't see them among the abandoned bodies. She prayed to whatever gods might keep them that they were still safe.

Their sole remaining raksaka held them back by the door until he was certain there were no gun wielding assassins lingering in the courtyard. But Aniri knew there could just as easily be someone lurking in the many shops that lined the large, open area. Although it appeared that everyone had fled for the moment or at least were keeping their heads down until the fighting passed. The three of them dashed along the perimeter, keeping to the edge to have at least one protected side. The entrance to the embassy was gated, with the building itself set back from the wrought-iron bars, but there were no guards posted. Either they had been caught up in the melee or they had pulled back inside.

Or possibly, her sister reached them first and asked them to withdraw.

Aniri banged on the locked iron gate. The grating sound of it echoed around the empty court-yard and made her skin itch with their exposure.

"Do we have a backup plan here, Aniri?" Ash was glancing nervously at the end of the courtyard where the main street jutted toward the center of town and where the fight had drifted.

"Not really." Aniri banged again, her heart climbing up into her throat with each metallic screeching sound.

Finally, a guard emerged from the recessed doors, gun drawn, and slowly crept toward the gate. Aniri waited until he got closer. She didn't exactly want to shout out that the Third Daughter of Dharia was demanding entrance into the embassy, along with the Prince of Jungali.

When the guard was close enough to see her, Aniri whispered hoarsely, "I'm the Third Daughter. You need to let me in before we get shot."

His eyes went wide. He quickly holstered his gun and retrieved a Samirian clockwork key from his pocket to unlock the gate. He locked it once more behind them and hustled the three of them to the doors of the Dharian embassy proper. Once they were inside, it didn't take long for Aniri to find Nahali. Her sister was striding out to the main lobby of the embassy just as they were coming in. She carried an iron determination with her that seemed to make everyone around her—embassy guards and staff—straighten as she passed.

"Nahali!" Aniri called, hurrying up to her.

"Aniri," she said, blinking and taking in Ash by her side and their lone raksaka. "I'm glad you made it away from the mob." She frowned. "Where is Seledri?"

"She and Pavan are making entreaties to the Queen."

Her frown deepened. "It would have been better if she came with you."

"Nahali, you can't attack the docks. Not now!"

Her sister's face settled into that hard look that Aniri remembered from their years as a child. The one she wore when she wanted to say one thing, but instead wore the face of a Queen. "I've already messaged Karan and ordered him to use the burning glass to destroy the Samirian Navy."

"Nahali, no!" Aniri's voice hiked up.

"Is there any way you can message them again?" Ash asked. "Tell them to belay that order—"

"I *could,*" Nahali said stiffly. "But I will not."

Ash pressed his lips into a thin line, looking as frustrated as Aniri felt. And she was about to tear out her hair. But she managed to keep from taking her sister by the shoulders and shaking her.

"Nahali, listen to me," Aniri said as calmly as she could muster. "Seledri and Pavan are going straight to the Queen. They are going to tell her everything. You have to give them time to order Natesh back to the capital."

Nahali's expression didn't change. "Natesh doesn't take orders from the Queen, Aniri. You know that. Force is the only thing he will pay attention to."

"He doesn't *care* about innocent lives being lost." Aniri curled up her hands and pressed them to her head. "He kills innocent people all the time. Don't you see? He'll just use the destruction of the navy for justification. Then he'll do anything he wishes."

"He's going to do that anyway." Nahali's face drew down. "He's going to bomb Dharia regardless, Aniri. I'm doing my best to stop him from invading as well."

Aniri stood toe-to-toe with her sister, her chest heaving with the frustration and anger pent up inside her. And the thing was… Nahali was probably right. Even if the Queen sent a direct order to the *Dagger* this very moment, Natesh would simply disregard it.

"There has to be something we can do." The hope was draining out of Aniri's body, and she suddenly felt light-headed. Like all the things she had endured up to this point had come to rest on her body and anchored it down, while her head floated high above.

Her home would be destroyed.

The *Prosperity* could wreak whatever retaliation it wanted, but that would only lock them into war. A war that would kill countless people in all three countries, until somehow Natesh was defeated. Or not… and then… her head snapped back to her body, and her vision focused on the grim face of her sister.

"We have to stop him," Aniri said. There was a quiver in her voice.

"Whatever it takes." Nahali nodded, and in that moment, Aniri understood. The First Daughter was effectively Queen. And she would keep her vow to defend Dharia no matter what, even if it took a war and lost lives and awful destruction. Because the alternative was to *not* stop Natesh… and that would mean three Queendoms under his rule. A rule of tyranny and despotism, the taste of which she had already gotten in his prison cells.

Ash must have realized it, too, because he laid a gentle hand on Aniri's shoulder.

"Is our mother safe in Dharia?" Aniri asked.

Nahali's iron face softened a little. "She is

secreted away, outside the capital. I cannot attest to her ultimate safety, should we not prevail."

"Then we have to prevail."

Nahali's slow nod drained tension from the air.

"What can we do to help?" Ash asked Nahali.

She turned to him. "Your Jungali sailors may yet carry the day for us," she said, her voice a little more soft now. It reminded Aniri of her mother's voice, when she was talking to a trusted advisor. That small change in tone swelled Aniri's heart.

"The *Prosperity* was a trade ship that was secretly built to be a death ship," said Ash. "Its only real weapon is the burning glass. Is that still its primary weapon or have you given it other capabilities since I last saw it?"

"It has the ability to carry and drop ordnance now," Nahali said. "There were substantial repairs that needed to be made as well. While that was under way, Karan and I made a few changes to the original design." This was her sister's mission, to ready Dharia for war, and Aniri prayed that she actually had time to accomplish that before hurrying to Samir on a diplomatic mission to save her sisters.

"Anything that can be used in the air?" Aniri

asked. "What we really need is something that can bring down a skyship."

"Exactly the discussion Mr. Karan and I had while retrofitting the *Prosperity.*" Nahali gave a small smile. "We had a few ideas, but nothing that can effectively be used against the *Dagger* in the sky. I'm afraid our actual offensive and defensive weapons options against a skyship like the *Dagger* are extremely limited. Even from the ground, accurately pointing our naval cannons to track a moving skyship is difficult. And the range of the ordnance is still a problem, especially when you're trying to hit a ship at any kind of altitude."

"What about the small balloons our mother used to defend Kartavya?" Aniri asked. "Those seemed to reach the *Prosperity* well enough."

Nahali nodded. "Those were able to rise to the heights necessary. But those were very imprecise. And, if you'll remember, highly ineffective."

Aniri just remembered them rocking the ship while she was on top of it. But she supposed they did provide little threat in the end. The ship was able to rise above them easily enough, once Garesh was defeated, and the bridge was under their command again.

Ash jumped in. "Could we simply put the cannons on the *Prosperity* itself?"

Aniri hiked up her eyebrows. When did he start thinking in terms of combat and not peace? But he was, after all, involved in the original design of the *Prosperity*. Even though he designed it for peace, Aniri knew he had given much thought to its uses for war.

Nahali shook her head. "We thought of that, of course, and I wish we could fly right up to Natesh and blow the *Dagger* out of the sky, but the *Prosperity's* not designed to withstand the recoil of a naval cannon, nor equipped to carry that much weight. At least, it can't do that and actually fly any distance."

Aniri nodded. "Because of the limited range and the fuel you have to carry."

Nahali looked surprised that she knew anything at all about skyships. But that wasn't what was whirring through Aniri's head. "When the *Dagger* flew their bombing campaign over Jungali's capital, they flew lower than usual. Probably so their bombs would fall exactly where they wished. But maybe, when they're making the actual bombing run on a city, they would be within range of our cannons?"

"Perhaps." Nahali sighed. "If we had mobile

cannons and were able to move them quickly and point them accurately, we might get a single shot or two off that was capable of defending the city. But even if we were able to somehow hit the *Dagger*, we would need to do more than punch a cannonball hole through it."

Aniri bit her lip. "The *Prosperity* was indeed rugged that way. It was blown half to bits in Jungali, and it was still able to fly."

"Precisely." Nahali's voice had taken on that eager tone she had when diving into the physics or mechanics that she loved. "What's needed is to think differently for aerial combat."

Aniri was suddenly glad that the future Queen of Dharia was so terribly clever. They would need someone clever to survive this war.

"Do you mean flying weapons?" Ash asked, his voice likewise eager.

Nahali smiled at that. "Perhaps. Definitely, given time and resources. Unfortunately, we have precious little of those. But in terms of what would bring down a skyship... even if conventional weapons are unable to effectively track an aerial target, and cannon balls aren't nearly as destructive as they need to be, there remains one thing no ship can survive."

Aniri frowned. "Sinking? For a sea-going vessel that's simple enough, but a skyship? You can punch a hole in the bag, but I thought it was designed against that. At least, you'd have to punch a pretty big hole."

Nahali raised one eyebrow. "Indeed. The balloon might withstand a very large hole or ten smaller ones… but there's nothing it can do against a flaming arrow."

Aniri's eyebrows flew to the top of her head. "Fire? You can shoot fire at a skyship?"

Nahali scowled. "Well, not exactly. But perhaps a clockwork device that could be fired at close range and would create a small fire on impact. Timing is still critical but—"

Aniri grabbed hold of her sister's shoulders, cutting her off. "You're a genius, Nahali."

She shrunk back from Aniri's hold, which made Aniri instantly release her sister, but an uncertain smile still graced Nahali's face.

"There are a number of ways to go about it, none of them tested," Nahali said. "But Karan may yet have some tricks that Natesh is not expecting."

"But you've ordered Karan to attack the Samirian ports," Ash pointed out.

"I've ordered him to depart from the Dharian

ones and head for Samirian shores," Nahali replied. "He knows the *Dagger* is on the way. If he can intercept the ship, he will engage it in battle. But if he can't, or even if he can, he's still on order to decimate the Samirian Navy as well."

"To prevent a ground invasion." The idea sent a chill down Aniri's spine.

"You saw what happened in the courtyard, Aniri. There are forces within the city, within Samir, and no doubt at the docks as well, who wish to see Dharia brought to her knees, if not destroyed. I've given orders to the Dharian Sea Navy to launch as well. If the *Prosperity* should fail, for any reason, we need to keep the Samirians from reaching Dharian shores."

Aniri nodded numbly. The war had started. The only question now was how much would be lost, in lives and homes and good will between the countries, before it was through.

"We should leave immediately," Nahali added. "The embassy has a network of transports that can smuggle us out of the country. I asked them to prepare it for us in advance, should we have need of it."

"You planned this ending from the beginning, didn't you?" Aniri wasn't angry about that—her sister's good planning might be all that would keep them alive through the war—but she realized it well and truly meant leaving Seledri behind. And if Natesh won, it would be her sister's death sentence as well as any other royals in his path.

Nahali was about to answer her, but an embassy guard, in full Dharian uniform, rushed into the lobby and dashed to her side. "Your majesty!" he said breathlessly. "There is another skyship!"

Nahali frowned like he had spoken an ancient curse. "What do you mean?"

His eyes were wide. "It calls itself the *Endeavor.* And it's sent us an aetheroceiver message asking if it's safe to dock at the palace."

Chapter Twenty-Four

THEY STOOD in the courtyard behind the Dharian embassy, staring up into the brilliant blue sky at the saddest excuse for a skyship Aniri had ever seen. Yet her mouth hung open in wonder at the sight of it. Ash and Nahali were likewise stunned, as well as the entire embassy staff, who had stuffed themselves into the tiny wall-enclosed garden within the protective confines of the embassy estate.

Nahali was busy giving instructions to the aetheroceiver operator who was seated next to her, the device clacking away in his lap. "This is the First Daughter. Identify yourself." Nahali pointed to the aetheroceiver. "Send that."

As he did so, Aniri shaded her eyes to take a closer look. It was identical to the *Dagger*—pitch-black skyship body with a blood-red gasbag on top —only the gasbag was shrunken, practically half the size of the *Dagger's* balloon, and the body looked like several chunks had been bitten out of it, leaving ragged edges where the wood was still broken. It looked even worse than the *Prosperity* after it had been half blown to bits. Aniri was amazed the thing was even afloat. Yet it hovered above the capital, near the palace, and directly over the Dharian embassy. The hope was on everyone's lips, yet no one spoke it: *was this Janak?* Had he managed to get one of the half-built Samirians' ships afloat?

The device clacked and whirred, and the embassy officer hastily scribbled the translation.

He handed it up to Nahali, who read it aloud.

JANAK, CAPTAIN OF DHARIAN SHIP ENDEAVOR

Aniri let out a huff of a laugh and nearly clapped her hands together. She shaded her eyes and waved up to the *Endeavor,* not caring at all if she looked like a fool on the ground to the ever-stoic Janak. A grin broke out on Ash's face. Nahali looked likewise pleased, but in a calmer, more digni-fied fashion.

When Aniri finally brought her gaze back down

from the heavens, she turned to her sister. "Nahali! Do you realize what this means?"

Nahali peered up at the *Endeavor,* her squint against the sun almost like a smile. "We can send Janak after Natesh."

"I should go with him," Aniri said immediately, not sure if she could come up with a plausible reason why. But she *needed* to be on that ship. To chase after Natesh, to finally have a chance to bring him down, and if at all possible, stop the *Dagger* before it destroyed her home.

Nahali squinted now at Aniri. "I was thinking that *I* needed to be on the *Endeavor,* to update Janak on the way as to our plans and to keep close contact with the *Prosperity.*"

"Nahali…" Aniri's eyes grew wide. "With *two* skyships… maybe we can take Natesh in the air."

"It certainly improves our odds." Her grin was gone, but there was a gleam in her eye. Aniri could almost see the clockwork in her sister's mind start to turn with the possibilities.

"We *both* should go," Aniri said quickly.

"We should *all* go," Nahali agreed, with a glance to Ash. "This will be our fastest ride out of Samir, I imagine."

Aniri nodded her agreement, and Nahali turned

away to instruct the embassy officer to send another message to the *Endeavor.* Aniri turned to smile at Ash, but his face was clouded.

Aniri frowned. "What's wrong?"

He took her hands in his. "You should go, Aniri. Stop Natesh. And if you can't, fly straight back to Jungali and take safe harbor there. Our people will welcome you. And your sister and mother, too, if you can get her safely out of Dharia."

"I… but…" She couldn't believe he was planning for them to *fail.* And somehow he thought all that would happen without *him.* "You're coming with us!"

He looked up at the *Endeavor.* It started to drift toward the palace balcony, no doubt preparing to dock on Nahali's instructions. When he looked back to her, he was holding something back, something painful in his pale, amber eyes.

She stepped closer and touched his chest. "I don't understand."

A clacking came through on the aetheroceiver, and he looked to it as though he already knew what it said. She frowned at it, but as Nahali's face drew down reading the message, Aniri's heart sunk.

"What does it *say?*" she asked.

Nahali pursed her lips, hesitated, then looked to

Ash. "Janak says they've dumped everything that was loose, chopped off what unnecessary parts they could, and they're running a skeleton crew. They can't take on board passengers, only crew."

Aniri darted a look back to Ash. He had already figured it out. Already thought it through. And had already shipped her out of Samir without him.

"Ash, no…" Her heart jumped up in her throat. "We're in this *together*, remember?"

He winced like her words sliced right through him. "That ship's barely staying aloft as it is, Aniri. But with a war raging, you'll be much safer in the air than on the ground in Samir. You can substitute for one of the crew. I know you can. And your sister *has* to go. She needs to conduct this campaign from the air if you're going to have any chance of defeating Natesh. I will find a way out of Samir through the embassy."

"No." Aniri was shaking her head. "I'll stay here with you."

"No! You will *not* stay." His voice was angry, but she knew it was just the pain coming through, the same pain that was ripping her heart into pieces. Ash took a breath and his voice calmed. "I need you to stay alive, Aniri. That's all I need, then I know things will work out just as they should. Go.

Destroy Natesh. Or simply escape Samir. Either way I will meet you back in Jungali." He closed the distance between them and cupped her cheeks gently in his hands. "And then I will make you my wife." Then he kissed her, softly, and held her, much more strongly.

She wanted to fight him, to refuse, but all she could do was cling to him. She couldn't say anything at all. And she couldn't believe he would send her off again, not after what happened in the prison cell. "I already lost you once," she whispered, choking back the tears.

His arms just held her tighter. Then slowly, he forced her away from him and held her at arms length. He wouldn't look at her, instead turning to face Nahali. "You will keep her safe. And return her to Jungali." It was a command.

Nahali's eyes were wide, but she nodded once. "I promise."

He released Aniri, still avoiding her gaze. Tears were glassing her eyes anyway, and words were stuck in her throat, but she couldn't believe he wouldn't even look at her.

Ash still held Nahali's gaze. "I will explain your mission to Pavan. I'll tell him you'll attempt to take down Natesh first, but failing that you will be forced to destroy the navy. We'll work from this end to message the docks and evacuate the people. I'll help gather whatever loyalists we can, see if we can forestall whatever fight there may be on the ground."

Aniri's mouth dropped open. He said he would leave. He said he would escape through the embassy. But he lied.

He was staying to fight.

That wrenched something deep inside her. "No!" Aniri lurched toward him, but her sister's hands pulled her back by the shoulders.

"We'll take him from the air if we can," Nahali said gravely. "You take him from the ground if we can't. Gods be with you, Prince Malik."

He gave her brief bow, hands pressed together, and turned on his heel, heading back into the embassy. Aniri couldn't form words, her mouth just opened and closed and released a wordless sob as he quickly strode away. She didn't even realize she was going after him until Nahali pulled her back again even more forcefully. Then her sister wrapped her arms around her and held her while Aniri's heart broke all over again. The deep emptiness of the night before in the prison was still fresh in her soul, and it carved out everything inside her again.

She could hardly breathe.

Nahali held her tight a moment longer, then pulled back to grip her by the shoulders. Her sister looked deep into her eyes. "You *will* see him again," she said, her voice thick. "Just as I will see my husband again in Kartavya. We must fight this war, Aniri. We must stop Natesh from destroying everything we love. Are you with me?"

Aniri sucked in great, shaky draughts of air. Pulling herself together at that moment felt like an impossible task, like bringing back together all the shards of a broken glass.

But she *had* to.

Ash had gone off to do his duty; she could do no less.

She stood straighter, on her own, without Nahali's firm hands holding her up. She gave her sister one, solemn nod.

Nahali turned to the waiting embassy staff, all frozen, watching the drama. "I need an escort to get us on that skyship."

Chapter Twenty-Five

By the time Aniri boarded the *Endeavor*, the urgent need to cry had subsided. She had wiped her face, but she truly didn't care if Janak or any of his raksaka serving as sailors aboard the ship saw her cry. It was all she could do to keep things together without worrying about that.

But when she saw Janak, disheveled and dirty with coal dust, she almost lost control again. She hugged him hard, which startled him momentarily, but she didn't let go until he had hugged her back. After a fashion. It was more of a reassuring pat on the back.

She released him only to spare him the indignity any further.

That, and they were already getting under way.

Aniri had taken the place of a captured Samirian sailor who had served as navigator. With Janak at the controls, and Nahali at communications with the aetheroceiver, the three of them were the entirety of the crew on the bridge. Nahali had also taken over as de-facto captain, something neither Janak nor Aniri quarreled with.

Aniri bent over the mapping table as Janak spoke loudly into the brass bell at the control panel. "I'm going to need full throttle, Mr. Devesh," he bellowed.

Aniri startled at the mention of Devesh's name.

"And start routing the heat through the bag," Janak continued. "We need to get aloft as quickly as you can."

"Devesh is working in engines?" Aniri asked. She was glad to hear he had survived the assault at the air harbor, but for some reason, she hadn't pictured him as someone who would be competent in engines.

"I'm working with the resources at hand, your supreme eminence," Janak said as he flipped the switches at several panels. He seemed unwilling to devote any more words to explanation as he hovered uncertainly over some of the controls. Devesh must have proved himself at the airharbor.

Regardless, Aniri could ill afford to question it, as she was having difficulty clearing her own mind to focus on the task at hand.

She bent over the table in front of her and tried to make sense of the maps.

A moment later, Janak asked, "Do you have a direction for me, my lady?"

"Are you in possession of a compass, Mr. Janak?"

"Aye, my lady."

"Then due west for now." She trailed a finger across the Samirian wind maps—they had a fair amount of detail, more so than the Jungali ones. Janak would have to keep adjusting the rudders to stay heading west, but she had no idea of their true destination. They were attempting to intercept the *Dagger* without any idea of where the ship went. Heading "west" would work for now. It would keep them headed toward the Samirian docks at the least, which was where Karan would be going as well.

Then there was the small matter of catching up with the *Dagger*, wherever it was headed. Natesh's ship was bigger, with a full load of fuel and a complement of capable crew. The *Endeavor* was barely afloat, and they'd be lucky to get it pointed in the right direction. But their ship was *light*… and that might work in their favor. Or Janak might have chopped off one of the essential bits to keeping them afloat and steady. But if they could catch a strong wind, that might help. It would be tricky finding the hidden streams that blew through the sky, like tempestuous highways that crisscrossed the air, laying in wait to help or hinder a sky-borne ship. Mr. Tarak had given her lengthy instructions on it, but putting his lessons to actual use wasn't something she expected to do on her own.

Aniri stepped up to the star navigator at the forward window of the bridge and used its small aetheroscope to scan the horizon, at least as far as she could see. But the mountain range that ringed the city of Mahatvak made the horizon very limited, and the *Dagger* had long since passed over it. Maybe once they were farther aloft she would be able to find it. The time was just past noon, so the sun was mostly overhead—not much for calculating a position with the star navigator, but once they were away from Mahatvak, she would have to give it a try. Without a good position they would be lost altogether. Aniri returned to the mapping table, where the aetheroceiver at the end clacked away.

Nahali was sending and receiving a series of messages.

"Can you get a position from Mr. Karan?" Aniri asked her sister. "It would help greatly in plotting a course."

"In just a moment," she replied, still bent over the encryption wheel.

Aniri stared at her sister. With her hair still plaited back, and her adventuring clothes no worse for wear from her time escaping the mob at the Samirian palace, Nahali still had a regal way about her, a Queenly presence, even as she focused intently on her work. Aniri couldn't remember ever working on something *together* with her sister before, even in play as a child. It was always Nahali in charge as Queen, and Aniri and Seledri as her subjects. But now, even though she was Captain, her sister had somehow changed. She seemed part of the crew and more comfortable there than Aniri could have hoped for. It brought a warm glow that fought off the trauma of her separation from Ash and the terrible duty they were about to perform.

Nahali finished her transcription and held the thin, curling strip of paper as she read. "Karan says he's at thirty degrees, fifty three minutes, nine seconds west by twenty degrees north." She looked up to Aniri. "Does that make any sense to you?"

"Yes." Aniri bent over the map and traced the cross-hatched lines to find Karan's position. She marked it with the charcoal pencil. "He's about halfway across the sea. I assume he's still headed for the Samirian ports?"

"That's his mission so far."

Aniri looked up. "Has he sighted the *Dagger* at all?"

"No."

Aniri frowned. "If we're going to catch up to Natesh, we're going to need more speed. He's got a head start on us, but not by much. I'm guessing twenty minutes since he left Mahatvak."

"That sounds about right," Nahali said.

Twenty minutes out, but which direction? Aniri straightened from the table to face Janak. "You arrived in Mahatvak soon after Natesh left. Did you see the *Dagger* at all? Maybe what direction they were headed?"

Janak frowned. "I'm sorry, my lady, we were keeping our sights on the ground, making sure we were staying aloft."

Aniri nodded then looked back to the map. Natesh might not have a tremendous start, and he was most assuredly heading for Dharia. But her homeland was enormous. That could be one of any number of headings. Yet... Natesh wasn't a fool. He would economize on fuel and take the most direct path to his destination, if he could.

But then she realized... "The *Dagger* has a longer range than we do, especially given how light we are on fuel. Even if we catch up to them, we're not going to be able to chase them across the sea. We won't have enough coal."

"We could refuel at the ports," Janak suggested.

Nahali edged around the mapping table to join in. "We can't be sure who has control there: the loyalists or Natesh's people."

"Agreed. But we won't be able to go any farther if we don't." Aniri stared at the wind maps, their position just outside of Mahatvak, and the stretch of Samirian countryside between the capital and the Samirian docks. "If I were Natesh, I would assume the docks were still a safe harbor. I would land briefly, refuel, then be ready to sail straight for Kartavya. That way I would be assured to have enough fuel for an extended bombing run over the Dharian capital and still be able to return home without having to stop again for fuel." She looked up into the grim faces of Nahali and Janak. "We need to catch him before he leaves Samir or we may not catch him at all."

Nahali's eyes narrowed. "Even if he's headed to the docks, is it possible for us to reach them before he leaves?"

"We're about to find out. Take us up, Mr. Janak." Aniri bent over her maps again. There was an air stream that blew west, a steady current that might boost their speed if they could find it and catch it. That would give them an increased speed for most of the distance between the capital and the docks. "I'll need about fifteen thousand feet of altitude and everything you've got on engines."

"Aye, my lady."

While Janak relayed the orders, Aniri plotted a course up to the slipstream, across the Samirian countryside, and then finally down to the Samirian docks. Then she calculated their fuel for all the maneuvers. They would burn just about everything they had getting there—which was great for staying light and blowing fast in the wind, but not so great for fighting once they got there.

She double checked her numbers, then asked, "What kind of weapons do you have aboard, Mr. Janak?" It was a Samirian ship; there should be some kind of weaponry. Maybe they could use Natesh's own armaments against him.

"Pistols, mainly."

She looked up to see if he was making a joke. The serious look on his face said *no*.

"Not even bombs?"

"No, my lady."

"You got rid of the armaments to get aloft."

"Aye, my lady."

Aniri sighed. She looked out across the receding Samirian landscape as they lifted higher and higher into the sky. No fuel. No weapons. Someday she was going to fly again in a skyship that wasn't half broken and barely aloft.

"You've not given me much to work with, Mr. Janak," Aniri said.

"Aye, my lady."

Nahali had her head in her hands and her elbows propped on the mapping table. Her fingers worked into her hair, and she seemed to be mumbling to herself. Aniri didn't interrupt, figuring she was either praying, cursing, or using that brilliant mind of hers to think of a way out of their predicament.

When Nahali finally looked up, she said, "Karan should have at least *some* weapons he can use against the *Dagger*. I believe he has ordinance he can drop, or he can use the burning glass if nothing else, assuming he can rise above the *Dagger*."

Aniri frowned, trying to follow her. "So we don't need to attack the *Dagger* ourselves. We just need to keep it around until the *Prosperity* arrives."

"Exactly."

Aniri smiled. "Well done, your majesty."

Nahali gave her an admonishing look, but it was fighting a losing battle with the small smile on her face. Aniri strode over to the forward window again and scanned the horizon. Still no sign of the *Dagger*, but they had just lifted above Mahatvak and ring of mountains surrounding it. She guessed the horizon was still only about 10 miles out. There was a small haze in the air that made it difficult to see, but still... nothing.

"What's our altitude, Mr. Janak?" Aniri asked.

"Two thousand feet and rising."

Aniri scanned the horizon again, this time using the small aetherscope as well. Nothing. She looked at the clear blue sky above the ship. A wisp of cloud scuttled past, headed west, curling and churning on the way. It was above them and to the north.

Aniri pressed her face against the window, trying to judge the distance. Then she hurried back to her mapping table. It wasn't on the wind maps, but Mr. Tarak had told her they were only broad guidelines. The sky tossed about as much as the ocean, and a navigator had to trust her eyes and her instruments as much as any map scribbled by a cartographer with a flotilla of paper lanterns.

"Keep taking us up, Mr. Janak," Aniri said, "and turn us north. I've got a tailwind I want to catch."

"Aye, my lady." Janak flipped some switches at the control panel, and Aniri could see the bow swing to the north. She hurried to the front again, scanning the air above the ship, but the telltale wisp was gone, and there was no way to see where the stream of air was. They would just have to hope that it was broad enough that they would rise into it —or that they would simply get lucky.

"Altitude, Mr. Janak?" she asked. Not that knowing their altitude would make a difference, but she needed something to fill the tense silence of the bridge other than the wind's gentle buffet against the window and the distant thrum of the propeller blades traveling through the ship.

"Fifteen thousand," he replied. "Should we level out, my lady?"

"Keep going," she said. "I want to see—" The

ship bucked as if they had hit something solid, and her face mashed into the window. Aniri braced her hand against it and pushed away, but then the ship jolted in the opposite direction, and her hand lifted from the glass. She tumbled backward to the deck. Her sister was likewise on the floor and just barely caught the aetheroceiver as it slid off the edge of the mapping table. The ship continued to jump and lurch. Aniri worked her way on hands and knees back to the window. Above her, the gasbag seemed to lean out over the bow of the ship, as if pulled forward by an invisible force.

"Hold our altitude, Mr. Janak." Aniri worked her way to standing, bracing herself against the glass.

"Your tailwind is a bit feisty, my lady," Janak said wryly. More seriously, he added, "I'm having trouble maintaining our course. The rudders are…" He paused, flipping some switches and watching some dials.

Aniri considered crossing the unsteady floor to help him, but a sudden bucking almost sent her tumbling again, so she kept her position at the window. "Just ride it as long as you can, Mr. Janak."

"Aye." He kept his gaze focused on the control panel.

Nahali wrestled against the shaking of the ship to lift the aetheroceiver back up on the mapping table. "I doubt the *Endeavor* was designed for this, Aniri." Her voice shook with the reverberations that were making the entire ship quake. It was as if a thousand tiny explosions were constantly buffeting the ship… along with occasionally a few larger ones that sent them all off their feet.

"I doubt it was meant to fly in the shape it is, either," Aniri said with half a grin. "Yet, here we are."

She nodded. "I will attempt to message Karan our intent to intercept Natesh at the Samirian docks."

Aniri dipped her head in acknowledgment, then remembered: at this altitude, she should be able to see a hundred miles or more. And at only twenty minutes ahead of them, the *Dagger* should be well above the horizon now. She gripped the star navigator to keep her balance and scanned the horizon once again. *There:* a tiny black dot near the horizon. She steadied herself against the tiny aetheroscope and swung it around to the south. It took several tries to keep the dot in the scope's sight, but once she did, there was no doubt: it was the *Dagger*.

"I have it!" Aniri cried. "The *Dagger* is to the

west and south, less than thirty miles out and below us, I think. Hard to judge from here."

"Should I change heading, my lady?" Janak sounded like he wanted out of the air stream as quickly as possible.

"No, Mr. Janak, keep your course," Aniri said. "I'll watch to see if it carries us too far to the north, but as long as we're in it, we'll make better time. And use less fuel as well."

"Aye." His voice was tense as he kept battling the rudders. Aniri could picture the poor, delicate fins of the skyship weren't meant for such abuse. She only hoped they could withstand it for as long as they needed to reach the shores.

Aniri kept the *Dagger* in her sights. "Soon," she whispered to herself. "Very soon, Natesh."

Chapter Twenty-Six

AFTER AN HOUR of harrowing journey in the jet stream, Aniri decided they had to drop altitude and head south again, else be carried too far away. The *Endeavor* was nearly to the coast, but too far north of the Samirian docks. She still had the *Dagger* in her sights, and Natesh was definitely making a stop at the docks. Once they dropped out of the stream, the ride turned instantly as smooth as glass. It was like floating in a dream compared to the last hour.

"Well done, Mr. Janak," Nahali said over her shoulder. She had joined Aniri at the window, but Janak was still at the controls, turning them southward.

"We've not yet arrived, my lady," he said, but it was a gentle rebuke.

Together, Aniri and Nahali watched as the *Dagger* slowly descended out of the sky toward the docks.

"You were right," her sister said. "He must be stopping to take on fuel. Do you think he's seen us yet?"

"He must not," Aniri said. "Or else he wouldn't be landing. How far out is Karan?"

"I'll get an update." She hurried over to the aetheroceiver and cranked it up. It clacked and whirred as she hastily sent her message.

"Are you quite certain we have no bombs on board, Mr. Janak?" Aniri asked, her gaze fixed on the *Dagger* as they inched closer, descending slowly as they went. "Or anything I could possibly drop on the *Dagger* when we arrive?"

"No, my lady." His voice was gruff. "Although landing on them has some appeal."

She dashed a look to her raksaka, and she knew that pinched expression as he avoided her gaze. He wanted Natesh dead as much as she did. And he would do whatever was necessary to achieve it. Aniri couldn't disagree in the slightest, but she'd rather not take everyone on the *Endeavor* with them in the process. "We've got the future Queen of Dharia on board, Mr. Janak."

"Understood." He still didn't look at her.

Aniri frowned. "I'm open to any other options, however."

The clacking from the aetheroceiver paused, and Nahali was madly scribbling her translation. After a moment, she said, "Karan estimates he's still fifteen minutes out."

"Then we'll have to delay Natesh for twenty." Aniri peered at the *Dagger* while Janak shouted orders down to engines to bring the *Endeavor* lower, then manipulated the controls to turn the rudder toward the docks. Natesh's skyship was perched at the end of a long pier, one of many that stuck out like fingers into the relative calm of the sea. The harbor was sheltered by an outcropping of mountains, such that the waves which buffeted the ships were small. She imagined the waves of air were likewise calm. It was a reasonable place to dock and refuel.

Nahali left her aetheroceiver and came to stand by Aniri at the window again.

"He has to notice us soon," Aniri said.

"Agreed. And Janak's idea of landing on the *Dagger* isn't entirely without merit."

Aniri lifted an eyebrow. "How do you mean?"

Nahali pointed to the skyship. "They're tied down at the end of the pier, presumably taking on fuel. Even if they cast off the lines holding them down, they're limited in the directions they can move. Normally, they would lift off and be able to travel in any direction once they got under way. But if the *Endeavor* were to hover over them…"

Aniri was nodding. "They wouldn't be able to lift directly. They'd have to go sideways first."

"It will be hard for them to turn with no wind, no forward motion. There's really only one direction they could go at first."

"Forward." Aniri could see it. "Hovering would be tricky, holding our position without being lashed. And we'd be limited in our movements, too, although we could lift if need be."

"At worst, we will all take a swim."

The corner of Aniri's mouth tipped up. "Is that a joke, Nahali?"

She pressed her lips into a grimace that was really half smile. "It was an assessment."

Aniri almost laughed, but they were approaching the docks, and their time was drawing short. She could even see the workers scurrying along the pier, resupplying the *Dagger*.

"Janak," she called out. "We need to come down as close as you can and sit on Natesh's head."

"Aye, my lady," he said. "But I think we're as likely to chew their bag with our propellers as sit on top of them."

Aniri threw a smirk to her sister. "That would work as well."

Janak scowled as he relayed the orders to continue cooling the bag to drop altitude. "I'll need you to be my eyes for the close maneuvering, my lady. And I'll warn you, my experience as a skyship pilot is extremely limited."

Aniri locked her gaze on the *Dagger* as they continued to approach. "All we need is to slow them down, Janak. And keep them low. If we can manage it, then the *Prosperity* can use the burning glass on Natesh when they arrive."

"Aye, my lady."

As Aniri watched, the movements on the pier grew more frenzied.

"They see us." Nahali's gaze was also locked onto the dock.

Aniri tore away for a moment to glance to Janak. "We need to come down faster."

"We're dropping as fast as we can," he said,

strain in his voice. He kept working the rudders. "We can only cool the bag so fast."

Aniri bit her lip and turned back to watch. They were going too fast forward yet dropping too slow—they were going to overshoot. "Slow the engines," she called.

Janak relayed the order, and there was a shift in the hum of the ship as the propellers wound down. It was enough that now they seemed to be on the right trajectory. Nahali gave her a nod, and they both watched as the *Endeavor* crept inexorably closer. They were only five hundred feet away from the dock now, both in altitude and incoming from the north.

Then the *Dagger* moved.

First, it drifted slightly away from the pier, its delicate rudders unfolding from where they had been tucked to its sides. Then it began to rise.

"They're on the move, Janak." Aniri's voice was strung tight. "We need to get ahead of them."

"Increase speed!" Janak shouted into the brass bell. The ship surged forward. They were still above the *Dagger*, and they sailed right over its billowing red gasbag, effectively cutting off their ascent, if only momentarily. Except now Aniri couldn't see where they were.

"Come about!" Aniri sprinted to the starboard side of the window and peered down, trying to see where they were in relation to the other skyship. The ship heeled over as it turned, but it was achingly slow. Janak had cut the engines as they turned, and it was killing their maneuvering ability as their fins grasped at the air to turn. Now that they were heeled over, she could see below the ship. But there was nothing but birds and seagoing ships and blue-green water below her. And the *Endeavor* was still drifting down. Then the *Dagger* edged into her view.

"We're still above them." Indeed, their turn had brought them back around on top of Natesh's ship, now only a hundred feet above and dropping fast in a tight spiral. The plumes of smoke and steam from the *Dagger's* engines billowed up and obscured her view. It was moving forward now. "Keep dropping!"

But it was no use. The *Dagger* was slipping out from underneath them.

She lost sight of them again as Natesh's skyship skimmed along the waves, puffing forward on the power of its engines.

Nahali was at the star navigator, for what purpose Aniri couldn't imagine until she called out,

"I've sighted the *Prosperity*. They're maybe a mile out."

"Message them," Aniri said quickly. "Tell them we're trying to keep the *Dagger* in the harbor, but they've got to get here *now*. Or Natesh is going to slip away. And we don't have fuel to follow."

A mile… a mile away with weapons, and here they were, right on top of the *Dagger* with nothing more than bullets and curses to throw their way.

Bullets.

As they spun, Aniri caught sight of the *Dagger* again. "They're headed due south and rising!" she called. "We need to straighten out and catch them before they gain too much altitude. Cut them off again. Force them to maneuver."

"Aye," Janak said, but his voice was strained. The *Endeavor* righted itself and stopped turning, but they weren't aligned yet with the *Dagger*.

"Do you still have those pistols, Mr. Janak?" Aniri asked.

"Aye, my lady."

"Then you need to get us close enough to use them."

He flashed her a look, but kept his hands on the rudder controls. "Hold this altitude," he shouted into the bell to engines. Then he looked back to Aniri. "What are you thinking, my lady?"

"That perhaps, if we keep chasing after the *Dagger,* we might get lucky and get close enough to board it."

"I think the odds are better on crashing into it." Janak's exasperated tone wasn't encouraging.

"I didn't say it would be easy. Besides, spooking Natesh might slow him down a little." Aniri's gaze was locked on the *Dagger.* "A little more speed and ten degrees starboard, Mr. Janak."

"Aye." He relayed the orders to engines. His voice competed with the clacking of the aetheroceiver.

Nahali stood, a curled strip of paper in her hands. "Karan says he can pursue Natesh or use the burning glass on the navy," she said gravely. "But he can't do both."

Aniri whirled to her. "If Natesh slips away from us, Karan has to stop him."

Nahali solemnly crossed the several feet between them and stopped in front of her. "If Karan engages Natesh and loses… we've lost the war."

"If he doesn't go after Natesh, and *we* lose him… Natesh will be free. We can't pursue the

Dagger across the sea, and the *Prosperity* won't catch him before he reaches Dharia."

"I know."

Aniri let out a sound of exasperation and curled up her fists. But she wasn't angry at Nahali. Her sister was only thinking it through to the natural conclusion. And she was right.

"We have to stop him," Nahali said. "Whatever it takes."

Aniri's eyes went wide. She meant they should ram the *Dagger*.

"Whatever it takes, Aniri," Nahali repeated.

"You're the *Queen*," Aniri said, a crack in her voice. "You need to survive."

"No," Nahali said. "The *country* needs to survive. The Queen is only a placeholder, a representative of what the country stands for. And I stand for opposing *this.*" She gestured to the *Dagger*, to Natesh, to all the destruction they both knew he would rain down on their people, either from the air or with his rule.

"Nahali, you have the *baby*," Aniri could hardly force the words out. "If we ram his ship... you could get hurt... you can't take that risk."

"Natesh will never let this baby live." Her voice was a cold fury. "You know that."

Aniri clenched her teeth and stared out the window at the *Dagger*. It was slowly gaining altitude. They had no time, no options, and no weapon but their half-crippled ship.

"Karan has to take the docks," Nahali said, her voice strained, but firm.

Aniri turned to look her sister in the eyes. They were the steely eyes of a Queen making the hardest decision she would ever have. Nahali didn't need her approval, and she wasn't asking for it. She had already made the decision… but she was seeking Aniri's agreement because it was a decision that had a good chance of killing them all.

It was something their mother would do, asking her trusted advisors, but taking the full responsibility herself. It was something a Queen would do.

"Yes, your majesty." Aniri's voice was thick.

Nahali gave a quick nod and hurried back to the aetheroceiver to relay the message to Karan.

Aniri met Janak's rock-hard gaze across the span of the bridge. She expected him to object, but he stayed silent, respecting the First Daughter's decision, even though it had to go against every fiber in his raksaka being.

"Bring us as close to the *Dagger* as you can," she said softly, but loud enough for him to hear over the clacking of the aetheroceiver keys. "You're not to let them escape under any circumstances. Is that understood?"

"Aye." But the words were a steely growl. He relayed the order to engines, and the *Endeavor* surged toward the *Dagger*.

Aniri watched as they closed in, hoping she hadn't just agreed to something that would kill them all.

Chapter Twenty-Seven

THE *ENDEAVOR* WAS light on fuel, light on navia gas in their balloon, and light on crew… but it seemed to Aniri like the heaviest of lead weights sailing through the air in its collision course with the *Dagger.*

Being light was an advantage at the moment: the *Endeavor* was able to accelerate faster than the *Dagger,* which was sluggish by comparison as it tried to gain speed and altitude ahead of them. They were trying to outrun the *Endeavor,* but they were held back by their ship's own mass and prowess.

"How's our fuel, Mr. Janak?" Aniri asked.

"Well enough for the task at hand."

Which likely meant they didn't have much at all. But as long as they didn't run out before they caught the *Dagger*, it didn't much matter. They were slowly gaining on Natesh's ship, running light and fast, and second by second, catching up to them.

Janak was shouting a string of orders into the bell horn to engines, and Nahali was sending the last of her instructions to Karan. They wouldn't need to message him again: he had his orders to take the docks and burn them to ashes with his burning glass. If the *Endeavor* somehow accomplished their mission of taking down the *Dagger*, and survived it, the *Prosperity* would have plenty of time to come fish them out of the water. Aniri peered down as the ocean continued to recede below them —soon it wouldn't matter who survived the collision of the two ships. No one would survive the fall from the sky.

She wondered it Natesh had any idea what they had planned—or if he would realize they were trying to ram his ship only moments before it happened. She hoped it came as an utter, horrific surprise. A breathless minute passed as they inched closer. Natesh must be guessing at their game by now.

The *Endeavor* began to turn slightly away from its intercept course with the *Dagger*.

Aniri threw a look over her shoulder to Janak at the controls. "What's your intent?"

"I thought we would come around from the side," Janak said tightly as he watched the *Dagger* up ahead and slightly below them. "The bridge is least protected, structurally the weakest. Nose to nose seems a good way to start a fight."

Aniri fought a smile. "Very well, then."

At that moment, two men rushed onto the bridge. Their sooty faces made them difficult to discern at first, and one she didn't know at all, likely one of Janak's raksaka-turned-crew, but the other was... *Devesh.*

Why were they on the bridge and not in engines?

"What are you—" Aniri hoped Devesh wasn't here for some foolish thing she didn't have time for.

Janak cut her off. "Defend her with your lives," he said roughly.

Aniri frowned, but before she could think of anything to say, both Devesh and the soot-covered raksaka took a position on either side of Nahali. She looked up from her final aetheroceiver message, startled.

"What do you mean by this, Janak?" Nahali's rebuke was harsh with angry surprise.

"Your majesty, you must retire to the captain's quarters, and do so quickly."

"I'll do no such thing!" But the men were already taking her by each elbow. She attempted to throw them off, but they didn't move. Dev only spared Aniri a short glance and an even shorter nod. He was going to ensure her sister and baby were safe. It touched her in a way that would have left her speechless if she had anything to say in the first place.

"First Daughter." Janak's tone brooked no argument. "We may all be risking our lives here, but under no circumstances will I allow you to die before me. The captain's quarters. *Now.*"

Her sister was furious, red splotches rising her cheeks.

Aniri lurched across the span of the bridge and took her sister by the shoulders. "It's your duty, Nahali. Protect the future Queen of Dharia at all costs." She gently placed a hand on Nahali's belly and urged her back into Devesh's arms. *"Please."*

Nahali's face was still mottled, but she nodded once, then turned and hurried out of the bridge with the men tight at her side. A weight emptied out of Aniri as she watched her sister go. The captain's quarters would not be any safer in falling from the sky than the rest of the ship, but at least she should survive the collision. And this way her sister would be one of the last taken by Natesh, should they fail. Aniri was sure that was the only reason Janak agreed to this plan at all.

"Aniri." Janak's voice was rough.

She spun back to face him.

"In the cabinet, next to the door. Weapons." He still had his hands full with working the rudder controls and watching out the bridge window as they came around toward the *Dagger*. They had only moments left.

Aniri ran to the door, threw open the cabinet, and found a half dozen pistols and several swords. She fumbled to load them, quickly realizing she had no time whatsoever for that. She got as far as two pistols loaded, stuffed both in her pants, one in front and one behind, then grabbed two short swords from the racks that held them. She dashed back to Janak's side, holding a sword out for him to take and sparing only a fast glance out the window.

They were so close she could see the panic on the *Dagger's* bridge.

Janak grabbed the sword from her hand, clasped her hand in his, and towed her from the bridge. They barely made it to the bulkhead door, and Janak was still fumbling to close it behind them, when the sound of screaming metal and exploding glass rent the air. An instant later, they were both thrown against the now-closed bulkhead door by the force of the impact. Their swords clattered on the steel riveted walkway outside the door. The howling of bent metal and popping of splintered wood kept going, like an angry, bellowing beast on the other side of the door. For a long stretch of seconds, Aniri thought it might break through and consume them as well. But a sudden lurch sent her and Janak tumbling to the walkway floor instead. The screeching slipped into an awful, larger, more all-encompassing sound: the whole ship was moaning.

"Have we broken the ship?" Aniri asked, breathless as she and Janak picked up themselves and their swords from the floor.

"The question is if we've broken *his.*" Janak attempted to open the door to the bridge, but it only moved an inch before being blocked. He wrenched and shoved and slowly the door gave way a foot, allowing them to squeeze onto the bridge. Once through, Janak moved with raksaka speed, climbing over the splintered wood and the over-turned mapping table. Only when he reached the point where the bridge window should be did Aniri see the full scope of the destruction.

The *Dagger's* bridge was now joined to theirs.

The glass was gone from both, with splinters sprayed all over the wooden decks and most of it lost to the sea far below. A gaping maw of twisted steel beams and broken wooden planks joined the two vessels together. It was as if Devkalaka, goddess of war and death, had taken the two skyships in her mighty hands and smashed them together, like a child with her toys. Janak summited the debris that heaved up between the tangled ships and entered Natesh's bridge before Aniri was halfway across theirs. She could see bodies on the *Dagger's* bridge, dead ones by the way they lay with their necks and limbs at odd angles, but there were also sailors still moving. Their shouts carried over the low moaning that shook both ships.

Aniri clambered over the wreckage after Janak, but he was already attacking the bridge crew. There were four of them, but they seemed unarmed. One surged toward Janak, but he cut the sailor down with his sword. A second, larger one took a fighting stance with a long jagged plank of wood, as if to hold Janak off with it, while the other two scrambled toward the door of the bridge. If they were going for weapons… Aniri reached the edge where the *Endeavor* was joined to the *Dagger*. A large gap yawned between the two ships, opening and closing as the surging wind and straining engines of the two ships fought their mating. The ocean glittered far below them, an impossible drop that no one could survive. But she'd neglected to give Janak one of the pistols, and he might soon be facing more than an unarmed bridge crew.

She leaped across the chasm.

Nearly tumbling to a deck strewn with broken glass, Aniri caught her balance on a twisted beam that had once been the edging of the bridge window. Just as she did, Janak dispensed with the large sailor in his way with a flurry of strikes with both sword and fist, but the two other bridge officers re-emerged with pistols in hand. They both fired at once. Janak moved with lightning speed. She lost track of him, but his sword gleamed from where it had fallen on the floor. He must have taken cover behind the wreckage that cluttered the bridge. Aniri hastily drew one of her pistols and fired, not at all sure she could hit the armed sailors, given the way the floor was shaking under her boots.

The officers, their pistols spent, ducked and ran from the bridge.

"Janak!" Aniri called over the wind gusting through the bridge and the ships' grinding in protest against one another. "Where are you?"

There was no answer.

She cast aside her empty pistol and clutched her sword tighter as she crept forward through the debris. The large mapping table was tipped over on its side. Half the control panels had been jarred loose and stood askew or outright fallen to the floor. The *Dagger's* star navigator hung from a bent metal post, dangling in the air amidst the twisted arms of steel and wood that once comprised the bridge's window frames.

"Janak," she called again, more quietly, as she stepped over a fallen control panel, its gears and linkages lying exposed to the elements. Her heart climbed into her throat, fearing the worst, when she heard a slight scraping sound. She followed the sound around the back of the tipped mapping table and found Janak struggling to rise up from the floor.

Aniri cursed under her breath and knelt to help him. Blood ran freely from his head, a gaping wound looking like something no one could possibly survive. She clutched his clothes in one hand, the sword still in the other, while she helped him balance as he stood. Aniri simply stared wide-eyed at him, amazed he was still alive.

Janak's hand went to his head, the wound an ugly stripe of flesh laid bare where his inky black hair should have been. When his hand came away bloody, he stared at it a moment, dazed, then rapidly blinked his eyes and cast his gaze about the bridge.

"Where are they?" he asked, his voice rough.

Aniri fought back tears. "Janak, you're injured—"

"Where *are* they, Aniri?" He braced himself on the table's edge and twisted around, looking for the bridge officers.

"They've fled."

Janak swiped the blood that was flowing down his face to clear his eyes. He seemed to have trouble focusing them. "They'll be back soon."

He searched the floor, found his sword, then stalked to the door of the bridge, stopping where the weapons cabinet would have been on the *Endeavor.* The layout of the *Dagger's* bridge was identical, or at least appeared to be in the twisted remains of it. She briefly considered helping him gather weapons, or at least locking the bridge door to keep the officers from returning, but she could see that it was hanging half off its hinges, torn loose by a buckled steel beam. Janak found a pistol and returned to her side.

"When they return, they'll want to regain control of the ship." His voice was thick, and a fresh flow of blood seeped down his face.

It took everything Aniri had to pull her gaze from it and look into his coal-dark eyes. "We need to take the ship down," she said. "Ditch it in the ocean."

He handed the pistol to her. "*I* will be taking the ship down. *You* will keep them from regaining the bridge while I do so."

She took the pistol and nodded. Janak stumbled on his way back to the control panels that were still standing upright. Aniri stood with her back to the wind-whipped gaping hole where the bridge window had been and faced the twisted-open bridge door. She set her sword on the upturned mapping table, standing behind it for some small measure of cover, then pulled the second pistol from her waistband. She held both pointed at the door, waiting for Natesh's men to regroup and reappear in its threshold.

Janak quickly assessed the damage to the control panels, cursing as he went. Then he looked back out the window. Aniri glanced over her shoulder and saw they were still gaining altitude, but the ship was heeling over and pointing back toward the Samirian coast. The two ships, clinging to each other, must be fighting over which had mastery of their path. And the delicate rudders, like fins on the sides of the ship, had to have been at least partially damaged in the crash.

Janak worked the controls, and the ship lurched. Aniri nearly lost her footing, but the screeching of twisted metal jerked her attention back to the *Endeavor.* The gap had widened. Janak kept at the control panels, and the ship jolted again. The protest was louder this time, with popping wood spraying splinters onto the bridge. The *Endeavor* seemed to jostle a little, moving independently of the *Dagger.*

He was trying to shake the ships loose.

She frowned. "Queen's breath, Janak, what are you doing?" she yelled over the noise.

"The Queen needn't go down with us, Aniri." His eyes never left the switches as he spoke.

Another tilt of the floor, even more vicious than the previous ones, sent her banging against the mapping table, almost losing her balance. The noise was horrific this time, and a second jolt in the opposite direction landed her on the floor. As she scram-bled to her feet again, the screeching subsided suddenly, cutting off like a switch. In the wake of the quiet that followed, a shuffling sound and shouts tumbled in from the hall outside the bridge.

Natesh's crew.

Aniri held her pistols steady, pointed at the door, sparing only a quick look for the *Endeavor* to see if Janak's maneuvers had done the trick. They were free of the ship! Then he slammed something on the control panel, and the floor tipped again—only this was no small jolt. The bridge kept tilting and tilting until they were heeled over so far that Aniri had to grip the edge of the table to stay upright. A glance to the outside showed them heading toward the Samirian coast in a spiral so tight that it would take them down into the water… if the land didn't catch them first.

Janak was fighting the skewed floor to scoop up his sword when Natesh's men came through the door.

Aniri fired, and she caught the first one, by the way he flew back into his fellow sailor. He only shoved aside his wounded fellow officer and moved with wicked speed toward her. She fired again, but fighting to stay upright with the tilting of the ship made her shot go wide, and he was practically upon her when he suddenly stopped short. The wideness of his eyes was all that told her why: he quickly fell to reveal Janak standing behind him with a bloodied sword.

But there were more coming.

Aniri's sword had fallen to the floor, and she was out of bullets. Janak whirled around and caught the next one by surprise, sending him to his knees with a sword through his chest. But the next was too fast. His flat hand chop caught Janak in the face and sent him spinning to the floor. Aniri scrambled for her sword and grasped hold of it, but these weren't just sailors… they were *raksaka*. She could tell by the way the sword was out of her hand and she was hauled to her feet before she even knew what was happening. The man who held her hands behind her back was iron-strong, and it was useless to struggle against his grip, but Aniri tried anyway. Another raksaka had beaten Janak into uncon-sciousness, and he lay unmoving on the floor at her feet. At least she prayed to the gods he wasn't dead. She couldn't tell with his face turned away, his body utterly still. But no shots had been fired, other than hers, and she didn't remember seeing a sword run through him.

The bridge was suddenly swarming with sailors and raksaka alike. They flowed to the control panels, righting them and madly flipping switches. Aniri stopped her struggle against the Samirian raksaka's hold as the *Dagger* slowly righted itself, flying straight and level and no longer in any danger of plunging into the sea.

Natesh strode onto the bridge, his head held high.

The last of her breath escaped her.

They had lost.

His sneer was bad enough, but the seething anger underneath it promised she would suffer for their attempt to stop him. But that hardly concerned her. At least Nahali was free. At least Janak had shaken the *Endeavor* loose before Natesh could board it and take her as well. They had failed to take down the ship, or Natesh, but Karan would make short work of his navy. Perhaps he already had. With the fight onboard the *Dagger,* Aniri hoped Natesh had been sufficiently distracted to not notice the *Prosperity* in its work. And now… at minimum, she could continue that distraction until it was too late for Natesh to do anything about it.

As Natesh approached her, she stood taller,

lifting her chin and giving him all of her hatred in one scathing, disdainful look.

Natesh shook his head, his smirk growing. "Proud to the end, Third Daughter." He chuckled. "I really have to thank you for being so *worthy* of an opponent. I think I might actually miss our little battles back and forth." Then his face lost all humor. "I don't, however, appreciate the damage to my ship." He took a step closer, looking her over. "Should I shoot you now or save it for later so I can enjoy the look on your face as I bomb your home into tiny bits of rubble?"

She pretended to give it some thought. "How about you wait until you return to Mahatvak, so I can see the look on *your* face when your mother disowns you for being a Royal Disappointment and hands the crown to Pavan?"

His face darkened. "You make *now* look so much more attractive." He stepped back and gestured to one of his sailors to hand him a pistol. It took a moment, but one was procured and handed to him. He pointed it at her head. "Funny, I keep finding myself in this position, Aniri, with a gun to your head. Only this time, you don't have anything left that I want. And since you won't live to see it, let me tell you how this will go. I will bomb your capital, then take what I want from your people. Next I will find your mother, the Queen, and ensure that she is quite and finally dead. Then I will travel to your docks and bomb your feeble navy until it is likewise a wreckage richly symbolic of Dharia's ultimate weakness against the rise of Samir's technological strength. The First Daughter of Dharia, wherever she is hiding, will be forced to surrender, and the Second Daughter and her Dharian-loving husband, my fool of a big brother, will meet their fate as traitors. Samir will take its place as the rightful head of all nations, and the humble Second Son and his Samirian wife will become King and Queen to ensure that Samir never again lives under the thumb of any country. We will restore peace throughout the land, and the people will have much rejoicing."

"Peace at the point of a gun in the sky." Aniri let the disdain drip from her lips. "How inspiring. Did you think that up all by yourself?"

Natesh gritted his teeth and cocked the gun. "On second thought, I'm not going to miss you much at all, Aniri."

She stared into his deceptively warm brown eyes, holding his gaze until the end. She wanted him to look her in the eye when he executed her.

But something else caught his attention, something over her shoulder, outside the skyship. Her heart sank, hoping they hadn't somehow turned the ship around so that the docks north of them were visible. Natesh's gun was still pointed at her head, but she didn't have his attention any longer. His eyes narrowed, then widened in disbelief. She struggled against the raksaka holding her, but then they both twisted around to see what he was gaping at.

The *Prosperity* was headed right toward them.

A huff escaped her. *How?* And *why?*

"Climb, you fool, climb!" It was Natesh's voice.

Aniri whipped her head back. He was at the controls, shouting at the sailor manning them. He was trying to gain altitude, and as Aniri looked back to the *Prosperity*, she could see why. It was still a couple thousand feet away, but it was bearing down on them from above… and the burning glass was active. It wasn't immediately obvious at first glance —the beam of light channeled by the beautiful copper wings of the butterfly on top was quite invisible as it shone all its strength down to the ground below. Only the *ground* wasn't being burned by the intense heat of that pure, concentrated sunlight…. the burning glass beam was plunging into the *sea*. A giant plume of steam trailed behind the *Prosperity*, rising from the water in a line that puffed straight back to the docks to the north. The clouds of steam obscured the port itself, but hints of the destruction could be seen in the spreading mist: blackened boats and piers, sliced in half with a charred knife of destruction.

And now that the *Prosperity* was headed their way… it was going to cut the *Dagger* in half as well.

Aniri almost laughed. Karan was going to stop Natesh after all. The crash must have slowed the *Dagger* down just enough. Dragged it off course far enough. They had succeeded in delaying Natesh and bought enough time for Karan to come after him as well. And now the *Prosperity* was bearing down on them with a flaming sword like Devkalaka herself. The only question was whether the *Dagger's* attempt to rise above the heat of that burning blade would succeed. Or if they could outrun or outlast the *Prosperity.* But Natesh's fervent shouts and shoving his sailors aside to work the controls himself told her he knew the desperation of that hope. Even the fact that Aniri and Janak would go down with the broken *Dagger* couldn't dim her deep satisfaction that Natesh would fall out of the sky with them.

Aniri struggled against the raksaka who held

her. He looked uncertainly between Natesh and the rapidly closing *Prosperity*.

"Let me go," Aniri said to him. "Let me attend to my raksaka." She peered up into his eyes, hoping she could appeal to some ancient code of honor among raksaka for their final moments. "If we're all going to die, I want to do it by my raksaka's side." He frowned, but surprisingly, he released her. Although he still hovered over her as she knelt next to Janak's body. Surely he didn't count her, a Dharian princess, as much of a threat.

Blood covered Janak's face, but as she bent her ear to his mouth, she could feel a tiny whisper of breath. He was still alive. She wanted him to *know*. To *see*. They had defeated Natesh, and even if it meant their deaths, too, she wanted Janak to know he had succeeded in the end.

"Janak," she said loud enough to be heard over Natesh's increasingly shrill voice. "Wake up." She shook him gently, and his brows pinched together. Whatever the Samirian raksaka had done to disable him, it must be causing some significant pain. "Janak, I need you to wake up, old friend."

He nodded as if she had given him the gravest of commands and curled forward, trying to muscle his way up from the floor. With her substantial help, he managed to roll up to sitting. She shifted, so he could see out the window. "The *Prosperity* is coming," she whispered in his ear. "Karan is bringing his butterfly."

Janak frowned at the blue sky out the gaping hole of the *Dagger's* damaged bridge, and she wasn't sure if he could see the skyship. Or understand her words. But he nodded slowly. Then his eyes roamed the room without turning his head, and she knew he was fully alert—taking in the surroundings, judging the threat. Probably making plans for their rescue even though it was hopeless.

Aniri smiled, her hand steadying him against the turn the *Dagger* was making. Natesh was no doubt trying to make a run for it. The *Prosperity* was behind them now, but they were so close it wouldn't matter. Karan would be upon them in moments.

"The only thing I regret," Aniri said to Janak, her voice close, only for him and not the raksaka looming over them, "is that you never told my mother you loved her."

He took a ragged breath and sat a little straighter, although she could see it was causing him pain. "I showed your mother I loved her every day."

"It's not the same thing." She also regretted not

having the chance to share a life with Ash, but at least they had made their love known in every way possible before actually being wed. "But for what it's worth, I think she knew."

"I may also have said something while she was under the vapors."

"You did not!" Aniri smiled. Janak couldn't have said anything at that moment that would have made her happier. "It's just like a raksaka to use stealth in declaring his love. You know, forthrightness is also a virtue."

He winced, then his gaze drifted to outside the window. Billows of steam were clouding the sky ahead of them. At first a wisp, then stronger, each gust of wind past the front of the skyship bringing more from the sea below. The *Prosperity* had to be right on top of them. Aniri braced herself for the dying scream of the skyship as it was sliced in two.

Nothing came.

Nothing but a sinking feeling. The same feeling she had in the pit of her stomach each time she started a descent to landing in a skyship—that unmistakable sense of losing altitude, a controlled plummet towards the earth. Only this wasn't very… *controlled.* They were sinking *fast.*

Aniri looked up to the raksaka guarding them.

He was likewise distraught, alternately watching the billows of steam growing ever thicker outside and the frantic Second Son with his sailors at the controls.

"What do you *mean*, you can't stop sinking!" Natesh shouted into a twisted brass bell that connected to engines. "Route more heat to the gasbag." He paused while a muffled squeak came through. "Of course it matters, you idiot." Another pause, then Natesh pounded his fist against the mangled control panel next to him. "Don't tell me that. Dump everything you have! We need lift, *now!*"

Meanwhile, the steam was getting so thick that it was invading the bridge. It was as though they were descending straight down into the stack of a boiler, clouds boiling thick and white all around them. As the steam grew more pronounced on the bridge, so did the panic. As well as the rate of their descent, if the sinking feeling in Aniri's stomach was any indication.

But they weren't truly *falling*.

What was happening? Why hadn't the *Prosperity* attacked? Couldn't they get a good slice out of the *Dagger* with all the steam while in flight? She frowned to show her confusion to Janak, but his body had gone tense. And he was slowly easing up to a crouch under the cover of the billowing steam. He looked with just his eyes to their fallen daggers several feet away, then tipped his head to her. Her eyes went wide. Did he mean for them to attack now? While Natesh and everyone else was distracted?

She nodded slightly, then prepared to move.

"What do you *mean?*" Natesh's voice was near hysterical now, shouting into the bell horn. "How can *steam* make us *fall?*"

In the beat of time that Natesh paused to listen for the answer to that question, a particularly thick gust of steam blew into the bridge, momentarily turning the entire deck white with its cover. Janak sprung from where he was crouched next to her, lunging in the direction of the sword and disappearing into the cloud. Aniri did likewise, grabbing for hers, blindly finding it in the mist, and swinging it back toward her Samirian raksaka keeper, in case he noticed her sudden movement. He appeared out of the whiteness and impaled himself on her rigidly held sword. She drove it the rest of the way through and hoisted herself up to standing as he fell to the floor. A stunned expression froze on his face as she quickly backed away, disappearing into the cloud. Shouts and grunts filled the bridge, and a shot rang out, but she couldn't see anything. All was whiteness and mist as the steam plumed even more into the bridge. Aniri felt her way across the debris, keeping her head down and her sword up. She ran into one sailor, but he was already stumbling backward, on his way down. He didn't move once he fell. She inched around the tipped mapping table and stepped over another fallen sailor. The grunts were less frequent now, falling silent one by one. She edged closer to the control panel where she last saw Natesh hovering over the brass bell shouting commands. She held her sword at the ready, and when a hand grabbed her out of the mist, she was ready. She swung her sword, but it clanged against a hidden panel of metal and bounced off before she could slay her attacker.

Janak yanked her close, his face appearing out of the cloud.

"Gods, Janak!" she said, dropping her sword arm.

Then their rapid descent came to a sudden stop. Both she and Janak were thrown to the floor, their bloodied swords flailing behind them. Something soft cushioned her fall, but Janak must have fallen hard on the floor. He grunted on impact and stayed where he fell, but then he slowly lifted his head to check on her.

"Are you all right, Aniri?" he asked, voice raspy with pain and effort.

"Yes," she whispered in reply, still expecting something or someone to come out of the mist and attack them.

But the ship was no longer moving. She lifted her head enough to look in the direction of the window. As she watched, the steam turned a blood red color, and then slowly cleared, thinning out like a dream dissipating into nothingness. The red gasbag of the *Dagger* lay draped over the gaping hole of the bridge. The bag had *sunk*. And the only motion of the skyship now was a gentle rocking back and forth.

They had *landed*. On the *ocean*.

All around them on the bridge lay the crew of the *Dagger*. Not a single one moving. Somehow Janak had snuck through the mist and caught every one of them unawares. And as she turned to look beneath her, she realized the soft thing that had cushioned her fall was Natesh's body. His face was frozen in surprise and anger. She drew back from it, scuttling over to crouch next to Janak.

"How is this possible?" she asked him.

"It turns out the Second Son is as susceptible to being run through with a sword as any man." He sounded immensely pleased with this fact.

Aniri nodded at Natesh's body, then shook her head at Janak, then peered again outside. "What I meant was… how is it possible that we're not dead as well?"

"I'm not certain, my lady," Janak said. "But I suspect that Karan, or perhaps your rather brilliant older sister, found a way to bring down the *Dagger* without splitting us in half."

"The steam." Aniri said it, but she didn't really understand it.

"I believe steam rises," Janak said, as though he were piecing it together for himself. "At least every time I've had occasion to observe it."

"That's because it's…" Realization dawned in Aniri's head. "Because it's *lighter than air.*"

"I can think of one other thing lighter than air." Janak adjusted his position until he was leaning against the control panel. It seemed to make him more comfortable.

"Navia gas."

"The question is whether navia is lighter than steam." Janak rested his head back and sighed.

"It would appear we've proven navia gas is

heavier than a giant steam cloud generated by a burning glass over an ocean of water." Aniri shook her head, still not quite believing it. "So what do we do now?"

"Now?" Janak asked. "Now, I think I shall take a short rest while we wait for the *Prosperity* to board us."

Aniri grinned. Then she settled next to Janak, leaning likewise against the control panel.

Impossibly, they were *alive*. And Natesh was not.

Whatever else came from here was simply a blessing from the gods.

Chapter Twenty-Eight

ANIRI STOOD BEFORE JANAK, straightening his collar. It chafed against his neck as if he had never worn the complete, formal royal uniform of the raksaka guard before. And come to think of it, the last time was probably at Seledri's wedding. Or possibly Nahali's.

And now for hers.

"Hold still," she said, shifting the elaborate fili-gree necklace that the raksaka donned only for the most royal of occasions. "You keep snagging the jewels on your jacket."

The heat from the fireplace in Ash's receiving room wasn't what was making her favorite raksaka's face darken with a reddish tint. They were back in Jungali, a miracle no smaller than the fact that she was about to be wed to the man she loved, but Janak appeared as though he was about to go into battle. His wounds from the one they had just survived were patched and covered, for the most part, but that wasn't was causing him distress.

It wasn't a mystery as to why. "If you don't tell her, I will."

"Somehow I think the Queen already knows you love her, Aniri." He was staring past her shoulder, out the window to the mountains, steadfastly avoiding her gaze.

"I am not making an idle threat, Janak." She stopped fussing with his uniform and propped her hands on her hips to stare him down. In moments, she would have to don her own wedding attire, but she wanted to have this matter settled before then.

Janak's stare was fixed on the distant Jungali landscape. "Once you are wed, I will return to Samir. I hear they're in need of good raksaka there. Perhaps I can serve Queen Seledri in some capacity."

Aniri sighed. Pavan and Seledri certainly could use him, but that wasn't why he wanted to go. Her sister and Pavan had never managed to speak to his mother, the Queen, before Ash had informed them of the bombing risk at the docks in Samir. The three of them, together with Akash's contacts on the docks, Riva's network of Free Tinkers, and Aniri's father's many connections throughout Samir, had managed to evacuate the ships before Karan and the *Prosperity* arrived to destroy them. Then the Queen Mother died soon after receiving the news of Natesh's death. Aniri didn't know what the Queen of Samir knew, or didn't know, in her final hours, but a nation mourning the loss of the Second Son and their beloved Queen still rose up quickly to proclaim Seledri and Pavan the new Queen and King of Samir. The Samirians were fond of their traditions, but as it turned out, they were more enamored of a stable monarchy. And Seledri's speech at the palace in Mahatvak, as well as Pavan's heroics in saving the people at the docks, both cemented their place in the people's hearts. There were still grumblings among some sections of the populace, but the overwhelming majority supported their new Queen and King.

"Queen Seledri will have you," Aniri said, "but I didn't think you were a coward, Janak."

His coal-black gaze whipped back to lock onto hers. But she knew there was a true fear quaking in his heart, and she was determined to have him face it.

"It's not cowardly to leave the Queen to her own choices."

"She is *not* going to welcome back my father with open arms."

His gaze dropped to his boots, shining black with new polish. "He's a hero now, Aniri. Come out of hiding to save his daughter and the Samirians at the docks. He's won his way back into your sister's heart. It's only a matter of time before he wins back your mother's as well."

"Seledri is his *daughter,*" Aniri said, exasperated. "And my father doesn't even *want* to return to Dharia. He wants to remain in Samir. To start a new life and be there for Seledri and Pavan and the baby."

"You're right," Janak said roughly. Slowly he raised his head to meet her gaze. "There's no place for me in Samir either. Perhaps Jungali would be better. When you are Queen, Aniri, you will need someone to train raksaka for the Jungali royal house. I would stay here with you, if you would have me."

"Gods, Janak!" Aniri threw out her hands in frustration, then took him by the shoulders. He stood rigid against her attempt to shake sense into him. "I expect you to visit me often. And possibly train our raksaka as well. But you do not belong in Jungali."

"What is this about not belonging in Jungali?" Her mother's voice jolted them both.

Aniri quickly dropped her arms and stepped back.

Janak went even more rigid, but turned to face her mother as she strolled into Ash's receiving room. "Your daughter was simply being stubborn again," he said. "Unfortunately, defeating a power-mad Samirian prince has only reinforced the habit."

Aniri shook her head, unimpressed with his attempt at diversion. "Mother, your raksaka wishes to leave Dharia." Aniri arched an eyebrow at Janak. *Gauntlet thrown.* She wanted to see him worm his way out of this.

Janak returned her glare.

"Is that right?" Her mother came to a stop before the two of them. She was impeccably dressed in her finest Queenly attire—woven-gold fabric, gold-laced corset, and clear, sparkling crystals from head to foot. She even wore the crown jewels, including a large, white diamond hanging down to her forehead. One would never have known she was on her deathbed not long ago. Aniri knew some of it was bravado, a royal showing for her wedding, but she also knew her mother had weathered the travel to Jungali well and seemed on the road to a complete recovery.

It was her mother's heart that concerned Aniri most now.

Janak was keeping silent.

"With all your adventures, Janak," the Queen said softly, "do you find Dharia too tame for your tastes now?"

Janak winced, and Aniri knew that had to cut to his core. The injuries he was still recovering from, acquired at the deadly hands of a Samirian raksaka, were nothing compared to the effect those words must have on him.

"No, your majesty." He seemed to have to work to get the words out. "But you will no doubt be busy with your Queendom. I'm sure you will hardly miss one raksaka—"

"As it turns out," her mother cut him off, "I plan to be substantially *less* busy in the coming months."

"My lady?" Janak's voice had never seemed weaker to Aniri. Not when he was dying on a skyship over Dharia. Not when he thought they were going to perish over the shores of Samir. Only when he'd held the Queen in his arms and thought *she* was dying, had his voice seemed so… lost.

Aniri held her breath, awaiting her mother's response.

The Queen took a breath. "I have two grand-children on the way." She smiled at Aniri. "And a Third Daughter about to be wed. I think it is time for me to lay aside the crown and let my very capable First Daughter start her rule."

Aniri let out her breath, but still waited for the rest to come. "Does Nahali know?"

"Not yet," her mother said. "But it's fitting that you two are the first to hear of it. Aniri, dear, you did more than just avert a horrible war that would have cost so many lives. You did exactly as I asked and helped Nahali become the Queen I knew she was capable of being."

"She did that all on her own, Mother." But Aniri smiled. Nahali would be so pleased. Even better, Dharia would have a strong, brilliant young Queen to go with their newly forged peace. She had truly earned her place, and better still, everyone knew it.

"And *you,* Mr. Janak," her mother continued. "You should be the first to know that I won't have need of an official raksaka any longer."

Aniri's heart seized. Janak's face had frozen into that stoic look that masked all the feelings she knew had to be roiling underneath.

"Of course not, your majesty," he said stiffly. "And I imagine you won't have need of an advisor, once you've stepped aside from your royal duties."

"No," her mother said gently. "Not an advisor either."

Aniri clamped her teeth tight to keep from protesting. Would her mother truly send Janak away? Simply because she was no longer Queen?

A lighthearted smile broke out on her mother's face. It was a bitter contrast to the ache that was tearing through Aniri's heart for Janak.

"In fact," her mother said, "I find myself very much in the position that my Third Daughter worked so hard to win for herself: free to marry for love." The delight in her voice was impossible to miss.

Janak dropped his gaze to the floor, his eyes half-closed in pain that Aniri could only imagine. Could Aniri have read this all wrong? Was her mother finally free of the years of lying about her father, free to go back to the man she continued to love, even when he had abandoned her? If she was no longer Queen, the affairs of her heart no longer mattered to the country. She was truly free to marry for love. Perhaps for the first time ever.

Only Aniri feared she might pick the wrong man… again.

Her mother stepped closer to Janak, invading that closed-off space he had created by averting his gaze. He twisted his head to the side.

"Janak…" Her mother lifted a hand to touch his cheek.

He had to look at her then, but it was with a blinking, twitching kind of look, as if she was causing him pain with her hand soft on his cheek. Watching them was certainly racing streaks of pain through Aniri's heart.

"I need someone who will always be by my side." Her mother's smile softened, but her gaze grew more intense. "Someone I can count on, in matters small and great, to be a steadfast friend. A trusted partner." She paused, as if she had more to say, but wouldn't let the words out.

Janak's expression opened, as if a new world had been revealed to him, and he was in wonder of it. "You deserve someone who would lay down his life for you."

"I want someone who will love me all the days of my life."

"Amala." Janak's voice was equal parts pain and hope. "Any man would be lucky to have the chance to love a Queen."

"You are not just any man," she said softly, as her fingertips traced a line across his cheek. "You are my raksaka."

The tenderness of her voice was unmistakable, at least to Aniri, but she held her breath as Janak remained frozen in place. He blinked, and Aniri was afraid he might pull back. Might not understand. But then he slid his arms around her mother's waist, gripped her to him, and kissed her with such passion that a blush and a joyful laugh rushed to Aniri's face at the sight of it.

She covered her mouth and quickly backed away.

They didn't notice.

Her heart felt like it might burst with happiness. Sweeping up her skirts and turning, she tip-toe ran to the back of Ash's receiving room, down the short hall, and to the far-corner closet. Once upon a time, Ash had pulled her inside and kissed her as wantonly as Janak was now kissing her mother. But today, Aniri knew only her handmaiden, Priya, lay in wait for her behind that secret door, no doubt fussing with all the last-minute adjustments to her wedding gown.

It was long past time for her to wear it.

Aniri threw open the door, and nearly burst out laughing at the scene. The room was barely more than a large closet, and it was stuffed with all kinds of wedding supplies stacked on shelves, but somehow the three women who had become her very best friends had crammed into the room… and they were enmeshed in an enormous puff of blue and white fabric that she could only assume was her wedding dress. Riva was deep under the dress, holding up the mannequin it was draped upon, while Priya stood on a small ladder to reach the top of it and make adjustments. Seledri had her arms full of the white filmy fabric, trying to keep the layers off the floor. At least the wedding arch and paper lanterns were gone or else there would be no possibility of the three of them and the dress all fitting in the room together.

"This isn't a dress, it's a living, tentacled beast," Riva grumbled as she fought her way out of the blue satin undercoats of Aniri's gown. The tinker was dressed for the wedding herself, although in a stern, black silk Samirian corset over a delicate blouse that closed tightly at her neck. Her skirt was slim, falling all the way to the floor, and Aniri almost didn't recognize her without her tools, breeches, and workshirt.

"I had similar thoughts when Priya first forced me through a fitting." Aniri's voice caught all three of the women's attention. Their smiles made her heart gladden even more, if it was possible to soar over the delight of her mother and Janak finally finding each other.

"It's about time you arrived, my lady," Priya called from her perch. Her deep blue formal attire was naturally perfect for a Jungali wedding. "Just how am I supposed to fit this without the Queen who's supposed to wear it?"

"I've put you through many trials, Priya." Aniri grinned as she stepped toward the three women and the dress. "I'm sure this won't be the last."

"Thank the gods you are here, Aniri," her sister said in a faux whisper loud enough to torment her handmaiden. "Priya was threatening to make Riva wear the dress."

Riva's eyes went wide, and she spun to face Aniri. "My lady, I would never——"

She cut herself off at the laugh Aniri was barely holding back. "Don't worry, Riva," Aniri said. "That's a torment I wouldn't foist on anyone."

"My lady, please remove that… *attire* you have." Priya gestured with disgust as Aniri's plain breeches and workshirt. "I'm not yet done with fitting you!"

Aniri had scrubbed and cleaned all residue of the trials and battles of Samir from her body, but she had yet to don royal clothes since her return just the day before. She and Ash were wasting no time in holding the wedding... life was too short, too unpredictable, and far too filled with unexpected traumas to take one second of it for granted. She had wanted to be wed the moment she had reunited with Ash at the Samirian ports, as soon as she had been reassured that he *lived*, that they had both *survived*, and that somehow the whole horrible experience was in the past. But until she had entered this very room, she hadn't yet felt like the adventure, for better and worse, was finished. She had clung to her clothes as if there was something yet to complete about it. Now, as she slowly peeled them off, it felt like the final pages of that story were closing… and a new one was unfolding in front of her. And these pages were made of sheer white fabric, royal blue raindrop crystals, and satin the color of the Jungali sky.

It was a dream that was finally coming true.

The effort of all three of them was required,

but they managed to hoist the dream-filled skirt over her head. It settled low on her hips, and her sister fastened the snow-white, heavily-jeweled corset that went with it. Her midriff and shoulders were bare until Riva brought the blue royal Jungali jewels and draped them around her waist and neck and fixed them in her hair. Riva's eyes were wide by the time she finished. She stepped back, nearly to the door, simply gazing at Aniri in her dress.

"Yer a wonder, my lady," she said, her voice filled with awe.

Just then, the door swung open, and Akash poked his head inside. "Hello ladies!" he said brightly.

"What are you—"

"Get out of here!"

Seledri and Priya chastised him like old women, but it was Riva's voice that caught his attention. Aniri didn't think it was just because she was closest to the door. His eyes went wide and approving at Riva's very feminine and formal attire.

"What are ye thinkin'?" Riva asked, incredulously. "Ye can't just bust in here. We're dressing a Queen!"

Akash grinned at her, then flashed his smile to Aniri. "A thousand apologies, my lady, but I was sent by your future husband. He told me this was a hazardous duty, but I had no idea—"

Riva made to shove him out the door, but he held up his hands and retreated.

Before he could escape, Aniri shouted over the clucking of tongues and tsking by Riva, "What did Ash want?"

"Just for me to check on you, my lady!" he called as Riva forced him back out the door and closed it firmly in his face. She leaned her back against it and shook her head in disgust and disbelief.

"He's a good man, Riva," Aniri chastised.

"He's a right presumptuous man," Riva shot back.

"He *was* rather brave at the docks," Seledri said with a smirk that made Aniri grin. "Facing down all those burly sailors bent on thwarting the evacuation. I'd say he was a proper hero. He'll make a fine addition to the court in Samir."

Riva harrumpfd, but Aniri shared a knowing look with Seledri. On the way back from Samir, they had compared notes and decided that Akash and Riva were definitely a match waiting to happen. And that match might get a small nudge from the fact that Akash would now be the official

Jungali Ambassador to Samir, by special invitation from the Queen and King of Samir for his service at the docks. Devesh had also earned his way into everyone's good graces, for all his help, not least on the *Endeavor*, so he would be welcome at the Samirian court as well, as a special advisor to the King. Hopefully he would refrain from interfering in business he should not, as Riva had once warned Aniri he seemed inclined to do. It was a second chance for Devesh that Aniri couldn't begrudge him. She only hoped he would use it wisely—and stay out of trouble.

"All I know is that we should be off," Priya said firmly. "I'll not have you be late for your own wedding, my lady."

"It can't come soon enough to suit me, Priya." Aniri lifted her skirts so they wouldn't drag and motioned the women to go ahead and open the door. Riva led the way, with Seledri and Priya clearing a path for Aniri. All three women were out the door, with Aniri following right behind, when suddenly Ash appeared at the threshold. Despite their cries and protests, he slipped past them into the room and closed the door, locking them *out*, and he and Aniri *in*.

"What are you—"

But then he cut her off with a kiss, and she didn't have to ask what he was doing: she *knew*. He had the same urgent need as she—to touch him, hold him, drown in his kiss. Ever since they had been reunited at the docks in Samir, she hadn't been able to stand being apart from him, not even for a few feet or a few minutes. His lips devoured hers, his hands roamed her bare skin wherever the dress didn't cover. All of it told her, he felt it too: a hungry need for each other that she doubted would ever be quenched.

"Gods, Aniri," he said softly as he swept his lips across her cheek, whispered in her ear, then nibbled down her neck. "I can barely stand it."

She bunched the midnight-black fabric of his royal wedding attire in her hands and urged him closer, even though he was already crushing the billowing white fabric of her wedding dress between them. She skimmed her hands up to his face and brought his lips back to hers.

"Barely stand what?" she asked in between kisses and tiny love nibbles that were lighting her entire body on fire.

His hands went to her hair, and it was good that she had convinced Priya to let it fall free, because he tangled his fingers in it, like he couldn't get enough of the feel. He paused for a moment, breathing hard as his lips hovered over hers. They were breathing the same air, holding each other tight, feeling everything intense and alive and *good*.

"I can't stand it when we're not together." His lips caressed hers with his words.

She held his face in her hands and pulled back just enough so that she could look deep into those cool amber eyes. Only they were on fire for her. She hoped he could see that same burning need in hers.

"From now on, whatever we do, we do it together," she said breathlessly.

"Always," he whispered.

Then he kissed her again and some more, and they forgot about the world for a brief blissful moment. And when they'd touched and held each other enough to calm their souls, they straightened their clothes and smoothed their hair. Then they laughed until the laughter subsided, and they could march solemnly out of the closet and on to the waiting wedding party.

ANIRI SUPPOSED there had been stranger things happen than a Dharian marrying a Jungali on a

Samirian skyship. But at that moment, surrounded by the people she loved, and standing in front of Sage Padma on the bridge of the *Dagger*… she couldn't imagine what those things had been.

They had followed the trail of white paper lanterns across Ash's highest tower and passed under the bleached-wood wedding arch—festooned with beads and ribbons and delicate white fabric—then boarded the black and red skyship that had until the day before had belonged to their most hated enemy. It was meant as a symbol of the peace that now reigned between the three countries, and the bridge was filled with exactly that. Nisha, Ash's sister-in-law, and her girls had brought a host of white flowers, and together, they represented all the love Aniri had for the Jungali people, as well as their prince. Her own sisters Seledri and Nahali, along their husbands, now Queens and Kings in their own lands, stood on either side of the altar. Priya and Karan were there: her handmaiden was already crying, and the massive tinker who had helped save the day in Samir was beaming and holding her hand. Soon they would have a wedding of their own. Even Riva and Akash stood together, a pair at least for the ceremony… one that was of necessity intimate in the small space, yet open to the entire mountain landscape of Jungali through a bridge that still lay broken from the ravages of a war barely averted.

And finally, her mother and Janak stood side by side, each glowing with a newly free love that made Aniri's heart soar. Even Ash had noticed something different about them. *Either there's a wedding in your mother's near future,* he had whispered to her on the way to the skyship, *or there are benefits of which I was not aware for certain raksaka.* Words which only made her heart laugh for joy even more.

She and Ash had exchanged their garlands, their vows, their rings, and long ago… their hearts. Now they stood before the priestess who would seal their love forever before the gods with a simple white ribbon. Sage Padma wrapped it around their wrists, looping once, twice, three times, until they were truly bound by it. They wouldn't unwind the slender piece of satin until they shared their wedding bed.

"You are now bound in the eyes of your families, your people, and your gods," Sage Padma pronounced with a smile as she clasped their ribbon-bound hands together with both of hers. "Let nothing separate what has been joined here today."

Ash looked deep into her eyes. "Together," he said.

"Always," she replied.

Their smiles gave way to their kiss. The roar of approval all around them was lost in the rush of love beating through their hearts.

Never had Aniri felt so loved, so joyful, and so completely and finally at home.

Make sure you subscribe to Sue's newsletter to find
out what she's writing next—and get some free
stories when you subscribe!

http://smarturl.it/SKQsnewsletter

Try Some Solarpunk

Hopeful Climate Fiction
https://lnk.to/HtBwebsite

CLOSET FULL OF TIME

Black Mirror-esque

A collection of short stories that speak to the feeling we're serving the machines instead of the other way around.

SINGULARITY

Hopepunk Sci-Fi

Eli is a legacy human, preserved for his genetic code, but he would give anything to ascend with the rest of humanity.

MINDJACK

YA Sci-Fi

When everyone reads minds, a secret is a dangerous thing to keep.

ROYALS OF DHARIA

Alt-India Steampunk Romance

The Third Daughter of the Queen must go undercover
as the fiancé of a barbarian prince to find a weapon
of war.

DEBT COLLECTOR

Cyberpunk

When your debts exceed your potential life earnings,
debt collectors come take your life energy and give it to
someone more "worthy."

FAERY SWAP

Middle Grade Fantasy

Finn becomes stuck the Otherworld when a runaway
faery prince steals his body.

Most of SKQ's books are available in audiobook.

Get a free box set of Singularity novellas when you

subscribe to SKQ's Newsletter.

http://smarturl.it/SKQsnewsletter

About the Author

Susan Kaye Quinn is a rocket scientist turned speculative fiction author who now uses her PhD to invent cool stuff in books. Currently writing hopepunk climate fiction, but her works include SciFi, YA, gritty future-noir, steampunk romance, and that one middle grade fantasy. Her bestselling novels and short stories have been optioned for Virtual Reality, translated into German and French, and featured in several anthologies.

www.SusanKayeQuinn.com